Seruna Savant

To Ed,
8/4/14
Timothy R. Oertel

Seruna Savant

Timothy R. Oesch

TATE PUBLISHING
AND ENTERPRISES, LLC

Seruna Savant
Copyright © 2014 by Timothy R. Oesch. All rights reserved.

No part of this publication may be reproduced, stored in a retrieval system or transmitted in any way by any means, electronic, mechanical, photocopy, recording or otherwise without the prior permission of the author except as provided by USA copyright law, and with the two exceptions stated after the appendix.

This novel is a work of fiction. Names, descriptions, entities, and incidents included in the story are products of the author's imagination. Any resemblance to actual persons, events, and entities is entirely coincidental.

The opinions expressed by the author are not necessarily those of Tate Publishing, LLC.

Published by Tate Publishing & Enterprises, LLC
127 E. Trade Center Terrace | Mustang, Oklahoma 73064 USA
1.888.361.9473 | www.tatepublishing.com

Tate Publishing is committed to excellence in the publishing industry. The company reflects the philosophy established by the founders, based on Psalm 68:11,
"The Lord gave the word and great was the company of those who published it."

Book design copyright © 2014 by Tate Publishing, LLC. All rights reserved.
Cover design by Joseph Emnace
Interior design by Jake Muelle

Published in the United States of America

ISBN: 978-1-63122-156-9
Fiction / Political
14.03.31

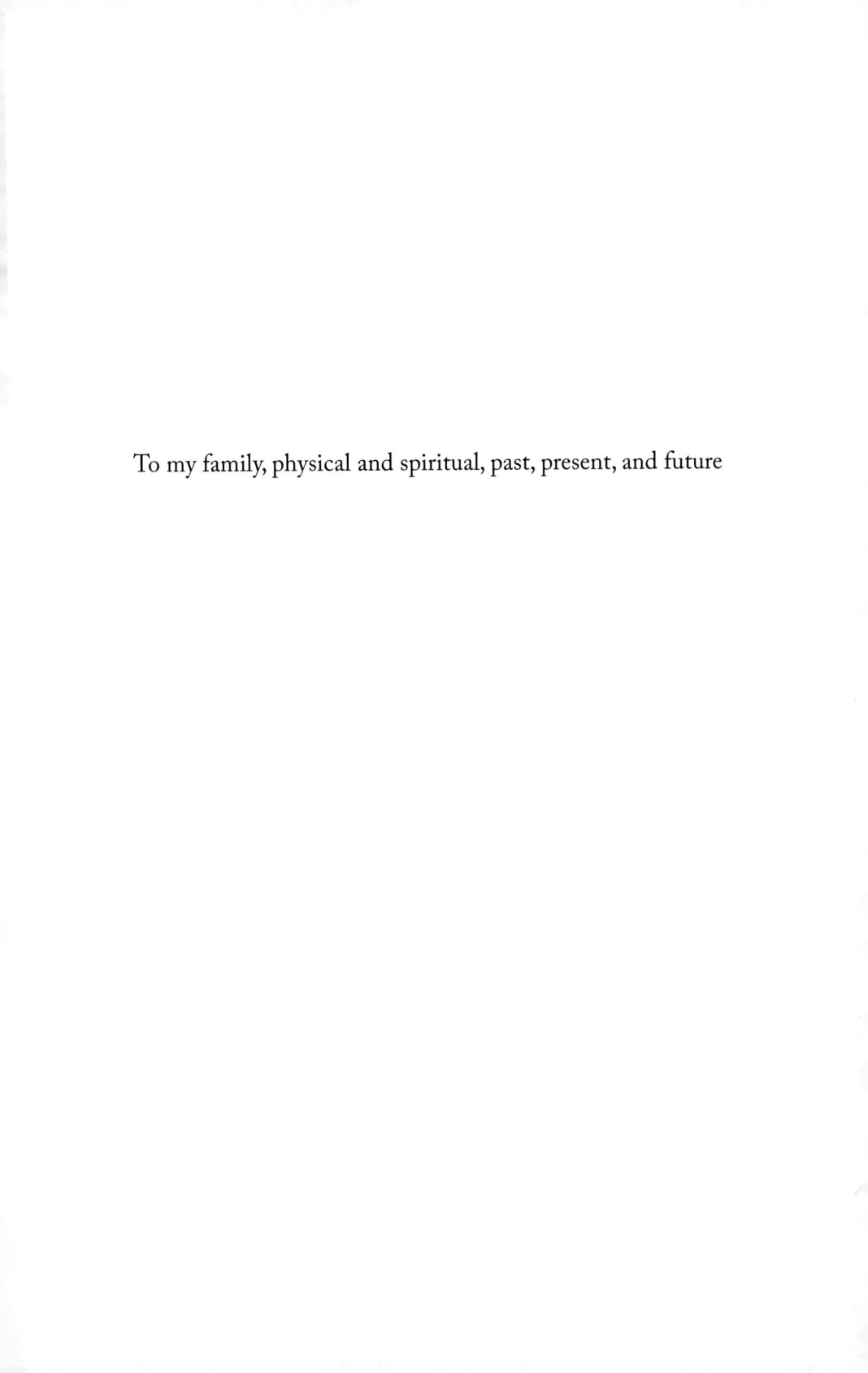

To my family, physical and spiritual, past, present, and future

Chapter 1

"So how does it feel to be the first woman to participate in the Challenge of Kingdoms?" Chirra asked, addressing her comrade from Southern Ivoria in the native language of Subterrania—the vast underground world with phosphorescent skies. She considered her friendship with Sheena to be unique and intriguing, for although the diverse kingdoms of Subterrania lie beneath skies of different color, and although the skin of human beings residing beneath each sky matches the color of the phosphorescent stone above, Sheena was an exception. She belonged to a migrant race that populated regions beneath the white sky of Ivoria and then became divided between the evil Kingdom of Vandolia and the benevolent Kingdom of Southern Ivoria. She and Chirra were close friends, having been roommates when they studied together at the acastoria in the jungle Kingdom of Equavere. This particular acastoria, or center for advanced learning, is a school renown for supremacy in the martial arts.

The two girls sat on the ground at the eastern edge of Lake Fushena. Above was a golden sky that gleamed like the throat of a twirpet, a small Arulian hummingbird with a crimson belly, blue wings, and an iridescent golden neck. Chirra wore a white tunic with matching moccasins, typical attire for unmarried Arulian females, whereas the married women in Arulia wore purple. Her abundant coal-black hair matched her dark eyes and long lashes, and her hair was strikingly beautiful in contrast with her golden skin.

A splash sounded a little distance to the south, followed by laughter and applause from a large crowd seated in the bleachers and standing along the banks of the shoreline.

"I've got to win," Sheena said. She stared out over the surface of the lake.

"There's no way you'll beat Horado. He grew up riding barqualls," Chirra remarked.

A loud voice permeated the atmosphere and preempted a rejoinder from Sheena. "Prince Vordon of Urmoonda scores twenty seconds and four hundred twenty-three microseconds," Chief Lamark announced. He was a better spokesman than the Arulian charftan, namely Charftan Arstro, and the charftan had graciously asked him to serve as master of ceremonies when Arulia was selected to host the Challenge of Kingdoms. "We now have a new leader in the event of barqual riding."

Hurrahs and clapping rose from the observers.

Chief Lamark's voice sounded again. "Second place now belongs to Rark of Chatazia at twenty seconds and ninety-two microseconds, and third place belongs to Kwitz of Draskar at eighteen seconds and three hundred eighty-one microseconds." There were additional hurrahs. "And next, it is my privilege and honor to call for Horado of Arulia."

Applause accompanied the sponsoring kingdom's champion as he strode to the edge of the lake.

"I don't need to beat Horado," Sheena replied, glancing at Chirra with steel blue eyes. Her flaming red hair tumbled over her shoulders and upper back when she turned her head. She wore a tight-fitting blue bathing suit that matched her eyes. "Horado was fourth in archery, which scores no points at all. All I need in this event is second place. I've figured up what I need to do in each event to win the entire competition, or at least what may give me a chance against Terrab."

Chirra stared at Sheena's profile. "Second place? So you're planning to beat Terrab at barquall riding?" Her voice was skeptic. "Once he takes hold of the barquall's pectoral fins, it won't ever be able to shake him loose."

Sheena turned her face and met Chirra's eyes. She cast a playful smile. "It is true that Equaverians are much stronger than the rest of us, but I happen to know something about Equaverians that gives me hope."

"What's that?"

"The green race has great strength, but they can only hold their breaths for seventy seconds at most."

"Really?"

"Yes. And as you know, if a barquall cannot throw a rider by thrashing and flipping, then it dives, and it usually stays underwater until it has to take a breath, which is about two minutes."

Chirra's brows rose. "That could give you a chance, especially considering all the times that we've ridden barqualls together."

Sheena nodded. "That's right. And if I get second place, and Terrab gets third, I'll only be twenty points behind him."

A dubious look captured Chirra's visage. "But twenty points? That's a lot of points when you're competing with Terrab."

"It only takes one second place win to get twenty points, and a first place win gives thirty points," Sheena retorted.

"I know, but—"

"And if we tie in the overall competition, then the tie is broken by another bout of archery, and I already beat Terrab in archery," Sheena added.

"Yes, I know, but what about Terrab's additional points? There are only two events left after this, and one of those events is a test of sheer strength."

A shadow passed over Sheena's expression. She shifted her body and peered into Chirra's eyes in a manner that seemed much too severe for concern over winning or losing an athletic competition. She presented a grave and desperate countenance, a look that troubled Chirra's heart. "Then I'll just have to hope for a miracle," Sheena spoke grimly.

The girls turned their faces as a whoop sounded from the edge of the lake. A blue mammal with a torpedo-shaped body, crescent tail, and large, stiff pectoral fins had been released from a pen that was situated on a shallow sandbar near the shore. On the barquall's back rode Horado, waving one hand in the air as the creature launched forward. He clasped both pectoral fins when the barquall began thrashing within the confines of a semicircle delineated by large buoys. A colossal net draped downward from the buoys to the bottom of the lake. Ivorian cameramen were positioned both above and below the surface of the water, three above and two below; and viewing screens were featured on tall poles that rose to either side of the bleachers.

Chirra turned back to Sheena. She shook her head. "Why? Why do you want to win this competition so badly? You're already the first descendent of an outlander to beat the native Ivorians and represent Southern Ivorian in the Challenge of Kingdoms, and you're already the first woman to be the champion of any kingdom whatsoever—so you're already a hero, are you not? So why fret?"

The shadow that had overtaken Sheena's countenance deepened into an air of pensive brooding. She sat in silence, locked eye-to-eye with her dear friend. She said nothing. The excited bravos and sounds of splashing were expelled from both girls' minds. And then inklings of comprehension took shape within Chirra's eyes.

"This has something to do with your mother, doesn't it?"

The look in Sheena's eyes deepened further. She still said nothing.

"Your father," Chirra blurted. "Your father's mission. This has something to do with your father's mission on the surface of the earth, his mission to help sick people." She paused and read the look in Sheena's eyes. "But how?"

Sheena dropped her face. Her body seemed to grow limp before Chirra's eyes. Chirra leaned forward and grasped Sheena by her shoulders. Sheena lifted her eyes.

"Please," Chirra entreated. "You know that I love you as my own sister. Please tell me."

Sheena lifted a hand and grasped Chirra's arm. She produced a hesitant nod. The two girls then released one another and sat face-to-face on the grassy bank. They addressed one another's eyes.

"You know about my mother," Sheena began.

"I know what you told me when we were roommates at the acastoria," Chirra replied. "When your father was murdered by evil men on the surface of the earth, it caused your mother to suffer some sort of severe mental shock. Something happened to her mind."

"That's right. She no longer recalls her previous life on the surface of the earth. In fact, she no longer recalls that the surface of the earth even exists. When her physicians try to bring these things back to her mind, she lapses into psychosomatic comas, not responding to anyone or anything for days. Her caregivers must be very careful about what they say around her, and they must also take special precautions in regard to any visitors, taking care that visitors will not say anything that disturbs her."

"And that's why she lives in the secluded cottage."

"Yes, that is why. Treshonda and Verma are Scintillian nurses that care for her at all times, and they have looked after me as if they were both my grandmothers. They do this because the Kingdom of Scintillia has great respect for my father and mother. They feel indebted to the service that my parents provided to their kingdom."

"You've told me about that before. Your parents identified the source of a poison that was seeping downward from the earth's surface. The poison was plaguing the Scintillian atmosphere and making the Scintillian people sick."

"Yes."

"So then, do you ever ask your mother about her previous life?"

"Never. When I visit her, we talk about her garden and her needlework and my schooling and any number of trite subjects, but we speak very little about my father, even though my mother has pictures of him all over the house. And we never talk about anything that has to do with the surface of the earth." Sheena paused and addressed Chirra with sober eyes. "And in addition to all of that, she's dying."

"What? Dying? How? She must scarcely be two hundred years old."

"Less. She should live for hundreds of years more, but her physicians say that she has a rare illness and that she will not survive much longer."

"A rare illness?"

A panged look swept Sheena's features. "They say she is dying of a broken heart and mental exhaustion, and they say that there is nothing that anyone can do about it, not even me. Her love for my father and her commitment to his mission, they say, were too great for her mind and body to endure the psychosomatic repercussions following the tragic nature of his murder."

"I'm so sorry," Chirra proffered. Sheena again dropped her face. Chirra gazed upon her friend's forlorn figure with an expression of sympathy, but then her visage changed to one of inquiry. "So how does all of that mean that you have to win the Challenge of Kingdoms?"

Sheena again raised her eyes. "It's complicated."

Chirra sustained a look of inquest. "I've been your friend for years. What could be more complicated than that?"

Chirra's remark drew a smile and then a chuckle. "Very well," Sheena conceded. She dropped her gaze to collect her thoughts and then lifted her face to meet Chirra's eyes. "When I was a little girl, my mother warned me to never touch foot within the realm of Cerulea. She permitted me to travel with my teachers and classmates to other kingdoms, but never Cerulea. She was even nervous when I visited kingdoms that bordered Cerulea, such as Equavere and Urmoonda."

"Really? Was she really nervous when you visited Equavere? We lived there for years when we attended the acastoria."

"Yes, we did, and yes, it really did make her nervous. My training in Equavere took some real persuading on my part. I had to point out that the acastoria is in the very heart of Equavere, not near the border of Cerulea and I emphasized the fact that Equaverian professors provide the best instruction in mural arts in all of Subterrania."

"Mural arts?" Chirra queried. "We both graduated with advanced instruction in the martial arts."

"That is true. But if you remember, I always took one course in mural design or mural painting or mural engraving."

"Oh yes, I do remember. Professor Trathbor all but offered to adopt you if you would change the focus of your studies to the mural arts. He thought you were such a gifted muralist that you could someday paint walls in charftans' palaces."

"And that is why I was not lying when I told Mother that I was studying in the field of mural arts."

"Fine. But why did it make your mother nervous for you to visit Equavere?"

"For the same reason that she would only agree to permit me to visit Urmoonda with my class back when I was twelve years old—if my teacher assured her that we would not approach the border of Cerulea. Both Equavere and Urmoonda border Cerulea, and my mother did not want me to ever cross the border of Cerulea."

A shrug and shake of her head preceded Chirra's next question. "But why was she opposed to your visiting Cerulea? The Ceruleans are wonderful and friendly people."

"The answer is quite simple," Sheena stated. "Although my mother makes no reference to the earth's surface and although no one around her can even mention the earth's surface, I think she subconsciously knows that the passageway to the surface of the earth is on the far side of Cerulea."

"And she does not want you anywhere near that passageway because she does not want you venturing to the earth's surface," Chirra surmised.

"Exactly."

Chirra broke eye contact and repositioned her legs, and then she again peered into Sheena's eyes. "So then, how does all of that have anything to do with the Challenge of Kingdoms?"

Sheena sighed. "Do you want the long answer or the short answer?"

"Well, tell me enough to help me understand what's going on."

There was a loud splash followed by a roar of applause. Both girls turned their heads long enough to espy a barquall leap from the water with Horado's legs wrapped around its torso and his hands clasping its pectoral fins, and then came another splash.

"It has finished its dive," Chirra noted. She looked back and again met Sheena's eyes. "Horado is just getting started. Go ahead."

"Very well. From the time I was a toddler, my mother taught me that my father was a hero and that he died fighting against evil men. I guess I assumed that he was fighting Vandolians. But I attended school just like other children."

"And you learned the truth about your father in school, right?"

"Yes, in a roundabout way. I think my teachers were coached to avoid mentioning anything about my father when I was in one of their classes, but my classmates were apparently told nothing. It was probably deemed wisest not to mention anything to my classmates—you could imagine what would happen if you told a group of six-year-olds to keep something secret."

"No doubt about that, I've worked with young children. So then, where did you attend school?"

There was a long pause. Sheena was cognizant of the fact that she was sharing information that she had theretofore kept confidential. She had convinced herself that discussing details about her father with personal friends might risk having one of those friends raise questions about her father with her mother, and she knew that such an occurrence might cause her mother to suffer a mental breakdown. But as she faced Chirra, she realized that there was another cause for her reticence—namely, her reluctance to discuss the extraordinary nature of her personal aspirations.

"I've told you that I grew up in a cottage on the southern tip of Lake Veroona," Sheena said. "And it just so happens that the largest population of native Ivorians in all of Southern Ivoria live in that region, especially in the area that lies between my cottage and the coast of Lake Tarsh."

"Yes, I know, and I still want to visit your cottage sometime."

"You must," Sheena replied. Her face took on a look of pleased excitement. "Please come anytime you take the notion. Lake Veroona is beautiful, and I can introduce you to some merfolk, and as long as you're careful not to mention my father or anything to do with the earth's surface, you will find my mother most cordial." She paused, and her visage returned to a more serious demeanor. "So anyway, I attended school in the village of Zortada, only a mile south of my cottage."

"And I assume that's where you learned about your father."

"Yes. Most of the children in my school were native Ivorians, but it was a girl of my own race who came and sat down beside me in the library. Her name was Wendra. I was ten years old. Without saying a single word, she placed an open book down on top of the table, right before my eyes, and then she just sat and stared at my face."

"A book about your father?"

"Well, no, not really. It was book of obituaries. One of the obituaries was about my father, and there were a couple of pages about him, and it mentioned his name. It was the first time in my life that I realized that I had never learned my own father's name: Mother always referred to him as *Father*."

"His name? Come to think of it, you've never told me your father's name. What is it?"

"Henry Borden."

Chirra stared at Sheena's face for several seconds before proffering another question. "If you didn't know your father's name, then how did your classmate know? How did she know that the article was about your father?"

"There was a picture."

"Your picture?"

"Well, yes, but my father and mother were with me, and Wendra recognized Mother. Wendra and I both enjoyed swimming with the merfolk, and Wendra had seen my mother on several occasions. So after she recognized Mother's picture in the book, she began reading, and she discovered that the baby in the picture was a girl named Sheena. We both became excited over her discovery, and we both read every word written about my family. The writer mentioned that my father was a courageous outlander who battled against environmental evils that plague the surface of the earth."

"An outlander? You mean your father was actually born on the earth's surface? He wasn't just a spy who ventured to the earth's surface from Southern Ivoria?"

Sheena's features tensed. "You're my dear friend, Chirra. Please do not be offended that I have kept a few things secret from you. My mother's condition—"

"I understand," Chirra interjected, briefly raising open palms to halt Sheena's apology. "So how did your father end up in Subterrania?"

Sheena shrugged and shook her head. "I have no idea. But the article said that my father worked with Dr. Azora to relieve human suffering in Scintillia, and it concluded by saying that his efforts to relieve the suffering of people on the earth's surface resulted in his murder in an outlander kingdom called the United States of America."

"He worked with Dr. Azora? You mean the famous Dr. Azora? Dr. Azora the professor—the chief director at the acastoria on the coast of Lake Tarsh?"

"Yes."

"Oh my," Chirra uttered. She nodded for Sheena to continue.

"And it also mentioned that my father and mother named me after a little girl who once lived in Quazaria."

"A little girl who once lived in Quazaria?"

"Yes. They named me after Sheena, the daughter of Shareesha."

Chirra's long lashes drew far apart. "The daughter of Shareesha? Does that mean you were named after the only child of the first Shareesha the Tiger Queen?"

"Yes."

"Oh my lands," Chirra mumbled. She stared at Sheena as if she were seeing her for the first time. Her brows drew together in thought. She slowly raised a finger and pointed at Sheena, and then she dropped her hand back to her thigh. "You're planning to be the third Shareesha, only without a tiger. You're planning to take up your father's cause and wage a one-woman war against environmental evils that plague the surface of the earth."

Sheena stared speechless into Chirra's eyes. She had never admitted to herself, in such frank terminology, the veracity of Chirra's proclamation, but she knew that Chirra's words were accurate. She responded to Chirra's assertion without breaking the bond between the two girls' eyes. "I went straight home from school and started telling my mother about the book in the library." A look of grief creased the corners of her eyes as she continued speaking. "Verma rushed into the room, and I remember seeing the look of dread on Verma's face. But much more than the look on Verma's face, I remember seeing the look that came over my mother's face and how her eyes lost all semblance of awareness, and I remember watching her crumple to the floor at my feet." A single tear appeared on Sheena's cheek. "And then I remember the sound of my own scream and how I dropped to the floor crying and shaking my mother's body and how Treshonda came and pried me loose and drug me outside while Verma tended to my mother."

A minute of silence followed. Tears became visible on both girls' cheeks. Their eyes remained bound.

Sheena continued, "Treshonda told me all about my mother's illness. Of course, I was already aware that my mother had help from Verma and Treshonda—I had never known anything different since I was a toddler—but I had never given any thought to my mother being ill. It terrified me. I asked Treshonda to tell me all about my father, but all she would tell me was that he was a wonderful man and that he loved me very much and that his name was a special secret and that my mother did not want me to tell his name to anyone and that I should never even say his name out loud. I ran away crying, and Treshonda let me go. She figured that I would go off and cry for a while and then come back home."

Sheena dropped her gaze downward for a few moments. When she raised her face, it was with a look of resolve. "I was a mature ten-year-old girl, almost as big as I am now, and I knew where to find Dr. Azora. I knew that he taught at the acastoria in Zireem. In fact, my class had visited the acastoria just a few months before when we went to Zireem for a boat ride on Lake Tarsh. Dr. Azora took the class on a brief tour of the acastoria while we were in Zireem."

Sheena paused thoughtfully. "And what I remembered more than anything I saw in the acastoria, was the way Dr. Azora looked at me. He looked at me different from the way that he looked at any of the other children. So later, after reading that Dr. Azora and my father worked together, I figured that Dr. Azora had been looking at me different because he knew my father. And that's why after running away from Treshonda, I put a bridle on Windsong and took off for Zireem to find Dr. Azora. I wanted to ask him about my father."

"You rode your horse bareback when you were ten years old?"

"I've always ridden bareback," Sheena responded. And then a wistful smile preceded her next words. "If I had known my way better, I could have reached Zireem without sleeping more than once. But as it was, I slept twice before meeting up with an Ivorian man named Irstrar. He asked me if I was well, and I broke down crying."

Chirra nodded, intrigued with the story and anxious to hear what happened next.

"So then I pled for Irstrar's help, and he took me straight to Dr. Azora. Then after Irstrar left us, I sat alone with Dr. Azora in his office at the acastoria. I was nervous about mentioning my father's name after the warning Treshonda gave me, but I figured Dr. Azora already knew his name. So anyway, I told Dr. Azora that I am Henry Borden's daughter, and I asked him all kinds of questions about my father's mission upon the surface of the earth, and I also asked him about my father's death. He answered all of my questions, for which I am forever grateful. And when our conversation finally drew to a close, he just sat and looked at me."

"He just looked at you?"

"Yes. The look on his face made me think he was about to say something the very next second, but we must have sat for almost a minute just looking at each other. And then when he finally opened his mouth and spoke, he said something that I will never forget. He said, 'You have your mother's face, but you have your father's eyes.' And when he said that I have my father's eyes, I knew that he was not just making a casual remark, he was planting a seed—a seed that took root in my heart and shaped my determination to carry on my father's warfare against the environmental evil that plagues the surface of our planet and causes untold human suffering."

Chirra wiped the tears from her cheeks and managed a smile. "Well, your plan to engage in warfare explains a lot, like why you were willing to humiliate the males at the acastoria in Equavere by graduating first in the martial arts class."

"It was a very close contest," Sheena rejoindered. "I didn't win a single strength event."

"So what? There were Equaverians in the class."

There followed a brief period of silence. Neither girl seemed to know what to say next.

Chirra reached out and grasped Sheena's hand and smiled. "Thank you for sharing all of that with me. I already felt like we were sisters, and now I feel like we're the closest and dearest of sisters." Then the expression on her face transformed to one of interrogation. "But hey, you still haven't told me why it's so important for you to win this competition."

Sheena laughed at Chirra's look of discomfiture and spoke teasingly. "You're quite right. And that was the primary substance of your original inquiry, wasn't it?"

Chirra answered with a contorted expression of curiosity.

"Very well then." Then her face gave way to a more sober mien. "That has something to do with a recent occurrence."

"Occurrence?"

"Yes. Several months ago I was strolling through the forest east of the cottage with Mother and Verma. We were picking pucas for Mother to bake a pie, and I think I know why Mother has always liked puca pie so well."

"Why is that?"

"I was reading about common foods in the United States of America. Dr. Azora told me it's the kingdom where both Mother and Father grew up. And there is a common fruit in that kingdom that looks and tastes almost exactly like pucas, and it's a fruit often used to make pies."

"I see. So then, you were picking pucas. What happened next?"

Sheena's face darkened. "It was horrible. My first two kills."

Chirra nearly choked. "What?"

Sheena nodded gravely. "News that there were two Scintillian women living in Southern Ivoria must have reached the palace in Esjumar. A Scintillian woman has never been captured by

Vandolian marauders, which is not too surprising since Scintillia is isolated from the rest of Subterrania on the far side of Draskar, so there is no telling how great a reward the Vandolian charftan offered for the delivery of a kidnapped Scintillian maiden. We were just about ready to head back to the cottage with three baskets of pucas when two armed Vandolians rushed from a thicket and grabbed Verma."

"Armed? With guns?"

"One had a gun, and one had a sword. They wore white shirts imprinted with golden skargs, though the skargs appeared more like legendary dragons from the earth's surface than the native beasts of Draskar."

"So Charftan Bohada commissioned the capture of a Scintillian female."

"No doubt."

"But don't they travel in groups of four?"

"Yes, but we learned later that two of the Vandolians were already slain by Ivorian watchmen. The watchmen thought that the other two were also slain and that their bodies sank into the depths of Lake Tarsh to be devoured by chukshara eels."

Chirra examined Sheena's eyes. "What happened? Was Verma injured? Were you hurt?"

Sheena shrugged. "Verma was roughed up a little, and my right foot was sore for a while. I kicked the gun a bit harder than I would have needed to, it sailed over the top of a puca tree."

Chirra voiced no further question, but she faced Sheena with inquisitive eyes.

"One man died by his own sword, though the sword was wielded by my hand," Sheena stated. Her voice was laden with remorse. "The other man died from a blow to the side of his head."

"They would have killed you, or worse," Chirra said, reading the expression of regret on Sheena's face. "Surely you've heard about the fates of women who fall prey to Vandolian marauders."

Sheena shuddered. "I know. But let's get back to your question about the competition."

Chirra nodded.

A few seconds passed while Sheena recollected her thoughts. "So then, after the fight, the three of us set out to find an Ivorian watchman. Mother mentioned nothing about my martial arts skills, even though Verma couldn't stop talking about the fight. Mother let Verma tell the Ivorian watchmen what happened, and then she let Verma show the watchmen where to find the slain Vandolian bodies. But when we got back to the cottage, my mother took me to her bedroom where the two of us could speak in private, and then she made a request."

"A request?"

"Yes."

There was a pause. The look that came to Sheena's face stilled Chirra's tongue, despite a mounting curiosity that swelled within her breast.

"I told you that my father was born upon the earth's surface."

"That's right."

Sheena drew a brooding breath. "Well, my mother was born there too."

"Really? So both of your parents are outlanders?"

"Yes. And after taking me back to her bedroom, my mother gazed into my eyes with an expression that truly made me feel like I was looking into the eyes of a woman from another world. And then came her request—a request that shocked me."

"What request?"

Sheena held Chirra's eyes. "She pleaded for me to promise that I would never cross the border of Cerulea and that I would never enter the Tunnel of Transformation."

"The Tunnel of Transformation," Chirra echoed. "So she was forbidding any access to the earth's surface, even by way of Quazaria."

"Yes, and I was tempted to point that out to her. But the look in her eyes restrained me. I did not want to see her lying at my feet in a psychosomatic coma."

"So what did you do?"

"Well, you know how I feel about promising anything. I think a person should stand by whatever that person says without having to make any promises. So I would not consent to making her a promise. But nonetheless, I agreed to her request so long as we both lived."

Chirra sat thoughtfully for a few seconds. "But you knew that she is dying."

"Yes, and so does she."

"Why do you say that?"

"I say that because she kept looking into my eyes with that same expression, that sophisticated expression, and then she asked me to agree that, after she died, I would not enter either Cerulea or the Tunnel of Transformation unless I obtained permission to do so from the Charftan of Southern Ivoria."

"Charftan Yarzon?"

"It's Charftan Yarzon *now*," Sheena said. "But at the time my mother spoke to me, it was Charftan Wilkins. My mother is a close friend with Yarzon, who as you probably know is Ivorian, and he had confided with her about his upcoming selection as Charftan of Southern Ivoria. Apparently Yarzon already knew that a sufficient number of chiefs and village ambassadors would vote for him. Most of us did not even know that Charftan Wilkins was resigning, or at least I did not."

"So I presume that you agreed to your mother's request."

"Yes, I did. I was quite certain that I could convince Charftan Wilkins to let me enter Cerulea. But it was only a few days later that I found out we had a new charftan, namely Charftan Yarzon. And when I found out about it, I trekked straight to his village to find him, but he had already moved into the palace in Spartana."

"And I bet you headed straight for Spartana."

"Yes, I did," Sheena stated emphatically. "Yarzon had visited our home several times, and I was familiar with him. He welcomed me into his office as soon as I arrived at the palace in Spartana, and then we talked."

Sheena stopped speaking, and her eyes seemed to drift. Chirra studied mixed expressions of wonder, respect, consternation, and fortitude that played upon Sheena's countenance.

Curiosity mounted within Chirra's breast. "So what happened?"

Sheena's eyes returned to her environment. She faced Chirra. "I had plenty to think about during my journey to Spartana. I slept three times, but I never slept well." A forlorn sigh broke the flow of her speech. "As you surely know, Charftans may rule for hundreds or even thousands of years, and Yarzon is Ivorian, so his expected life span is much greater than mine. I love my mother dearly, but I almost felt betrayed as I came to the realization that she had persuaded me to make a commitment that could confine me to the realm of Subterrania for my entire lifetime."

"She thinks she is protecting you," Chirra proposed.

"No doubt," Sheena conferred. "But I want no such protection. I'm not a child. I want to follow the path that my heart leads me to follow, so long as I can do so with the Creator's guidance and blessing."

Chirra gave a nod. "Of course. So then, what happened in Charftan Yarzon's office?"

"Well, it was obvious that my mother and Yarzon had already discussed the matter. I asked Yarzon for his consent to venture outside of Subterrania after my mother died, and he seemed to know exactly why I needed to ask for his permission."

"And?"

"He just shook his head and said no. I pled like I had never pled in my entire lifetime, or at least not since I was little girl—back when I begged my mother to let me go with my class to Urmoonda. But Yarzon would not budge. I could sense his sympathy, and I am sure that he will be a marvelous ruler, but

I was almost beside myself with frustration. I was at a loss for words. I just sat and stared. And then it happened."

"What happened?"

Sheena leaned slightly forward and held Chirra's eyes. "He told me that he had watched me grow up and that he had the greatest respect for me, but that there was no way I could survive the battle that I was determined to wage upon the earth's surface."

Chirra gave a startled jolt. "So he knew? He knew your plans?"

"My mother must know. Somewhere deep within that ailing mind of hers, she must know a lot more than one can tell from her outward demeanor. And she must have told him."

Chirra was spellbound by Sheena's eyes. "So then what happened?"

"I think I started hyperventilating. I felt desperate. And then from nowhere, as if inspired by some force beyond my own being, I found myself speaking words that shocked me."

"What words?"

"I looked Yarzon straight in the eyes, and then I asked him if he would grant permission for me to venture to the Earth's surface if I succeeded in taking first place in the Challenge of Kingdoms."

Chirra rocked back on outstretched arms and gazed at Sheena's face. "So that's why you have such a passion to win. Yarzon granted your request."

"At first he just looked at me as if I had inherited some sort of mental infirmity from my mother. But then he produced a smile that made it obvious that he considered it absurd for me to think that I had any chance of winning; and he told me that if I won the competition, then he would permit me to journey to the surface of the earth by any route whatsoever."

Chirra felt both excitement and foreboding as Sheena finished speaking. It was exciting to witness her friend's determination, hope, and enthusiasm and to reflect upon the great accomplishments that Sheena had already achieved. But now that she knew the depths and sincerity of Sheena's motive for winning the Challenge of Kingdoms and now that she perceived how heartrending it would be for Sheena to finish in second place, the prospect of Sheena vying with a warrior such as Terrab of Equavere cast an ominous shadow over the future events of the day.

"You know," Chirra said, "both the first Shareesha and the second Shareesha served the welfare of peoples right here in our own realm of Subterrania."

Sheena had no problem deciphering the purpose of Chirra's comment. Chirra was seeking to provide consolation because Chirra expected Terrab to win. Sheena's face dropped downward.

"I'm sorry," Chirra spoke, perceptive of Sheena's feelings. "You may yet win, by some miracle or whatnot. And even if you do not win, there is another competition in seven years."

Sheena raised her face. "I have much to be thankful for, even if I never set foot in Cerulea or pass through the Tunnel of Transformation. But I believe that my heart and spirit are inspired toward the goals I pursue—inspired by the Spirit of my Creator." For several moments, she peered into Chirra's eyes, and then she smiled. "And as I have worked these many years to prepare myself for the mission toward which I believe the Creator is guiding me, I consider myself truly blessed to have worked alongside a friend such as Chirra of Arulia."

Chirra returned Sheena's smile. "And I am blessed to have a friend such as Sheena of Southern Ivoria."

A rise in the cheering from the stands drew the girls' attention. They espied Horado riding toward shore with one hand raised above his head, waving at the crowd. His other hand was propped leisurely against the back of the barquall."

"He has tamed his barquall," Chirra observed. "That is a rare feat."

Then the cheers converted to laughter as Horado was hurled forward and splattered against the surface of the lake. A crescent tail splashed and vanished above the barquall's diving body.

Horado swam forward and then walked onto the shore, laughing along with the crowd. Several Ivorians with stylish cameras filmed his approach.

"He has a good sense of humor," Sheena remarked.

"Oh, yes, he really does," Chirra concurred. "He's a very nice man."

Sheena faced Chirra. Chirra blushed and shrugged.

Chief Lamark's voice hushed the clamor. "Horado of Arulia scores sixteen minutes, four seconds, and seventy-nine microseconds. We now have a new leader in the event of barquall riding." Applause erupted, and the applause continued for nearly a minute before Chief Lamark could resume speaking. There were observers in the crowd from every kingdom of Subterrania apart from Vandolia, but the Arulians, who were sponsoring the competition, outnumbered all other attendees. Finally Chief Lamark was able to speak above the noise of the crowd. "Second place now belongs to Prince Vordon of Urmoonda at twenty seconds and four hundred twenty-three microseconds, and third place belongs to Rark of Chatazia at twenty seconds and ninety-two microseconds." There was some additional applause, but Chief Lamark quickly concluded. "And next, it is my privilege and honor to call for Terrab of Equavere."

Due to the reluctance of Equaverians to step beyond the borders of their own kingdom, there were few Equaverians in attendance. But Terrab still received a respectful degree of ovation. He was well liked, and he was in first place. He waded out to the sandbar where several barqualls were penned. His green swimming shorts were bulkier than the loincloths he generally wore in Equavere.

"So I guess you and Horado are acquainted with one another," Sheena teased. She would be competing after Terrab, and she wanted to lighten the nature of her conversation with Chirra before attempting to ride a barquall.

"We've met," Chirra replied.

Chapter 2

"With one competitor remaining, Horado of Arulia is still our leader at sixteen minutes, four seconds, and seventy-nine microseconds," Chief Lamark's voice sounded. The crowd cheered with enthused expectations of a victory for the sponsoring kingdom's champion. But there was some degree of uncertainty to their cheers, for one competitor remained, and she was a competitor that had already astounded them. The Rules Council had decided that the first female to ever qualify for participation in the Challenge of Kingdoms should be permitted to take the last turn in every event. They doubted she would win anything, but they were pleased to think that she would provide an additional factor in attracting spectators.

Chief Lamark continued his announcement. "Second place now belongs to Terrab of Equavere at one minute, thirty-eight seconds, and two microseconds, and third place belongs to Prince Vordon of Urmoonda at twenty seconds and four hundred twenty-three microseconds." There were the usual cheers, and then Chief Lamark resumed. "And next, it is my privilege and honor to call for Sheena of Southern Ivoria."

Chirra gave Sheena's arm a supportive squeeze. Sheena stepped out into the water. She had received a hearty degree of cheering when her turn came in the first event, especially from the younger women in the crowd, but now the cheers that escorted her were infused with awe—she was a woman, she was a descendent of outlanders, and she was in second place with only two more events remaining. Her achievements in the competition were deemed more than amazing; they were considered downright supernatural. The cheers succumbed to a still hush as she positioned herself on the back of a barquall and took hold of its pectoral fins.

Sheena brought Chirra's advice to mind: "Just pretend that you've leapt onto the back of a sleeping barquall like you always do." An Arulian attendant opened the gait to the pen. The barquall thrust forward. To Sheena's surprise, the barquall swam forward to deeper water and then dove. She barely had the presence of mind to draw a breath.

"Whowooah!" The barquall merely dove deep enough to launch back upward and break into the air where it corkscrewed so forcefully that Sheena's long red hair whipped around behind her head like a pouch on the end of a twirling sling. "Whoopee!" she cried out with exhilaration as the barquall landed with a splash and then began twisting, thrashing, and bouncing up and down off the surface of the water like a skipping rock. The crowd went wild. Chirra laughed until she almost cried.

It was difficult to tell one adult barquall from another, but it was common knowledge in Arulia that there was one barquall unlike any other, a barquall bequeathed the name Whiplash. Whiplash appeared and acted like any other barquall—that is, until someone mounted his back. The council had considered giving a competitor a second ride if that competitor ended up on the back of Whiplash since it was reportedly impossible to remain upon Whiplash more than five seconds. It was finally decided, however, that no two barqualls were exactly the same and that the Challenge of Kingdoms was, after all, a series of games, and that it would be best not to complicate the games with too many rules. Thus, Whiplash remained an eligible barquall.

Sheena drew a quick deep breath before Whiplash's second dive. The underwater cameramen, wearing sophisticated scuba gear, found it difficult to keep Whiplash and Sheena within the frames of their viewing lenses. Oohs and aahs swept through the spellbound crowd of spectators. Whiplash swam downward to the deepest point of the lake that was contained within the net, about twenty feet beneath the surface, and lay still. Sheena's brilliant red hair captured light from the cameras and hovered about her head. The atmosphere above the lake grew still and quiet.

"That's long enough," Chirra whispered to herself. She began to wonder if Sheena knew how deep Whiplash had taken her. Murmuring started up among the onlookers and grew in intensity. One of the underwater cameramen turned off his camera and started swimming in Sheena's direction.

Suddenly Whiplash darted ahead and then shot straight upward. The cameraman who was still filming beneath the water could only capture blips of a streaking blue creature mounted by a white woman with red hair. Then Whiplash and Sheena broke through the surface of the water with Whiplash performing three complete flips in midair before crashing back into the lake. It was during the completion of Whiplash's first flip that Sheena's body flew up and back, sailing westward over the buoys and disappearing beneath splattered water. Then the sounds of splashing subsided. Silence gripped the environment.

Sheena's red hair appeared above the surface of the water. An explosion of applause followed. She turned around, treading water, and waved to the crowd. Chirra breathed a sigh of relief. Chief Lamark's voice became audible.

"Sheena of Southern Ivoria finishes second at two minutes, twenty-three seconds, and four hundred eighty-two microseconds."

Cheering continued as Sheena swam to shore. A small platform was set up at the edge of the lake, centered before the crowd. There were three tiers to the platform with the center tier higher than those to either side. Horado was directed to stand upon the center tier, with Terrab to his right. Sheena made it to shore and was positioned to Horado's left.

"The event of barquall riding is completed," Chief Lamark proclaimed. "The next event, namely the Challenge of Wits, will commence at the scheduled time. And now it is my privilege and honor to announce the winners. Third place goes to Terrab of Equavere, second place to Sheena of Southern Ivoria, and first place to Horado of Arulia." Chief Lamark's voice was eclipsed by sounds of celebration and applause before he completed the word *Arulia*.

When the three champions stepped down from the platform, Chirra ran forward to Sheena. "Let's get you out of here," she said. "Are you injured?"

"A little sore," Sheena admitted. She glanced down at a bruise on the back of her left thigh.

"Oh my. Did Whiplash get you with his tail?"

"I think the surface of the lake got me," Sheena replied.

"You need cool pressure. Otherwise it might swell. Come on."

Chirra had assumed roles as Sheena's agent and trainer. They walked south to a group of small tents and entered the tent assigned to Sheena. Chirra picked up one of several towels. "You can dry off and change clothes while I dowse this towel in cool water. I'll be right back."

A meal was delivered to the tents where the athletes were camped. Meanwhile, the main body of spectators traveled east to the village of Muelta. An outdoor amphitheatre was situated just west of village, and the amphitheatre had accommodated all the athletic competitions prior to the barquall riding, and it would accommodate the remaining two events. Villagers in Muelta made certain that ample food and lodging were available to all the guests and competitors. An air of excitement instilled the atmosphere; the local champion had just taken first place in barquall riding, and the only woman to ever participate in the Challenge of Kingdoms had performed a mesmerizing ride on the back of Whiplash. The Rules Council was most pleased.

"Wake up. Breakfast is served," Chirra said, shaking Sheena's shoulder.

Sheena awoke and sat up. Fruit and nuts were arranged in a platter beside her, along with some bread and meat. There was water to drink. Additional foods and drink were placed beside Chirra, who sat cross-legged near the open flap of the tent. Sheena gazed absently ahead, trying to recall the substance of the dream she was experiencing when she was awakened.

"What is it?" Chirra asked.

Sheena glanced toward Chirra and then again gazed forward. "I was dreaming. I was talking to Mother, only—"

"Only what?" Chirra prompted.

Sheena faced her friend. "Only she was really talking. I mean, she was talking like a normal person, and we could talk about anything."

Chirra held Sheena's eyes. "Perhaps, someday, that will happen."

Sheena gave no reply. She looked down at the food beside her. "The Creator has blessed us," she spoke.

"The Creator has blessed us," Chirra repeated.

The two girls ate without additional comment in regard to Sheena's mother. For the most part, they discussed the next event in the competition. Many of the more intellectual spectators considered the Challenge of Wits the most intriguing event in the agenda. There were differing and unique events each time the Challenge of Kingdoms took place, depending largely upon the sponsoring kingdom and the members of the Rules Council, but the Challenge of Wits was always included as one of the events. And even if a competitor won nothing else, a laudatory homecoming was guaranteed when a kingdom's champion won the Challenge of Wits.

Arulian volunteers cleaned up after breakfast and took down the tents as the participating challengers headed east toward

Muelta. Lush green grass that flourished around the Arulian borders of Lake Fushena gave way to a beautiful forest of blue, crimson, and silver. Forest trees in Arulia were generally thick-trunked with long, sprawling limbs and lobular leaves. Birds were abundant and brightly colored. Gliding squirrels, black-bodied with bushy red tails, chattered, leaped, and soared overhead as the two girls passed beneath branches.

By this time the amphitheatre was familiar to the girls. They made their way to an elliptical Ivorian module that was situated just south of the stage entrance. Great tiers of benches, composed of solid limestone, rose before the stage and continued upward to the outer edges of the amphitheatre. The benches were already filled with spectators, and a spokesman was addressing the crowd. An Ivorian attendant stepped before the solitary door to the module as Sheena and Chirra approached.

"My name is Darzkor, and I will be conducting the entering and exiting of each participating champion," the attendant said. He gave Chirra an occasional glance, but he spoke to Sheena.

"Very well," Sheena said.

"As you have been informed, everyone within the chamber is to maintain strict silence. The chamber is soundproof. Any champion that forgets and speaks will lose points. An Ivorian by the name of Chukhoya is positioned inside to record any infractions. The chamber is equipped with a toilet facility. Do you have any questions?"

"No questions."

Darzkor looked at Chirra. "You may take a seat inside the amphitheatre."

Chirra gave Sheena a hug and departed. Darzkor nodded to Sheena and opened the door to the chamber. Sheena stepped inside. The interior of the module made her feel as if she had entered a hollowed cavity within a giant white pearl. The walls, floor, and ceiling were composed of a smooth white substance reminiscent of porcelain. Deep-padded lounge chairs lined either side of the module, and they appeared to be fused with the walls. An interior wall and door were situated at the left end of the module, obviously the toilet.

An Ivorian seated at the end of the module to Sheena's right nodded and signaled for her to sit in an empty chair beside him. There were numerous nods and smiles as she settled in the chair and looked about the chamber. Seven of the other competitors were already seated: Horado of Arulia—a land of canyons and forests beneath a golden sky; Xarron of Cerulea—a country of mountainous woodlands and grassy plains beneath a blue sky; Rark of Chatazia—a mysterious and beautiful realm of colossal caverns beneath a black sky; Kwitz of Draskar—a rocky dessert stretching more than three thousand miles beneath a crimson sky; Terrab of Equavere—a lush, teeming jungle beneath a green sky; Lorso of Scintillia—a kingdom of quaint forests and rolling hills beneath a sky of the same color as the sky above Vandolia and Southern Ivoria, namely a white sky; and Prince Vordon of Urmoonda—a territory with barren sandstone dunes abutting multicolored arboreal wonderlands beneath a red sky. Like Sheena, the other competitors wore tunics and moccasins; that is, all except for Terrab who was barefooted and wore a loincloth. Three phosphorescent orbs were suspended below the center of the ceiling to provide light. The only detectable sounds in the chamber were the sounds of persons breathing.

A few minutes passed, and then the door opened. Sounds from the adjacent amphitheatre poured into the chamber, and in stepped Elroth of Chireem—a majestic region of marble bluffs and crystal pools beneath a silver sky. Like most of the others, he wore a tunic and moccasins. There were only two empty chairs remaining; and as with Sheena, Chukhoya nodded for Elroth to be seated in one of the empty chairs. Time passed slowly.

Terrab of Equavere was first to be summoned from the chamber. The utter silence within the chamber was made evident whenever the door to the outside opened. It was Darzkor who stepped just inside the chamber and pointed at Terrab. Silence returned after Terrab and Darzkor exited, and the door was again closed. Roughly twenty minutes later, Darzkor returned and pointed at Xarron of Cerulea.

The competitors were beckoned from the chamber one by one until only Chukhoya and Sheena remained. No one had spoken a word inside the chamber. At last Darzkor returned and pointed at Sheena. Chukhoya followed behind as Sheena stepped outside the module. She did not know if she were permitted to speak, so she remained silent. Another Ivorian, a woman, stood outside the doorway holding some sort of black garbs in one hand.

Darzkor signaled for Sheena to halt. Chukhoya walked away toward the amphitheatre without comment.

"The rule of silence continues until you are permitted to ask your first question," Darzkor stated. He gestured toward the other Ivorian. "This is Evera, and she will secure a blindfold around your eyes. The blindfold is to remain in place until your event is completed. Evera will lead you by the hand, and I will follow close behind."

Sheena watched as Evera threw a black scarf over one shoulder and straightened a pair of black velvet blinders. Then Evera moved behind her. "Very well then, close your eyes," she said. Everything went black. Sheena felt Evera tightening the blinders, and then she felt her position and tie the black scarf over the blinders.

Evera clasped Sheena's left hand. "I'll give you instructions as we go," she said. "Remember, do not speak a word."

Sounds of chatter increased in volume as Evera guided Sheena up the stone steps to the stage of the amphitheatre and then led her to the center of the stage. Evera grasped Sheena's shoulders. "Now turn this way, toward me," she said. A scooting sound followed. "Very well, there is now a chair just behind you. Sit down in the chair."

Chirra looked on from the front row of the center section of the amphitheatre. Below the steps on either side of the stage were

Ivorian cameramen. To Sheena's right stood a Cerulean man who held the reins to a unicorn. The unicorn was beautiful, with a blue body and golden hooves, mane, and tail.

Chief Lamark rose from the front row of spectators and climbed the steps to the stage. A microphone was clipped to the neck of his tunic. He positioned himself to Sheena's left. "It is now my privilege and honor to introduce Sheena of Southern Ivoria," he announced. Then he turned his torso toward Sheena.

"Sheena of Southern Ivoria," Chief Lamark said, speaking loudly enough for all of those in the amphitheatre to hear his voice. "To your right is a citizen from one of the nine original kingdoms of Subterrania. That citizen has with him either a plant or animal that is native to his kingdom. You are permitted to ask that citizen one question at a time in regard to the plant or animal he has with him. When you would like to guess the identity of that plant or animal, you may do so, but if your guess is incorrect, you lose ten points in your overall score. Nod if you understand."

Sheena nodded. "Very well," Chief Lamark continued. "You may not compromise your blindfold at any time, you may not rise from your chair, and you may not move your chair. Please voice your questions so that they may be plainly heard, and I will repeat each question to those in attendance. Once that question is answered by the citizen to your right, then it counts as one question. The competitor that rightly guesses the identity of the plant or animal to your right and who does so after asking the fewest questions wins the Challenge of Wits. Three minutes and twenty seconds of thought are permitted before each question, and I will give you a warning if your remaining time of thought reaches one minute, and I will give you a second and final warning if your remaining time of thought reaches ten seconds. Failure to pose a question prior to three minutes and twenty seconds will be counted as an incorrect guess. You may proceed."

Chirra leaned slightly forward on the stone bench where she sat. Sheena had said nothing about what sort of strategy she would employ in the Challenge of Wits no matter how much Chirra prodded, but she had responded with a cunning smile that spurred Chirra's curiosity. Terrab, who sat to Chirra's right, was in third place in the Challenge of Wits, having identified the unicorn with his first guess after asking six questions. Lorso of Scintillia was in second place with a correct guess after five questions, and Elroth of Chireem was in first place with a correct guess after three questions. If Sheena could somehow win the Challenge of Wits without voicing any incorrect guesses, then Terrab would drop to fourth place in the Challenge of Wits and receive no points, and Sheena would move ten points ahead of him in the overall Challenge of Kingdoms.

Lines of concern creased Chirra's forehead. The only clue given to Sheena was that she had to guess the name of a plant or animal from one of the nine original kingdoms of Subterrania. Some persons viewed Quazaria as a kingdom of Subterrania, but including Quazaria would yield ten kingdoms rather than nine kingdoms, so the question itself excluded Quazaria, and besides that, no Quazarian had ever taken part in the Challenge of Kingdoms. Vandolia and Southern Ivoria comprised what was originally Ivoria, explaining why there were originally nine kingdoms rather than ten kingdoms; and of course, no one from the evil Kingdom of Vandolia was permitted to participate in the Challenge of Kingdoms.

The lines of concern across Chirra's forehead changed to perplexity. Sheena had dropped her face downward and was sitting perfectly still. Time passed. The audience looked on in quiet suspense. Chief Lamark peered down at the time piece on his left wrist and then looked up at the audience as if he were about to speak.

And then, suddenly, as if bursting into existence from an invisible loudspeaker that was suspended above the amphitheatre, a spine-tingling sound pierced the atmosphere. Chief Lamark crumpled to his hands and knees on the stone stage. Chirra's hands caught hold of the bench beneath her and barely prevented her body from toppling over backward. No one had noticed Sheena draw a slow, deep breath. Her masked face rose simultaneously with a bloodcurdling scream.

"Ho, boy!" a terse cry sounded from Sheena's right, a cry mixed with sounds of clopping hooves and vibrant, high-pitched whinnies.

A smile formed across the lips below Sheena's mask, and every eye in the amphitheatre became fixed upon that smile. She drew another breath, and many hands braced themselves on the edges of benches. Chief Lamark, who had risen back to his feet, widened his stance to better his balance. But instead of another scream, there issued from Sheena's lips the low sound of a horse's neigh. She cocked her head to her right. There was no response.

Then Sheena drew another breath, and this time she issued a vivacious whinny in a manner peculiar to unicorns, a whinny she had mastered in a soundproof audio booth in an Ivorian library. A nearly identical whinny sounded back. Again she smiled. Chirra also smiled, and she wiped a tear from beneath one eye. It was obvious that Sheena had solved the riddle.

"I would like to proffer a guess," Sheena said.

There was a pause. Chief Lamark gazed about the audience, and then he scanned his eyes across the faces of the Rules Council, a group of eight men and women who were seated on the first row to his left. There was nothing but smiles and nods from the Rules Council. Then he looked at Sheena and spoke. "There is no rule that prevents a contestant from submitting a guess after asking zero questions."

He turned and glanced back at the council members, almost winking, and then he looked out over the audience and spoke grandiosely. "If you succeed in guessing correctly, Sheena of Southern Ivoria, then it will not merely mean that you win the Challenge of Wits in this Challenge of Kingdoms, which is a great accomplishment in and of itself. It will also mean that you become the very first person in the history of the Challenge of Kingdoms to score a correct guess after asking zero questions. You may give your first guess."

Chief Lamark's proclamation brought gasps of excitement and expectation. Chirra was certain that Sheena knew the correct answer, but she still held her breath.

"I guess that the creature to my right is a unicorn."

Two seconds after the word *unicorn* passed from Sheena's lips, the crowd was on their feet. The applause that followed was the greatest that had taken place during the entire competition. And notably, no one clapped harder or cheered louder than Terrab of Equavere.

"You may remove your blindfold," Chief Lamark proclaimed, having to speak very loudly for his voice to rise above the applause.

Sheena pulled off the blindfold and searched the audience for Chirra, expecting to find her dear friend seated somewhere near the front of the amphitheatre. She smiled and cried and waved as she met eyes with exuberant spectators. And then one brow rose quizzically as she noted that Chirra was seated in her spot—the front, center bench was reserved for the competitors, and Chirra was seated between Terrab and Prince Vordon. She rose from her chair and bowed, and then stepped down from the stage to take a seat.

"We now have a break as the stage is prepared for the final competition," Chief Lamark announced. "Please be back in your seats in thirty minutes. And while the stage is being prepared, music will be provided by the Silkatta Sisters of Scintillia."

Sheena expected Chirra to rise and relinquish her seat as she approached, but instead, it was Terrab who stood up.

"Congratulations, my worthy challenger," Terrab said. "I now finish fourth in this test of intellectual brilliance, which means you are the overall leader by ten points." He smiled at Sheena and tersely bowed.

"Thank you," Sheena replied. She had become acquainted with Terrab while training at the acastoria in Equavere. In fact, he taught several of her martial arts classes.

"Please take my seat so that you and Chirra can visit with one another until I return."

Sheena held Terrab's eyes. All the competitors were good sports and were generally polite, but it was taboo for someone else to sit in a seat that was designated for one of the competitors. "That is most gracious."

Terrab broke eye contact and again bowed, and then he strode briskly away.

Sheena slowly sat down in Terrab's seat while staring at Terrab as he walked toward the front, right tier of stone benches.

"You were wonderful!" Chirra exclaimed, clutching Sheena's arm.

"Thanks," Sheena responded. She glanced at Chirra, but then her eyes returned to Terrab. He was leaning over the first row of benches and talking to the members of the Rules Council. The stadium was alive with chitchat and with the bustling sounds of attendees rushing to the toilet or going after food and drink, so Sheena was not able to hear what Terrab was saying. But whatever he was saying, it was obvious that he had captured the full attention of the council members.

"Did you know that two of the Silkatta sisters really are sisters?" Chirra asked.

"Yes," Sheena replied. She looked up at the stage where several Scintillian musicians were positioning small chairs in a semicircle and sitting down. Each held a musical instrument. Some of the instruments were stringed and were played with bows, while other instruments were equipped with reeds or mouthpieces. The musicians were both male and female. Four women entered from stage left just as the musicians finished sitting.

Sheena commented further, "Learla and Mofetsa are not only siblings, they're bona fide descendants of the original Silkatta sisters."

"Oh, so you must be familiar with this group," Chirra remarked. She made no comment about a large metallic device that was being hauled onto the stage by several Arulian attendants. The device consisted of a rectangular, metallic base about three feet wide and fifteen feet long, with a silver metallic cylinder rising to a height of approximately four feet at one end of the base.

"Very much so. My mother listens to their music almost every day," Sheena said, still speaking to Chirra but looking back at Terrab. "Hey, look, it's Charftan Elkondro and Charftan Arstro," she noted. "They're with Terrab. And there goes Chief Lamark. They're talking." She turned her face back to Chirra. "Why would the Charftan of Arulia, the Charftan of Equavere, the champion of Equavere, the Rules Council, and Chief Lamark all be talking with one another?"

A sheepish expression came to Chirra's face. She gave no verbal response.

"What is it? You know something, I can tell," Sheena coaxed.

Chirra's face cleared. "It has something to do with the rules governing the strength competition," she sputtered while proffering a seemingly naïve shrug. Then she looked back to the stage. "Oh my, look at the outfits."

Sheena followed Chirra's gaze to the forefront of the stage. The four female singers were lined up before the musicians. They stood about four and a half feet tall with white skin and golden hair, much like Ivorians in appearance but of smaller stature. A great blue flower with large petals was fixed to one side of each of their heads, secured by a silver brooch that complemented a silver satin tunic. Broad blue sashes were tied about their waists, perfectly matching the color of the flowers in their hair, the moccasins on their feet, and the irises of their eyes.

"You say it has something to do with rules?" Sheena posed, starting to look back at Chirra, but then the music and singing commenced. Both girls turned their faces forward and fell silent.

The Silkatta Sisters were equipped with silver Ivorian microphones that were barely visible on the fronts of their tunics, but the sounds of their voices poured over the entire amphitheatre. Sheena loved music. She was an accomplished soprano vocalist, but she could not sing like one of the Silkatta Sisters. In fact, no other race above or below the surface of the earth could match the beautiful tones of Scintillian singers. Many of the Subterranians that repeatedly journeyed to the Challenge of Kingdoms every seven years did so mostly for the entertainment that was provided between events and after the events were concluded.

The Scintillian ensemble moved from one musical piece to another so rapidly that Sheena had no opportunity to ask Chirra additional questions. As the music continued, her mind wandered to thoughts of her mother and to recollections of her upbringing. She had been blessed with a wonderful and happy childhood, despite the unusual environment of her household and her mother's mental handicap. Recordings produced by the same singers and musicians who performed before her eyes had often pervaded the rooms of the quaint cottage where she grew to womanhood. She gave little regard to the metallic apparatus that the Arulian attendants had finished positioning in the center of the stage. The base of the apparatus stretched from left to right before the audience, with the metallic cylinder rising from the far right end of the base.

Then the music stopped, and applause filled the atmosphere. Everyone stood, clapping and cheering. The musicians and singers bowed and exited the stage.

"You're fifty points ahead of third place," Chirra said as she leaned and gave Sheena a hug. "It's between you and Terrab now. Enjoy yourself. And may the Creator be with you always."

"Thanks, and may the Creator be with you," Sheena said. She remained standing, gazing inquisitively as Chirra walked away. There was something odd about Chirra's speech and demeanor. Then Terrab appeared. The two of them switched places so that they were standing in front of their appropriate seats. He smiled and nodded, peering into Sheena's eyes.

"Dr. Azora is right," Terrab stated. "You have your father's eyes."

For several seconds, Sheena just stood and stared back into Terrab's eyes in startled silence. "You knew my father?"

"Yes."

She shook her head in puzzled inquest. "Then why—"

Chief Lamark's voice sounded out loudly, interrupting Sheena's inquiry. "Would those who are not yet seated please take your seats. The final competition is about to begin."

The crowd grew quiet. Terrab leaned and spoke into Sheena's ear. "I'll speak with you after," he said, and then he sat down.

Sheena sat down also. She glanced upon Terrab's profile with bewildered curiosity, and then she joined him in facing ahead at Chief Lamark.

"The machine you see behind me is called a quadrospool," Chief Lamark announced. "Before our first contestant takes the stage, Irkmon of Equavere will come forward and explain how the machine operates."

Chief Lamark moved to one side as Irkmon stepped up onto the platform. Irkmon walked to the end of the machine where the cylinder rose from the base and placed one hand on top of the cylinder as he faced the audience. A silver thread encircled his neck with a small cartridge suspended upon his chest—an Ivorian microphone. There was little clothing for attaching the microphone since, like Terrab, all he wore was a loincloth. He was shorter and squatter than Terrab, with longer hair, and although all Equaverians were known to be strong, Irkmon appeared to be exceptionally strong.

"The quadrospool was invented at the acastoria in Equavere," Irkmon commenced. His voice was deep and gruff, yet friendly. "This particular quadrospool is sensitive enough to measure the strength of little girls from Scintillia and tough enough to measure the strength of grown men from Equavere." He paused long enough to pat the upper surface of the cylinder. "A dial on the face of this pillar records how much force is wielded on a rope of woven steel that winds around a spring-loaded drum within this pillar. The spring is strong enough to withstand the pull of a berquhor, namely one of the giant-horned reptiles that roam the deserts of Draskar." Again he paused, this time leaning forward and grasping a metal bar wrapped in crisscrossing strands of leather, a bar that hung against the upper, inner surface of the cylinder.

"This bar is attached to the steel rope," Irkmon said. He released the bar and then rose and pointed to the rectangular base. "A competitor must stand upon the metal band. He or she then grasps the bar and braces his or her feet against the surface of the metal band. Fifteen seconds are then allotted for the contestant to pull back on the handle with as great a force as he or she can muster, and time will be kept by Evera of Arulia. No shoes or gloves are permitted, and the competitor may not apply any powder, cream, or anything else to his or her hands or feet. If the competitor touches the floor outside the border of the metal band, then his or her turn ends immediately, even if fewer than fifteen seconds have elapsed."

Irkmon then nodded to Chief Lamark and exited the stage. Chief Lamark took Irkmon's cue and walked to the center of the stage. He glanced at Sheena long enough for her to meet his eyes and then looked out over the crowd. Sheena sensed something.

"Before our first contestant comes to the stage, that is to say Kwitz of Draskar, I need to make a further announcement in regard to this event," Chief Lamark said. He did not look at Sheena again, and she had the impression that he was purposely avoiding her inquisitive stare. "The metal band upon which the competitors stand has been roughened to give more traction for the soles of the competitors' feet. If desired, a competitor may choose to have this roughened surface covered with bachawa leaves."

Sheena's face was not the only face that evinced puzzlement. An outbreak of curious gossip stirred the spectators.

"It is now my privilege and honor to call upon Kwitz of Draskar," Chief Lamark proclaimed, and then he stepped down from the stage and took a seat on the right front row of the amphitheatre.

Kwitz rose from his position to Sheena's left and headed for the stage. He was the shortest of the competitors at four feet and ten inches in height, but his talent, strength, and agility were sufficient for him to begin the last event in third place. He had shoulder-length black hair and crimson skin, and he was the only contestant who wore a beard and moustache.

Sheena leaned toward Terrab and positioned her lips near his ear. "Why would anyone want bachawa leaves beneath their feet? Aren't those the kind of leaves we used at the acastoria to cover the floor in order to simulate fighting on a slick surface such as wet stone coated with algae?"

Terrab answered without facing Sheena. He kept his eyes on Kwitz. "I advise against your choosing the leaves. The surface of the metal band is not very painful to the feet, even though it has been roughened, and as you can see, Kwitz is not choosing the leaves. There is no reason why a woman's feet cannot withstand the same surface as the feet of men."

Sheena leaned back and looked up at Kwitz. An expression of defiance took form upon her countenance: if the Rules Council thought that they needed to cover a metal surface with leaves just because a woman was on the roster, then they needed to do some rethinking. She dropped her face and brewed over the matter for a few moments, and then she drew a breath and looked back up at Kwitz. Apart from the fact that she was assigned to take the last turn in each event—a courtesy that she endured for the sake of honoring male chivalry—she had been treated equally and fairly in each of the preceding events. All that she would have to do in order to end the competition in the same vogue would be to decline the leaves. She rested her mind on the matter and focused on the scene before her.

Sheena observed that Kwitz's rough garment barely passed as a tunic. A wide strip of animal hide hung over one shoulder and suspended a sort of skirt that hung to his midthighs. The garb was secured around his waist by a second strip of hide. Without a doubt, he was the most muscular-appearing of the contestants. He positioned himself on the metal band and took hold of the metal bar, and then he nodded toward Evera, who was seated beside Chief Lamark.

Evera stood and walked to the edge of the stage carrying a glass sandtimer. She held the timer over the front lip of the stage with the sand in the bottom compartment. "Make ready!" she called out. It was obvious that she wore a microphone. "Go!" she shouted as she inverted the timer and set it on the stage.

Grunting sounds issued from Kwitz's throat as he pulled backward.

"Amazing," Terrab spoke.

Sheena glanced at Terrab's face and then looked back at Kwitz. She knew that Terrab could defeat anyone who was not Equaverian, and she surmised that Terrab was impressed by Kwitz's strength in consideration of the fact that Kwitz was a member of a different race. Muscles bulged beneath the crimson skin of Kwitz's arms, legs, and thighs. He drew the metal rope more than half the length of the metal band, and then his body was drawn back toward the cylinder.

"Stop!" Evera cried.

Chief Lamark and Irkmon, who were sitting next to one another, both arose and stepped up onto the stage. Kwitz permitted his body to be pulled back to the cylinder and then he released the bar. He stepped off the metal band and faced the crowd as Chief Lamark and Irkmon both examined the dial on top of the cylinder. The two of them whispered to one another, and then Chief Lamark stepped forward to address the crowd.

"Kwitz of Draskar has just achieved the highest score of any competitor, apart from an Equaverian, in all the history of the Challenge of Kingdoms," Chief Lamark announced. He then had to wait until applause subsided before announcing Kwitz's score. "The score is eight feet, nine inches, and thirteen sixty-fourths of an inch."

Sheena could not help but note how white Kwitz's teeth appeared in contrast to his crimson lips as he cast the audience an exuberant smile. Additional applause continued for almost a minute.

"It is my privilege and honor to call upon Rark of Chatazia to compete next," Chief Lamark's voice sounded.

Kwitz, Chief Lamark, and Irkmon exited the stage as Rark made his way to the quardrospool. The process of competing on the quardrospool then repeated itself several times. First there was Rark of Chatazia, then Xarron of Cerulea, then Prince Vordon of Urmoonda, then Lorso of Scintillia, then Elroth of Chireem, and then Horado of Arulia. There was applause after each contender, and each contender seemed to be pleased with his individual effort. None of the contenders requested that the metal band be covered with bachawa leaves.

Sheena's mind wandered while watching the others compete on the quardrospool. At times she found herself contemplating how it was that Terrab had known her father and what Terrab might be able to tell her about her father, and at other times she discovered herself pondering over all the events that had taken place during the Challenge of Kingdoms. She was trying to conjure up a plan on how to best train so that she could defeat Terrab at the next Challenge of Kingdoms. Champions who won the Challenge of Kingdoms were permitted to participate again until winning the competition three times, and then, after three victories, they were retired from the competition and their names were entered on a special plaque featured in the Hall of Memories, a renowned museum in Urmoonda. This would be

Terrab's second time to win the competition. If nothing else, she figured that she might be able to win the Challenge of Kingdoms in fourteen years, after Terrab had won three times and was no longer eligible.

As usual, the applause that came after Chief Lamark announced Horado's score was extensive. Then there was more applause when Chief Lamark announced that Kwitz remained in the lead with Prince Vordon second and Rark third. When the noise of applause subsided, Chief Lamark spoke again. "And now it is my privilege and honor to call upon Terrab of Equavere to compete," he said, and then he exited the stage.

Cheers rose as Terrab stood. Terrab hesitated and then turned back around and leaned over to speak into Sheena's ear. "Ten more points would give you a score that ties the highest score ever achieved in the Challenge of Kingdoms. You have powerful thighs and legs, and I think you have a good chance to defeat all of the others apart from Kwitz and Prince Vordon. And remember what I taught you back at the acastoria—a good sport should give his or her best effort." He then turned and strode away before Sheena had any chance to respond.

Sheena was discombobulated for several seconds, staring at Terrab as he stepped up onto the stage. But then the obvious explanation for Terrab's words dawned within her mind. Several factors fit together: first was the fact that Chirra was seated beside Terrab, second was Chirra's odd speech and behavior, third was Terrab's conversing with the Rules Council, and last was Terrab's comment about her eyes. She continued staring at Terrab as he took a position before the quadrospool. She deduced that Chirra divulged her plan to take her father's place and explained to Terrab that she would have to win the Challenge of Kingdoms in order to be permitted to do so, and she deduced that Terrab decided to grant her the opportunity to fulfill her ambition. She soon learned that she was right.

"I choose to have the metal band covered with bachawa leaves," Terrab proclaimed.

Sheena's heart began throbbing against the inner wall of her chest. Terrab's strategy was obvious. He wanted to lose the event, yet he did not want to break his own advice about giving one's best effort. With an official rule that permitted bachawa leaves to be placed on the surface of the metal band, he could give his very best effort and still lose. And if he lost, then her mother's impending death would open the gateway for her to journey to the surface of the earth.

Three Arulian attendants, two male and one female, appeared from a dressing room. Each of the attendants carried a bucket that was heaped full of leaves, leaves gathered from bachawa trees that grew outside the amphitheatre. They worked together, scattering glistening silver leaves on the surface of the metal band. The leaves were rounded, with a small point opposite the stem; and they were large, about the size of a man's open hand. When the end of the metal band nearest the cylinder was covered with leaves, the attendants stood along the opposite side of the quardrospool from the audience, still holding their buckets. And then Terrab mounted the quardrospool and took hold of the bar.

"Ready," Terrab spoke with force. He needed no Ivorian microphone for his voice to carry to the farthest row of the amphitheatre.

Evera came forward with the sand timer. "Go!"

Terrab's body tensed, and both legs shot upward into the air. He plopped down onto his buttocks and then rose instantly with two attendants tossing more leaves onto the metal band where he was attempting to stand. A few giggles and chortles broke out among the crowd, and many more observers held their breaths to restrain laughter. Then Terrab ran backward for several steps without moving more than a foot: leaves flew up over the cylinder, and the attendants frantically flung more leaves beneath his feet. And then came a fall that would immortalize Terrab in the chronicles of the Challenge of Kingdoms thereafter, a fall that featured a backward flip followed by a sprawled-out belly-flop onto the metal band.

A virtual explosion of laughter erupted. The entire amphitheatre succumbed to hilarity. Members of the Rules Council looked at one another, laughing and nodding. They had been nervous about permitting bachawa leaves to be used in the quardrospool competition, but such well-received entertainment as that performed by Terrab could only boost the popularity of the Challenge of Kingdoms.

"Stop!" Eva hailed.

Terrab's right foot had come down just outside the edge of the metal band, thereby disqualifying him from any further efforts. He released the bar and rolled to a sitting position, facing the crowd and laughing along with them. Sheena both laughed and cried. She wiped trickling tears from her cheeks. The additional years of training that she had been contemplating would no longer be required: she was winner of the Challenge of Kingdoms.

The Arulian attendants began scooping up leaves and returning them to the buckets while Irkmon and Chief Lamark examined the dial atop the quardrospool. Then Terrab stood to his feet as Chief Lamark stepped up beside him.

"The champion of Equavere," Chief Lamark began, and then he yielded to further laughter, sparking additional laughter in the audience. Finally he choked down his mirth and managed to speak. "The champion of Equavere and previous winner of the Challenge of Kingdoms has scored four feet, seven inches, and forty-nine sixty-fourths of an inch, putting him in eighth place in the quardrospool competition."

Terrab bowed to hearty applause and then stepped down from the stage. Before sitting in his designated spot on the front row, he permitted Sheena a hug. She released her arms and gazed into his eyes. There were no words spoken between them: Sheena could never have found mere words to convey her appreciation for Terrab's unselfish gift, but her eyes bore heartfelt thanks. Her father's mission was now her own.

Chapter 3

"You did not have to request bachawa leaves just because I did," Terrab remarked. "You could have tied the highest score ever achieved if you had not asked for the leaves."

Terrab sat beside Sheena in a small recess in the face of a cliff. Below lay a gorge that featured a pristine river coursing through lush forest vegetation. The atmosphere carried fresh botanical fragrances following a recent rain.

Sheena shifted positions but gave no reply. The recess where she sat with Terrab was a hideaway that Chirra and Sheena had discovered while rock climbing several years before, and it was a perfect location to get away from the nearby village of Muelta and carry out a confidential conversation. The final ceremony in the Challenge of Kingdoms, a ceremony to commemorate the winners of various events and to honor the overall champion, was due to take place the following day. Six days of festivity had already passed—days filled with music, cinema, drama, art exhibits, feasts, and dancing—and one of the favorite cinema presentations was a film that featured Sheena riding Whiplash.

Terrab waited for Sheena to respond. Sheena had asked him about her father following the competition on the quadrospool, but he had requested that she grant him some time to meditate and refresh his memory before sharing information about her father. Sheena consented. After what Terrab sacrificed on her behalf, she was more than willing to temporarily harness her curiosity. Now, as she sat beside him in the spot where she and Chirra had chatted in confidence in years past, it seemed likely that she would engage in a conversation that would transform the nook in the cliff into a hallowed site of memorable revelation.

"So what?" Sheena finally rebutted. "You could have topped the highest score ever achieved if you had not asked for the leaves. I gave it my best effort, and only one male had to endure being beaten by a female on the quadrospool, a male who could have easily won the event and the entire competition."

Terrab chuckled. "It was clever of you to hold the bar behind your back and run forward. I could not help but laugh at how frazzled the attendants became while they were trying to keep bachawa leaves beneath your feet, and I think Elroth was almost sweating—you came within three inches of matching his score."

"I gave it my best effort, and I'm glad that I did not embarrass Elroth," Sheena stated. "I was given what I desired before I began my turn on the quadrospool. Again I thank you. With all my heart, I thank you."

"You earned your victory," Terrab retorted. "You were ahead of me when we came to the last event, and then you beat me at that event. And besides, you had to defeat the champions from seven other kingdoms in order to win."

Sheena accepted Terrab's declaration in silence. She gazed out over the beautiful gorge, wondering whether or not her father had ever visited Arulia and had looked upon the same scenery. She dropped her face downward upon the deep blue fabric of the tunic that enfolded her knees: her mother was fond of acquiring apparel that matched her eyes.

Terrab sensed Sheena's altered mood. "So then, I guess you want to know why I never mentioned your father."

"Yes," Sheena said. She spoke without looking up.

"I did it out of respect for your mother."

Sheena raised her face and met Terrab's eyes. "My mother?"

Terrab nodded. "Yes, your mother. Dr. Azora and I were standing together after your father's ceremonial funeral, still at the cemetery site, and your mother approached us."

"Funeral? I thought he was slain on the earth's surface and that his body was destroyed by his murderers."

"True enough, but there was a funeral nonetheless. A monument was raised in his honor in the cemetery near the Palace Museum on Lake Ultreelle."

"The Palace Museum?" Sheena's voice carried a tone of incited curiosity. "Mother forbade my venturing anywhere near that museum."

"I am not surprised by that," Terrab said. His lips parted to speak something further, but then he faltered, seeming to change his mind. When he spoke next, Sheena was left with the impression that he left something important unsaid. "Your father's monument is near the tombs of Chief Zake and Chief Alania, two of the greatest military leaders that Subterrania has ever known."

A look of intrigue beset Sheena's countenance. "I've read much about Chief Zake, and I've read even more about Chief Alania—the second Shareesha the Tiger Queen. She was also Princess Alania, a title she carried with her from the earth's surface. It is reported that she wielded a sword better than any other human being who ever lived, male or female."

"I have no doubt of that," Terrab affirmed. "And she was a lovely person and the perfect hostess."

Sheena reflected upon the fact that Equaverians live much longer than the descendents of migrant outlanders and that Terrab had lived during the era of Chief Zake and Chief Alania. Then a wrinkle creased her brow. "Why didn't Dr. Azora tell me about my father's funeral?"

Terrab hesitated before replying. "Dr. Azora has answered every question you have asked him about your father," he stated flatly. "That was his agreement."

"Agreement?"

"Yes. Your mother was carrying you in her arms when she approached us after the funeral. Your hair was as red then as it is now."

"And my mother made some sort of agreement with Dr. Azora?"

Terrab broke eye contact and gazed outward. He looked back at Sheena before answering. "It was obvious that your mother suffered tremendous grief. She was not as she is now. She was sane, but her sanity bore the burden of an anguished heart." He stopped speaking long enough to capture the full regard of Sheena's eyes. "She asked both of us to agree that we would never mention your father to you or anything about our ventures with your father upon the earth's surface."

A panged look captured Sheena's visage. Her stomach tightened. "So you both worked with my father, and my mother did not want you to mention him? Why? Mother loved Father."

Terrab read Sheena's expression. He raised an open palm and shook his head. "No, do not misinterpret my words." He dropped his hand. The sincerity in his eyes deepened. "Beyond all doubt, your mother bore immeasurable love for your father. Her impassioned love for her husband may have been as great as any woman has ever held for any man in all the history of mankind."

Sheena absorbed Terrab's words and drew the veracity of his proclamation from his eyes. Her stomach eased. "Then why did she say that? Why did she ask you not to mention my father?"

Again, Terrab shook his head. "The Creator is greater than any evil that plagues the earth. But He has granted, for a time, that the kingdoms of this earth and the citizens of those kingdoms may serve what gods they will, whether the true God who grants eternal life or a false god who devours the soul. We are in the midst of a great battle between good and evil that reaches both above and below the earth's surface, and your mother and father wholeheartedly engaged themselves in the battle against evil upon the earth's surface."

Sheena continued to address Terrab with questioning eyes. She nodded for him to continue.

"I think it was your eyes that gave your mother such great fear that you would become a warrior and rise to battle in your father's stead," Terrab said.

"My eyes?"

"Yes. Your eyes have the exact shape and color of your father's eyes, apart from the red lashes that enframe them. And when I gaze into your eyes, I sense the same indomitable resolve that I sensed in past times when I gazed into your father's eyes. There was much ado in Quazaria, though it was little known on this side of the Dimensional Chasm, about the flaming hair and steel blue eyes of a baby girl who was conceived in Quazaria and who was not of the Quazarian race. There have only been two human beings who, for a time, were carried inside their mother's wombs within the world of Quazaria and who were not of the Quazarian race. The first such child was born there."

Sheena's mouth dropped open. "Quazaria? My mother lived in Quazaria while she was pregnant?"

"Yes."

"So my father lived there too?"

"Yes."

"And you say only two pregnant women from outside Quazaria have ever lived there? Only two?" Sheena dropped her face in thought for a while and then peered back into Terrab's eyes. "So that's why my parents named me Sheena. There have only been two foreigners carried within their mothers' wombs within the realm of Quazaria, and I was the second one."

"That is correct. The first Sheena was the daughter of Shareesha, namely the Shareesha who befriended Gwarzon the Tiger and became the original Shareesha the Tiger Queen."

"Yes, I know." The look on Sheena's face evinced a thousand questions, questions that whirled within her mind without taking expressible substance. Then she settled her thoughts sufficiently to evoke an inquiry. "So did Dr. Azora agree to my mother's request?"

"To an extent."

"An extent?"

"Yes. He said that, until you revealed that you had discovered your father's identity, he would only answer specific questions that you asked about your father."

Sheena's eyes regarded Terrab from beneath puzzled brows. She pondered his words for several seconds and then responded, "But that doesn't make sense. How could I ask specific questions about my father if I did not even know my father's identity? I discovered my father's identity before I asked Dr. Azora anything about him."

"Did you?" Terrab posed. "Dr. Azora has confided with me over the years. He says that you have asked many specific questions about your father, and he says that he has answered all of those questions."

Terrab's words further puzzled Sheena. She shrugged and shook her head. "It is true that Dr. Azora has answered many questions about my father, but he only did so after I found him and told him about the obituary I read in the school library when I was ten years old. Like I said, I discovered my father's identity before asking Dr. Azora anything."

Up to that point in the conversation, Terrab and Sheena had looked back and forth between the fascinating scenery and one another's eyes as they conversed, but now Terrab set his eyes solely upon Sheena's face. "So then, do you really think that you discovered your father's identity?" he asked.

"Yes, Henry Borden," answered Sheena; but Terrab's demeanor and steady gaze brewed a sensation of uncertainty within the pit of her abdomen.

"And your mother's name is Mary Borden?"

"Yes," she answered weakly.

Terrab dropped his eyes downward. This further disconcerted Sheena. She had lived in Equavere for many years while training in martial arts, and she knew the Equaverian people to be forthright and decisive. She had rarely seen a member of the green race embroiled in contemplative silence during the course of a conversation.

Terrab raised his eyes. "My response to your mother was different than that of Dr. Azora. I simply told her that I would honor her words."

"You mean at the funeral?"

"Yes."

"So that's why you've never mentioned my father?"

"That is why."

Sheena tilted her head inquisitively. "Why are you talking to me about my father now? Why did you tell me that I have my father's eyes?"

"I am talking with you now because another person has wooed my honor. A young woman has worked long and hard for many years to earn the right to wage warfare in her father's stead, and that woman has persuaded my heart."

Sheena felt a quickening throb within her chest. "Very well then, why do you make me feel doubtful about my own identity? Am I not the daughter of Henry Borden and Mary Borden?"

"Well, yes and no."

"You mean I'm adopted? Was it another woman who carried me in her womb in Quazaria?"

Terrab shook his head. "No." Then Terrab again dropped his eyes.

"What is it?" Sheena urged.

When Terrab next raised his eyes, he bore a look of irreversible resolve. "Your father is Justin Collins, and your mother is Rachel Collins."

Sheena stared at Terrab's face. "Justin Collins?" Her face became drawn in contemplation. "The name sounds familiar. Should I know him? Why did the obituary say his name is Henry Borden?"

"Have you never studied the history of Quazaria? I thought you had a special interest in Quazarian warriors."

Rachel's face appeared perplexed for a moment, but then her eyes went wide. She brought a hand to her breast and gasped. "No, it cannot be," she uttered. Her voice seemed the verbal embodiment of incredulity. She turned her eyes away and cast her gaze toward the gorge below them without focusing on anything.

"Can it not? Think back to your father's picture in the obituary," Terrab said, addressing Sheena with steadied patience. "Did he not have a bandana wrapped around his forehead? And what about all of those pictures of your father that your mother has hanging on the walls of your home? Do any of those pictures reveal the vermaskian cylinders that were implanted across his forehead, or is his forehead always hidden?"

Sheena's breast rose and fell. It seemed apparent to Terrab that she was hyperventilating. She looked back toward him with desperation in her eyes. Her face presented an image of sheer shock. When she spoke next, her voice quivered. "Is my name really Sheena?" she asked. She was obviously on the verge of crying.

Compassion creased the green skin at the corners of Terrab's eyes. "Yes. You were named after both the daughter of the first Shareesha the Tiger Queen and after your own mother. Your name is Sheena Rachel Collins."

Sheena sat in silence, wooing Terrab for more information with the earnest of her eyes.

Terrab succumbed to Sheena's eyes. "When your family moved from Quazaria to Southern Ivoria, your parents decided to assume new identities rather than deal with the hullabaloo that would accompany the known presence of a Quazarian warrior.

They claimed to be migrants from the earth's surface, which was true, and they claimed to have aided Dr. Azora on the earth's surface, which was also true."

Sheena dropped her face into open palms and broke out sobbing. "So my father was shot in the back without warning, along with Chad and Ouana," she choked between sobs, reciting facts that she had learned during studies of Quazarian history. She spoke without raising her face from her hands.

"Yes. In one fatal ambush, perpetrators of an evil plot took the lives of all three Quazarian warriors who had not taken the Quazarian Vow—the only Quazarian warriors free to wage warfare outside the world of Quazaria," Terrab expounded. "And to this point in time, the void that was left behind when those warriors were slain has never been filled."

"And my father was the only Quazarian warrior in all of history who was not a member of the Quazarian race," Sheena asserted, still sobbing with her face cradled in her hands. "He is one of the most wonderful men who ever lived, and I never even got to meet him, not when I was old enough to remember. And I've lived all of these years without even knowing who he is."

Terrab gave no response to Sheena's proclamation. He turned his face to the Arulian landscape and let her weep. His heart was pierced by cries that bore the grief of a fatherless childhood and by wails that bemoaned the murderous cause of a mother's broken health. He marveled that such a tenderhearted young woman could become champion of the Challenge of Kingdoms. At last her crying abated. He turned his eyes upon curtains of red hair that shrouded a mourning woman's hands and face.

With her head still bowed, Sheena lifted a fold of her tunic and dabbed tearstained cheeks. Then she straightened and faced Terrab. When she spoke, her voice was composed. "In my studies of the United States of America, I came to suspect that my father, who I knew as Henry Borden, was murdered by some renegade villain who was commissioned by the United States government.

But now, since you have informed me that my father is in truth Justin Collins, I no longer consider the role that the United States government played in my father's murder to be merely a suspicion. From what I have learned, it is well established that the government of the United States of America was responsible for the murders of Justin Collins, Chad of Quazaria, and Ouana of Quazaria."

Terrab marveled at Sheena's self-possession. "That is correct," he said. "But you must understand that the government of the United States of America is complicated and fluctuating. There have been both good men and evil men in that government throughout most of its history."

"And in my studies regarding Quazarian warriors," Sheena recommenced, "I learned that Rachel McMurray, who would later be Rachel Collins, was rescued from a high-security prison. She was rescued by the same three Quazarian warriors who would later return to the earth's surface and be slain."

"That is correct. She was liberated from Brockman Penitentiary," Terrab confirmed. "And to my knowledge, Brockman Penitentiary still exists. It's a prison of sorts, a place to stash away political dissidents who pose genuine threats to the government's order of business."

"And the threat my mother posed was that she knew too much, right?"

"Yes. She once sat in a living room where a woman named Marie Collins disclosed information about an air pollutant that wreaks devastating illness upon the inhabitants of the earth's surface."

Sheena faced Terrab for several seconds before responding. Her jaw tensed. "I have studied all that is known about Marie Collins and about her husband, who was murdered, and about her son who I now know to be my father." She paused and drew a breath. "So then, Marie Collins is my grandmother."

"Yes."

Sheena resumed speaking. "And I have studied all aspects of the environmental pollutant discovered by Dr. Henry Collins and about its effects upon human health. Dr. Azora aided my education in all of these matters, and he did so in confidence, respectful of my mother's mental frailty."

Terrab nodded. "I know."

"You both knew," Sheena blurted. Her voice became impassioned. "You both knew who I am and why I studied and trained with such earnest and what I someday hope to accomplish. And all of this time, you have permitted me to believe that my father is Henry Borden and that my own name is Sheena Borden."

There were several tense moments of silence, and then Terrab looked steadily into Sheena's eyes. "We wanted to wait until you were ready to know yourself."

Sheena stared back. She and Terrab continued gazing into one another's eyes. "So am I ready?"

"We both believe so."

Another period of silence lapsed. "Very well. I can believe that I am almost ready," Sheena averred. Her expression changed. "I will meet with Dr. Azora when I return to Southern Ivoria, but there are a couple of questions that I hope you can answer for me now."

"I will answer if I can," Terrab said.

"Did my mother identify herself as the wife of Justin Collins when she attended his memorial service?"

Terrab hesitated. "No. She shed many tears, but she maintained the identity that she assumed when your family moved to your present home."

"And the only name on my father's memorial is Justin Collins?"

"No. The inscription on the memorial stone states that Justin Collins is survived by his wife, Rachel Collins, and his daughter, Sheena Collins."

"Sheena Collins," Sheena reiterated. "That's why Mother didn't want me to visit the museum."

"I would think so. Sheena is a rare name in Southern Ivoria. It is more common in Quazaria. Your mother was probably fearful that the memorial stone would lead you to consider the possibility that Henry Borden and Justin Collins are one and the same."

"And she was fearful that I would take up my father's cause on the earth's surface if I found out that I am the daughter of Justin Collins."

"I believe that is true, but I believe she was fearful of your rising up in your father's stead for other reasons."

"Because of my eyes?"

"I think that's part of if."

"What else—" Sheena began, but then she stopped short. Startled expressions came to both Terrab's and Sheena's faces.

"It's Chirra," Sheena said.

A faint cry carried over the edge of the cliff and into the canyon: "Sheena! Sheena!"

Sheena cupped her hands to her mouth. "We're here!" she shouted out. Then she and Terrab climbed back up the face of the cliff and met Chirra.

"What is it?" asked Sheena.

Chirra was breathing hard. She wore an anxious expression. "It's your mother," she said.

Sheena gasped. "She's dying?"

"Yes. A man named Sir Barnwald is here. He's at the south entrance to the amphitheatre. He brought your horse."

Sheena turned to Terrab. "Sir Barnwald is our nearest neighbor. I must go." She glanced at Chirra and then looked back at Terrab. "Will you ask the Rules Council to let Chirra stand in my place at the awards ceremony?"

Terrab faced Chirra, who nodded, and then addressed Sheena. "Of course. May the Creator be with you."

"And with you," Sheena returned.

"Yes. And you should have seen his face when I thanked him."

Sheena's brows rose. The mother she had known for so many years would have done anything but thank Charftan Yarzon for presenting a way for her daughter to venture to the earth's surface. "You thanked him?"

Rachel nodded as her face assumed a deeply serious mien. "Yes, and I can explain that." She broke eye contact with Sheena and peered aimlessly downward. Then she raised her eyes with an expression of uninhibited intimacy. "Many years ago, when you were only months old, I felt my heart weakening after learning of your father's death. I sensed that I was dying. I would have welcomed the transfer of my spirit to a better and eternal realm where I could once again be with my husband, except for one thing—my infant daughter. I was determined to complete my role as a mother until that daughter was grown."

The underlying message in her mother's words troubled Sheena's heart. "I've still got a lot of growing to do, Mother, and you're so young."

A lighthearted laugh took Sheena by surprise. "Young? To the contrary, no one who I ever knew upon the earth's surface would still be alive if I returned to the home of my youth. Even the children of the children who I knew would have died of old age. No, my dear, I do not count living to one hundred and seventy-seven years of age as being young."

"But I'm still here, Mother," Sheena pled.

"All the more reason for me to let nature take its course. All the more reason to let my broken heart free my spirit." Rachel again clasped Sheena's wrist. She peered more deeply into Sheena's eyes. "You are a grown, mature, and wise young woman. I have long believed that the Creator has chosen you for a special mission, even if I have suppressed cognizance of that belief beneath a cloak of mental infirmity. My insanity was real enough, but it was something I willfully chose. I chose insanity in order to quell the anguish of my broken heart and preserve my physical existence until you reached womanhood."

Sheena delved into her mother's thoughtful eyes, eyes that evinced no hint of mental imbalance. "You believe the Creator has chosen me for a special mission?"

At first, Rachel's only response was a knowing smile. "Don't you?"

Sheena and Rachel studied one another's eyes and expressions. "Yes."

Rachel gave a slow nod. "I have no doubt of it. And there are a few things I want to make sure you know before you set out on a quest to the surface of the earth. I have fought hard these past few hours to sustain my mortal existence long enough to look upon my daughter through sane eyes and to speak with her."

Sheena began shaking her head and opened her mouth to speak.

"No," Rachel interrupted, releasing Sheena's wrist and raising an open palm that halted Sheena's speech. As she placed her hand back down on the bed, her face became more sober than Sheena had ever before witnessed. "My heart beats through willful and wakeful effort. When I next close my mortal eyes to sleep, I do not think that I will open them again. Please permit me, now that I am myself, to converse with you this one time."

Her mother's petition touched Sheena's heart. She made no verbal reply. Tears, a smile, and a nod bid Rachel to continue.

"No doubt you have learned how Justin Collins brought invaluable information to the inhabitants of the earth's surface, doing so while suspended in midair beneath a Quazarian spacecraft."

"Yes, I have," Sheena replied. "But the government of the United States of America generated propaganda claiming that the event was a hoax and that the information given was erroneous."

A troubled look captured Rachel's visage. "Yes. It was uncanny how easily the government of my homeland manipulated the cluster of moons. Sheena sat at the south side of the table with Dr. Azora to her right and Charftan Yarzon to her left.

Mere hours had passed since the memorial service conducted in tribute to Rachel Faith Collins. There were no attempts to withhold her identity. The funeral was eloquent, with Scintillian music and with commemorative dialogues from Sheena, Verma, Treshonda, Dr. Azora, Terrab, Golchuron of Quazaria, and Charftan Yarzon. Rachel's body was buried beside the memorial tomb of her husband, Sheena's father, Henry Justin Collins. Sheena had slept once during preparations for the funeral. She was quartered in the museum, in the bedroom that had once been occupied by Shaquina, the daughter of Chief Zake and Chief Alania.

There were five other persons seated at the table in addition to Sheena, Dr. Azora, and Yarzon. These included Golchuron of Quazaria, Terrab of Equavere, Charftan Zimstar of Scintillia, Charftan Nukeel of Cerulea, and a Southern Ivorian spy named Leah, who brought information into Subterrania from the surface of the earth. The purpose of the meeting was to arrange and coordinate specific details for Sheena's mission, the mission to bring relief to untold masses of suffering human beings on the surface of the earth. Sheena did not want to delay her departure. She had trained and studied in preparation for this mission for well over a hundred years.

The group was in the midst of discussion, with Dr. Azora addressing the others.

"The airborne poison acts as a hapten," Dr. Azora explained, "adding a carbon and nitrogen to native bodily proteins and triggering a host of autoimmune diseases, including fibromyalgia. The type of autoimmune disease that is triggered can vary from one person to another, and some persons may be afflicted with two or more autoimmune diseases. Furthermore, the poison interferes with the use of oxygen by living cells, afflicting susceptible persons with fatigue, memory problems, and irritability. It also lowers serotonin and dopamine levels in the brain, causing depression in some, and leading to autism in vulnerable children who are found to have less than fifteen percent of the poison's major metabolite in their urine." He halted his speech and looked from face to face before making his next statement. "But we have determined that Sheena should not mention any of these things during the first phase of her mission."

Charftan Zimstar was first to respond. Like all Scintillians, he had ivory skin, golden hair, and blue eyes. He was slight of stature and wore a blue tunic with a silver disc suspended on his breast, a disc engraved with images of musicians and musical instruments. "Not mention them?" he retorted. "How can she fulfill the purpose of her venture without mentioning the devastation to human health caused by the airborne poison?"

"A good point," Dr. Azora conferred. "And I assure you that we have plans for her to address all of the airborne poison's effects. We simply consider it wisest to do so in a gradual and tactful manner."

"I see. Well, as you surely know, my kingdom is donating a large number of Scintillian diamonds to this young woman. We are hopeful that our generous contribution will help alleviate suffering upon the earth's surface, just as efforts by this young woman's father and mother brought relief to the native citizens of Scintillia. So then, can you be more specific as to why you are delaying the release of critical information?"

Dr. Azora proffered an amiable nod before responding. "We are fearful that disclosing all of the ailments caused by the airborne poison will result in dismissal of the information altogether."

"Dismissal by whom?"

The others at the table, including Sheena, looked on with interest as the conversation between Charftan Zimstar and Dr. Azora continued.

"To begin with, we would fear dismissal by the professional we have selected as Sheena's primary contact. If he were presented with such a great quantity of information, with so many ill effects attributed to a single air pollutant, we fear that he would simply discount all of the information as dubious conjecture."

"Who is this professional? And besides the fact that there is a great deal of data, do you have any other reason to believe that he would dismiss the information?"

"Yes, we do. The professional is an endocrinologist in the United States of America. He was educated in public institutions within that kingdom, and there is little doubt that his mind was implanted with prejudice against any information that conflicts with viewpoints of the educational hierarchy of that kingdom. Educational institutions in his native kingdom are thoroughly controlled by the central government, and the citizens within that kingdom have little cognizance of the brainwashing they receive during their years of schooling. We believe that Sheena will face a tough challenge when she seeks to break through the mental handicaps instilled within the mind of the endocrinologist, even though she will only address the single disease we have decided to initially bring to light, namely that of diabetes."

Charftan Nukeel, a native Cerulean with blue skin and hair, leaned forward and placed folded hands atop the table. "What, if I may inquire, is an endocrinologist? And what is diabetes?"

"Diabetes is a prevalent disease upon the earth's surface," Dr. Azora answered. "As the air levels of the poison have increased, so has the incidence of diabetes. Diabetes can cause many problems, problems that vary from vision loss and kidney failure to fatigue and depression. Sensitivity to the airborne poison is often inherited, so the prevalence of diabetes tends to run higher in certain families. And as would be expected of a disease caused by an airborne poison, diabetes is more prevalent where there are higher levels of air pollution."

Charftan Nukeel was not a scientist. He shrugged and nodded. "Very well. And what is an endocrinologist?"

"An endocrinologist is a special physician who treats diabetes." Dr. Azora paused and nodded toward a woman with long brunette hair and brown eyes. He then readdressed Charftan Nukeel. "Leah is one of our most capable spies. She attests to the integrity and trustworthiness of Dr. William Bartholomew Johnson. He is wholly committed to serving the purpose of the Creator throughout his brief life span upon the earth's surface."

Charftan Nukeel nodded. Dr. Azora turned his face to Charftan Zimstar, who likewise nodded.

Dr. Azora then looked about the group. "Leah will guide Sheena through the passageway to the earth's surface and take her to our headquarters in Switzerland. There, Sheena will be provided with identification and travel papers, and then she will receive further training, including instruction in driving an automobile. When her training is concluded, Leah will travel with Sheena to a city in the United States of America called Houston. From there, Sheena will drive several hours to reach her destination, and then she will seek to gain employment in Dr. Johnson's medical clinic."

Terrab spoke up. "Will her training also include warnings about the sun that casts radiation upon the surface of our planet, and about plants and animals native to her destination?"

"Yes," answered Dr. Azora.

Charftan Yarzon added, "And we have already initiated such education through resources contained in our kingdom's libraries."

Next to speak was Golchuron of Quazaria. He was smaller in stature than any of the others at the table, but there was no one who commanded greater respect. His keen blue eyes looked at Leah and then at Sheena and then settled upon Dr. Azora. "You mentioned Dr. William Bartholomew Johnson's brief life span upon the earth's surface. I presume Sheena is aware that she will age about ten times faster during the period of time she resides upon the earth's surface."

Dr. Azora studied the expression on Golchuron's bronze face. No one at the table, apart from Golchuron himself, had any idea how old the Quazarian professor might be—Quazarians are not a fallen race and they do not die of old age unless they choose to live outside the boundaries of their own universe. "Of course," Dr. Azora replied. "Sheena is fully aware of the sacrifices and risks her mission entails."

Golchuron spoke again, "And I also presume that Sheena has received the full series of immunizations against the truth serum that is used upon the earth's surface to extract information from prisoners, is that correct?"

"Correct," Dr. Azora confirmed. "She has received all of the immunizations that are typically given to Southern Ivorian spies, including immunizations against the most common anesthetics used in tranquilizer darts."

"Very well. Has she received proper training to work in a medical clinic?"

"Yes. She has completed training in clerical functions, nursing, and laboratory tasks."

"And has she mastered the native language where she intends to perform her mission?"

"Yes."

Sheena felt Golchuron's stare. She met his eyes. "Your father was one of my favorite students," Golchuron said. "All of Quazaria supports your efforts. May the Creator be with you always."

"And with you," Sheena replied. "Thank you."

Chapter 4

"Insulin? But, Will, I've been doin' ever-thang you've been tellin' me fer the last two whole years. Besides all the meds you've got me takin', I've been doin' the cinnamon and the chromium and the vitamins and all that. I don't really hafta start stickin' myself with needles, do I?" Bill pled.

Few of Dr. Johnson's patients called him Will, but Will Johnson, MD, was not the type to make a fuss over the way people addressed him.

Dr. Johnson looked up at Bill Peebles from the stool where he sat in the exam room. Bill was perched on the end of the examination table with his shirt off. He was the last patient on a busy day. "Now, Bill, I told you when I first started taking care of you that you really needed to be on insulin. It's only because of your efforts at exercise and diet that you've made it this long without it."

Bill dropped his eyes downward toward his pudgy belly. He was a gruff old rancher with sun-baked skin, but he had a compassionate heart and a spirited sense of humor, and everyone liked him. "Well, if it means I won't hafta be havin' a foot cut off, or be goin' on one of them fake kidney machines, then I guess I'll jest hafta put up with it."

Will Johnon, MD, was known for his encouraging bedside manner and positive outlook on life, but a sober expression came over his countenance. "I'll do all I can, Bill, but I can't make any guarantees. Earth life is short, and we just have to do the best we can with the imperfect bodies we have."

"I know," Bill responded. "We can all be lookin' forward to a better body in heaven. But I ain't thar yet, and I'd like to keep right on walkin' on my own two feet and seein' outa my own two eyes till my graduation. And I'm not in any big old rush to graduate."

Bill's droll demeanor drew a smile to Will's face. "I guess after all the money you've spent on boots, we'll have to try and keep those feet intact."

A feigned look of indignation beset Bill's visage. "Boots are downright important! What's a man gonna spend money on anyhow if it ain't on boots?"

Dr. Will Johnson laughed as he stood and handed his patient a prescription for insulin. "Insulin class is Wednesday at four o'clock. You can leave after you get your shirt on. There's no copayment today, but I expect some more of those homegrown tomatoes."

"First, the darn government makes us buy insurance, and then they hit us up with copayments," Bill grumbled.

Will smiled. He turned and stepped to the door.

"Thanks, doc," said Bill.

"My pleasure," Dr. Will Johnson replied. He closed the door to the exam room and then walked a short distance down the hallway. His office door was open. He sat down at his desk and started working on a stack of patient charts.

A tall, grey-haired woman wearing nursing scrubs walked into the office and sat down in one of three chairs in front of Will's desk.

"Great work today, Katie," Will said, hardly looking up. "I'll be a while, so just lock up when you leave."

Katie Clem sat and gazed with sympathetic eyes. She was a retired nurse, or at least she was retired until hearing that a young endocrinologist was opening a clinic in Pineville, Texas. Pineville, her hometown, had never had an endocrinologist. She had wondered what sort of endocrinologist would come to one of the poorest communities in the State of Texas and start a new medical practice, especially when that endocrinologist was the only son of the governor of Texas, and when she met Dr. Will Johnson, she knew that she had found a compelling reason to reenter the work force.

"Are you okay?" Katie asked.

Will looked up. It was unusual for Katie to simply plop herself down in his office and strike up a conversation. "I had some tough patients today, especially with having to tell Bill Peebles that he needs to start insulin shots. But I'll be all right."

Katie shook her head. "No, I mean about Jill."

Will shrugged. "Better to find out now than later, like after getting married to her."

"I always thought that girl was out after money," Katie declared. "Whenever she came around, she had her nose in the books, checking how many patients you were seeing per day and how much money you were bringing in and whether or not you were meeting government quotas."

"Those quotas treat people like cattle."

"Bill might argue with you about that," Katie rebutted. "He says he gives his cattle a lot more respect than the government gives us."

Will smiled. "I think Bill knows more about politics than most college professors." Then his face sobered. "I guess you're right about Jill. You should have seen the look on her face when she found out I moved into a mobile home."

"I can imagine. She thought the son of the state's governor, a physician to boot, was a ticket to high society. And it took her two years to figure out that she couldn't manipulate your professional career."

A shadow passed across Will's face. "I was always honest with her."

"Yes, you were, and a girl like Jill interprets honesty as weakness and gullibility. She thought she could change you and manipulate you." Katie straightened in her chair. Her face took on a look of admiration. "I thank God she was wrong. Men like you are rare and far between. If I were thirty years younger, well, and if my husband were dead, then the other ladies in town would have to fight me off to even get close to you."

Will chuckled and looked down toward his desk. He drew a breath and released a wistful sigh. "She sure was personable, and she sure was good-looking."

"Sure enough, she was personable, whenever things were going her way. And I used to think she was good-looking too until a few minutes ago."

Will looked back up. "Until a few minutes ago? What do you mean? What happened?"

An intriguing expression emerged upon the face of Dr. Will Johnson's only full-time employee. "I mean that I used to think a lot of women were good-looking. I even used to think that I was good-looking, once upon a time. But that was before my eyes set themselves on what strolled into the reception room just a short time ago."

Will's eyes glanced through the open doorway to his office. He again faced Katie. "Someone's out there?"

"Someone or something," Katie returned. "I've never seen anything that seemed so downright perfectly beautiful." A look of awe donned her visage, a look that made Dr. Will Johnson's skin tingle with curiosity. "Maybe she's an angel, I just don't know."

"An angel?"

"Yes. An angel that wants to work as your receptionist."

The look of curious wonder on Will's face became intermingled with disappointment. "But we can't afford a receptionist. At least not yet."

The look of awe on Katie's face transformed into a smile. "I told her that. She wants to work for free."

Will's face evolved through expressions of incredulity and suspicion. "Did my dad send her?"

"No," Katie stated firmly, shaking her head. "I wondered the same thing. She came here from Switzerland, aiming to serve people who suffer from diabetes."

The incredulity on Dr. Will Johnson's face deepened. "How do you know she's telling the truth?"

"I asked her that," Katie returned. Then her countenance changed. She leaned forward and stared into Will's eyes. "You should have seen her face. You'd have thought that I asked her if she was the daughter of Satan. She looked at me as if I had just made the greatest insult against her personal moral character that anyone could imagine. And then, do you know what she said?"

Will found himself captivated. "What?"

Katie drew a breath and continued staring into Will's eyes as she spoke in a dramatic tone of voice. "May my heart keep my lips from speaking a willful lie albeit the vilest man on earth wields the gravest of tortures against my mortal flesh." Katie lifted open palms and then slapped them down against her thighs. "Those were her exact words. I was so outright flabbergasted that I grabbed my pen and wrote down what she said before I had a chance to forget it. And just before I came in here, I read it over several times. Reading it makes me feel good, like there's really some decency left in this world. Can you believe it?"

"Those were really her exact words? Even the word *albeit*?"

"Yes." Katie leaned back, still locked eye-to-eye with Dr. Johnson. "And, Will, you should have seen her eyes. She was telling the truth, I know she was."

Dr. Will Johnson stared in silence for almost twenty seconds. "Did you ask her how she plans to feed herself if she works for free?"

"No, not after I asked her where she's staying."

"Why? Where is she staying?"

"You know that place Burt Kingsley used to rent out on that private lake?"

Will's eyes widened. "It costs a fortune to rent that place."

Katie shrugged her shoulders. "Well, she didn't rent it, she bought it."

"What?"

"Yeah, that's right. And she apparently likes lakes, 'cause she bought the lake too, and all the property Burt owned around the lake."

"He must have three hundred acres around that lake."

"Not anymore, he doesn't. She just got through buying it all. I asked if she had the deed with her, and she pulled the deed out of her purse and showed it to me. And then it finally dawned upon me to ask her something practical."

"Something practical?"

"Yes." Katie conjured up a playfully sincere smile. "Her name's Sheena, and she's single and unattached. And I told her you'd be glad to speak with her, though you might not be in the best of spirits since you just got through breaking up with your fiancée, making you single and unattached just like she is. And I may have mentioned that you're average height, slender but athletic, and have dark brown hair and gorgeous blue eyes."

Will was speechless. He stared out the open door to his office. Katie rose and brushed a few wrinkles out of the top to her scrubs. "Well, I've done my part," she said. "I'm going home. I'm sending her in here, and then I'm going home. The rest is up to you."

Katie smiled to herself as she walked down the hallway toward the reception room, imagining the expression that would appear on Will's face when Sheena stepped into his office. Then her smile gave way to an expression of concern. Bill Peebles' voice was audible, and she certainly did not want Bill to frighten the young woman away before Will had a chance to meet her. She entered the reception room.

"Whoa doggies, Katie, have you met this here woman?" Bill asked in a high-keyed voice. "Her name's Sheena, an' she's wantin' ta work here!"

"Yes, we've met," Katie replied, smiling toward Sheena and speaking in a calm voice.

"Well, if she's gonna be workin' here, I think ya'll better be gettin' a bigger parkin' lot."

"Thank you, Bill," Katie said. "Now I guess we'd best be going and let Sheena interview with Dr. Johnson. He's waiting for her in his office."

Bill turned to Sheena. "It's the third door down that thar hall on yer right." He paused and looked Sheena over. "And if ya don't mind answerin' jest one question, how on earth is it a woman with hair like yers don't have no freckles? Didn't yer mother let ya out in the sun?"

Sheena glanced toward Katie and then looked back at Bill and smiled. She had bumped into Bill when she reentered the reception room after stashing her purse in the trunk of her car. "As a matter of fact, sir, my mother never wanted me out in the sun until shortly before her death."

Bill's face withered into an expression of puzzled curiosity.

"Come on, Bill," Katie coaxed. "I think that will do for prying into this woman's personal affairs. We'd best be going."

"'Twas a pleasure, ma'am," Bill said, curtly bowing as he spoke.

"Thank you, sir," Sheena replied, performing a perfect curtsy.

"Great curds of goats' milk," Bill muttered, staring back at Sheena as Katie took his arm and ushered him out the door.

Sheena turned to the passageway that led to Dr. Johnson's office. She drew a deep breath and shook the tension from her limbs. Several briefings were conducted in regard to Dr. William Bartholomew Johnson before she departed from Subterrania. Information presented during those briefings included his education, his hobbies, his keen interest in American history, and the fact that he was engaged to be married. The recent revelation that Dr. Johnson was no longer engaged and was an available bachelor gave her a nervous sensation in the pit of her stomach. She opened the door and strode down the hallway.

Will faced the open door to his office. The footsteps that resounded through the clinic sounded strong. Then she appeared.

"Hello, my name is Sheena. I presume you are Dr. Johnson?"

Will glanced over the tightly clad, muscular figure standing before him. She wore a one-piece, knee-high, blue satin dress with a wide blue belt. Her high-heeled shoes were the exact color of her dress, and both her shoes and dress matched her eyes. Thick, long, wavy red hair hung down over her shoulders like a hood of fire. A single strand of white pearls was suspended around her neck. He had never seen anything so stunning.

"You can call me Will," he finally responded. "Please, come sit down."

Sheena stepped forward and sat down in the center chair before Will's desk. She noted that he was casually dressed, wearing a button-up shirt with an open collar, and a lab coat, and she noted that Katie was right, he had gorgeous blue eyes.

Will folded his hands on top of his desk. He felt at a loss for words. "So what can I do for you?"

Sheena responded in a steady and confident voice that gave no indication of the queasiness in her abdomen. "I would like to fill the position as your receptionist. I am aware of your clinic hours and the requirements of the position, and I find them acceptable."

Will twiddled his thumbs subconsciously. For a moment, he wondered if he were dreaming, but then he recalled his full day of work at the clinic. This was no dream. "And you are aware that we do not have the funds to pay you anything?"

"I have been informed of the taxes incurred for earning money in this country, and I desire no such complication. Under no circumstances do I want you to pay me anything."

"I see. Well, may I ask why you want this job? Where are you from?" Will met Sheena's eyes. He found himself hoping that, at least in part, he played some role in this woman's decision to work in his clinic. He had never before experienced such attraction to any female, not even to his recent fiancée. Then a troubling thought struck his mind: *what if she is an angel?* He realized, though it would be a marvelous thing to be working with an angel, that he truly hoped she was a human female.

"I grew up in a forest cottage near a lake. My sponsors wish to keep their location and identities secret."

"Your sponsors?" Will posed, feeling his heart quicken from the assurance that he was conversing with a flesh-and-blood woman.

"I am a missionary, of sorts, and I will refer to those who commissioned my coming here as my sponsors."

"A missionary? So what kind of missionary?"

"To begin with, I am a missionary to those who suffer from diabetes, and to those vulnerable to acquiring diabetes."

"Then you've come to the right place," Will declared. "I welcome you."

Sheena smiled. For a while, the two of them just sat and gazed into one another's eyes. There was a communing between their eyes. They both became aware of an inner sense that they were kindred spirits. And before another word was spoken, they both realized that they shared a mutual admiration for one another. Sheena had never before experienced the feelings that swelled within her chest as she gazed into Will's eyes, and Will had never known anything as potent as Sheena's ardent stare. Neither one of them knew what to say next.

Sheena finally blushed and dropped her eyes. "Thank you."

"When would you like to start?" Will asked. His senses were too overwhelmed to think of anything else to say.

Sheena lifted her eyes. "Tomorrow morning."

"Great," Will said. Then he suddenly realized that he had not inquired much about a woman who would be helping to care for his patients and manage the business of his clinic. "Before you leave, may I ask a few questions?"

"Of course."

"Well, how old are you?" An expression of embarrassment took form on Will's face. "I mean—"

"I'm over eighteen," Sheena inserted, smiling at Will's discomfiture.

"Of course, very good," Will stammered. "And, well, of all places in the world, why are you here? Katie said you came from Switzerland."

Sheena's and Will's eyes remained connected as she responded. "Evils that contribute to the rampant plague of human suffering that you refer to as diabetes are not just physical. They are also social and political. One reason I was sent to this clinic is because your father holds a powerful position of public leadership."

Will's face wilted. Sheena had no trouble interpreting his look of disappointment. She could not help but smile. "But that was not the major reason that your clinic was selected," she added. "The major reason is you."

Sheena could not have said anything that would have elicited more stirring emotions. She may just as well have said "I love you." Her zealous stare penetrated deeper into Will's eyes. He felt a quivering sensation sweep throughout his body. "Me?" he reiterated.

"Yes, you—a son of the Creator, dedicated to serving both the spiritual and physical needs of suffering men, women, and children, bowing to no idol and compromising nothing. I was astonished to learn that such a man exists upon the surface of the earth."

Will had seen movies that featured love at first sight, but such a concept was something he had always categorized as fantasy. Not anymore. If it were in God's will to grant one desire during the span of his earthly life, he knew beyond doubt that he was looking at her. And there was no mistaking the look in her eyes. "Do you have any plans for supper?" he asked.

Sheena again smiled, and for several seconds, she and Will simply looked at one another. Then she dropped her lips toward the pearl necklace that hung from her neck. "Beshaatah shuntoosi."

Will stared in silent wonder. The pearls ignited like round white fireflies, increasing and decreasing in intensity in varying sequences and patterns. They were beautiful.

"*Cahmsta* Mildred Purser," Sheena said. She raised her face.

"Mildred?" Will inquired, meeting Sheena's eyes. He could not understand the other words Sheena spoke, but Mildred Purser was a lady he knew well.

Sheena nodded, granting another smile.

"Hello, Mildred here," a woman's voice sounded.

Will stared back at the pearls. Mildred's voice sounded as clearly as if she were standing in the room.

"This is Sheena. Would it be too awful much trouble to prepare for a guest? I'd like to bring Dr. William Johnson home to dinner."

Will looked back and forth between Sheena's face and the pearls. Sheena continued smiling and faced Will as she carried on the conversation with Mildred.

"Will! Gosh, no it wouldn't be any trouble. Didn't take 'um long ta get smart to ya, did it? Say, I'll put the two of ya in that private dinin' room. What time ya want dinner?"

"Would seven o'clock be all right?"

"Yep, gives me time ta pick up some blackberry cobbler and ice cream. That's Will's favorite dessert."

"Thank you, Mildred. And please feel free to spend the night in one of the guest bedrooms."

"For real?"

"Of course. Pick one with its own bathroom."

"Uptown! I'm gonna like this job, I'll tell ya that."

"I hope so. Let me know if I can do anything else for you."

"How about marryin' up with Will and settlin' down here in Pineville?"

Sheena hesitated. Her smile gave way to a look of nervous uncertainty. She and Will delved more deeply into one another's eyes.

"You're on speaker phone, Mildred," Will piped up. "Now why don't you just do the cookin' and let me do the proposin'?"

"Will! Hey! This 'un's the best 'un yet, by a long ways. Don't let 'er get loose."

A gap of silence followed.

"That may be the best advice anyone's ever given me," Will said, addressing Sheena more than Mildred.

"Of course it is! Now I'd better get ta shopin' an' cookin'. Adios, you two."

"Good-bye, Mildred," Sheena said. A faint click sounded. "Cahmsta bauk," she spoke, and the pearls returned to their former appearance, opaque white.

Another gap of silence followed. Sheena's and Will's eyes yielded shared astonishment over their obvious attraction to one another. This time Sheena broke the silence. "Mildred was there when I purchased the house from Burt. I offered her a raise if she would continue her employment."

"I'll bet she was tickled pink," Will said. He glanced at Sheena's necklace. "Your pearls are a voice-activated cell phone."

"Yes, among other things."

Will scrutinized the pearl necklace. It was lovely, but there was no clue that it was anything more than a necklace. He raised his eyes. "I feel like I'm sitting face-to-face with Batgirl."

Sheena had studied the English language and American history for fifty years. She was well versed in regard to superheroes. "Well, have you ever thought about being Batman?"

A look of exuberance captured Will's visage, and he straightened in his chair. "I've always wanted to be Batman. What language were you speaking?"

"I was attempting to add some Texas flavor to fundamental English."

Will grinned. On top of everything else, Sheena had a sense of humor. "No, I mean the other language, the language you used when you were directing your necklace to turn on and off."

Sheena knew that the very existence of Subterrania was a sacred secret. She also knew that no native Subterranian was ever known to migrate to the earth's surface and marry an outlander. It was very apparent that she and Will were enthralled with each other. What would happen if she married this man? Would she tell him where she came from?

"It's a secret language," Sheena said.

"From a secret land?" Will asked, speaking in a teasing voice. The look that came to Sheena's face erased all thoughts of teasing from his mind. "No," he uttered, staring hard at Sheena. She was obviously very different than any person he had ever met before, and he had never seen anything like the pearls that she used to communicate with Mildred. He assumed that she was human, but was she an alien human? "Your not from, that is to say, some other world or planet, are you?"

Sheena voiced no objection. Her face pled acceptance.

"Oh my," Will said. "Where is it?"

Sheena maintained eye contact with Will as she sat in thought. One of the thoughts that passed through her mind was far removed from the subject matter of her conversation with Will: it was the realization that she wanted to avoid death, at least for a while. She knew her mission was dangerous—very dangerous—and that she could be killed in an instant, just like her father before her. She did not fear death, and prior to meeting this man, she did not shun death. She knew that the Eternal Kingdom, where both her father and mother were already residing, was far better than anything in the temporal worlds. But now her heart was drawn toward remaining in the temporal realm long enough to become better acquainted with the man who sat before her.

She stood to her feet and walked around the desk. Will stood to meet her. She came close enough that he could feel her breath when she spoke.

"Bringing truth to this world can be dangerous. If you involve yourself with me, you may soon be dead."

Will absorbed Sheena's profound statement and stood in solemn contemplation. For two long minutes, their eyes communed, Sheena pouring her heart and resolve into Will's eyes and Will determining what sort of response would rightly reflect his inner convictions and his emotional response to Sheena's presence. "For me to live is Christ, and to die is gain," he said, quoting from the Bible. "I would rather live one more day of mortal life in God's perfect will than experience a hundred more years of mortal existence apart from his will."

Sheena ventured into Will's eyes and placed her hands on his shoulders. She shook her head and smiled. "I can hardly believe it. You're just like my sponsors hoped you would be." She drew her face an inch closer and lost herself in his eyes. "And more than I could ever have thought possible, you're the man that I have always hoped and dreamed I would one day meet."

Will was curious about the identity of Sheena's sponsors and about where she came from, but his heart and mind were consumed by her presence. A kiss was something he deemed rather serious, but it was all he could do to keep from throwing his arms around Sheena and drawing her lips to his own. "Really? I am?"

"Yes, you are. And please excuse what I'm about to do, but I have no way of knowing how long I'm going to live in this world, and I've always dreamed that someday I would meet a boy that I really wanted to kiss, and I've never kissed a boy in my whole life, and—"

Will saved Sheena the effort of further explanation. Their lips met, their eyes closed, and it seemed that their hearts and souls passed into a new dimension. It was not a material dimension—a dimension that could be measured in length or time. It was a spiritual and emotional dimension that transcended anything corporal or temporal and united their hearts and souls like the blending of two rivers en route to the sea. When their lips parted, they gazed into one another's eyes with the pervasive impression that only death would prevent their eventual matrimony.

"How could this happen?" Sheena asked. She gazed into Will's eyes for several seconds before again speaking. "I love you."

Will shrugged and shook his head, never breaking eye contact with Sheena. "I know we've just met, but it seems like I've known you all my life, or maybe, I've wanted to know you all my life." His expression became one of reverent contemplation. "With God, one day is as a thousand years, and a thousand years are as one day. This is a very special day. I love you too. And what's more, I believe that your mission, as you call it, is also my mission. Sit here in my chair."

Sheena sat down in Will's padded chair while he brought a wooden chair to her side. He sat down and faced her. "Okay then, you mentioned my father. What role might he play in our mission?"

A gracious smile broke out across Sheena's face, and it was all she could do to keep tears from appearing on her cheeks. The words "our mission" carried a meaning that did not escape her cognizance. "We can discuss your father's role after supper," she said. "For now let's talk about us. What kind of music do you like?"

Sheena laughed at Will's story about trying to ride a cow to impress a little girl and then being bucked off into a mound of manure. "And come to think of it, if I'm remembering right, she had red hair," Will added. Sheena laughed again, and Will laughed with her. They were waiting for dessert after a scrumptious dinner of roasted chicken breast, mashed potatoes and gravy, pinto beans, cranberry salad, green beans, and collard greens. Will had insisted on driving Sheena to her new home, saying that he would pick her up for work the next morning.

Will and Sheena had talked during the entire drive to Sheena's new home, discussing the typical topics that an engaged couple would be expected to discuss, even though there had not yet been an official marriage proposal. Mildred was rapturous. She served food and drinks to the little table in the private dining room and listened to everything her ears could perceive. She could not help but feel a part of the blossoming romantic relationship; after all, she had selected a pink tablecloth and placed crystal candleholders in the center of the table where she lit white candles. She even dimmed the lights in the chandelier that hung above the table.

"Now that's a dessert fit to take a blue ribbon at any fair in Texas," Will commented as Mildred sat bowls of blackberry cobbler and ice cream on the table.

"You two just take yer time an' holler if ya need anythin'," Mildred said. It was obvious that Will's comment pleased her. She turned and walked back toward the kitchen.

Will smiled toward Sheena. "This is a treat worthy of timely indulgence. How about discussing my father's role in our mission while we start on the cobbler?"

"Sure," Sheena said. "I'll be right back."

Will waited until Sheena returned to the table with a small notebook and sat back down. Then he took a bite of ice cream and blackberry cobbler as he observed her.

Sheena opened the notebook and placed it to one side of her dessert. She faced Will. "My sponsors think the best way to explain your father's role in our mission is to first review a little American history. Are you game for a few questions?"

"United States history questions?" Will asked. The tone of his voice was one of hopeful excitement. He considered himself a virtual sage when it came to the history of his nation.

"That is correct," Sheena answered. She glanced at the open pages of the notebook and then looked back at Will. "We will begin with presidents. I will give a clue about a particular president and see if you can identify him. If you cannot, then I will give additional clues."

Will found himself very pleased with the prospect of impressing Sheena. "Okay, I'm ready."

"Very well. What president was the founder and first rector of the University of Virginia?"

Will answered without hesitation. "Thomas Jefferson."

"Very well," Sheena said with a nod. She smiled playfully. "That was too easy for you. How about this, what president won the battle of Buena Vista?"

Will's skin paled. His forehead grew furrowed as he pondered Sheena's question, but then his face cleared. "Zachary Taylor," he said, and then he lifted a scoop of ice cream and blackberry cobbler to his mouth and faced Sheena with an expression of triumph.

Sheena stared in silence. She likewise took a helping of dessert, saying nothing until she had swallowed it. "That was amazing," she conceded. Then her face took on a serious air. "What president wrote an executive order, in his own handwriting, for the execution of more than thirty native American Indians without any civil trial, referring them as Indians and half-breeds."

Will's eyes widened. He gave no reply.

Sheena resumed speaking. "The same president invited a group of darker-skinned persons of our race to the White House, and then he attempted to persuade them to move out of the United States and relocate in Liberia, thus setting an example for all of the other darker-skinned persons of our race who resided within the United States."

Will's eyes became interlocked with Sheena's eyes. "Darker-skinned persons of our race? Are you referring to the black race?"

Several moments passed before Sheena answered. "I have visited the kingdom of a black race," she conferred. "It is a noble and beautiful race with golden eyes, golden hair, and smooth black skin like the polished surface of basalt. They are a separate race from us."

There was something about the way Sheena pronounced the words *separate race* that spurred Will's curiosity. "A separate race? What do you mean?"

"If you or I were to marry one of them, we could bear no young. Where I come from, all men and women who dwell upon the surface of the earth are considered members of the same race, even if there is some variance in size and color."

Sheena's words roused Will's heart and mind to thoughts far removed from American history. His gaze into Sheena's eyes deepened. "So you did come here from another planet, right?"

The sound of a dish crashing to the floor disrupted eye contact.

"Just a plain serving dish, nothing fancy," Mildred's voice sounded.

Will and Sheena ignored the interruption and again met eyes. "Please, I wish I could share more about the place I come from, the place where I grew from infancy to womanhood, but I plead for you to understand that I cannot. Those who have sent me here have put their trust in me."

A troubled crease formed in Will's brow. "But we are of the same race, are we not?"

Sheena's expression eased into a smile as she perceived the nature of Will's underlying concern. "Oh, yes, very much so. I do not believe we would have any difficulty bearing young."

The crease disappeared from Will's brow. He blushed and smiled in return.

Then Sheena's face sobered in thought. Finally her lips parted to again speak. "It is true that I come from someplace very different from this world; but I'm here now, and I intend to remain here."

"Will felt a thrill pass through his body at the insinuation of Sheena's words. "And you intended to remain here before you ever met me, am I right?"

"Yes."

"Why? Why is the mission of helping people who suffer from diabetes so important to you? Is there diabetes where you come from?"

"There is virtually no diabetes where I come from," Sheena answered. "I believe that you and I share the same aspiration, namely to fulfill the Creator's perfect will throughout our entire lifetimes, whether those lifetimes be a thousand years, a hundred years, or one day." Sheena peered more intently into Will's eyes. "And since I have arrived here, my heart has come to know an additional reason to stay."

Will gazed into Sheena's eyes with wonder and admiration. He could not help but mull over how fortunate he was to have passed through several failed romantic relationships and to have remained single long enough to meet the woman who sat across the table from him. Then, relaxing his posture and accepting the fact that he hoped to someday wed a woman who apparently came to Texas from another world, he redirected his mind to the substance of their conversation. "So then, are you saying that you do not believe that Indians and Blacks and Whites are of different races?"

"You are well versed in the Word of God, are you not?" Sheena asked.

"Yes."

"Does the Bible ever mention God creating races upon the earth?"

Will sat and stared. His mind churned in thought. Sheena waited in silence, like a teacher pausing to see if a student can come up with a correct answer without any outside prompting.

Finally Will responded, "He confounded human language in order to prevent the human population from unifying in a humanistic society that failed to acknowledge and serve the true Creator, namely himself."

"Granted."

Will thought some more. "God's Word makes it clear that all human beings are spiritually alike and are spiritually equal through the regenerating blood of Jesus Christ, but it also makes it clear that God purposely created human beings, on the physical level, to be male and female."

"Also granted," Sheena said. She again waited in silence.

Will perceived that he was being tutored. "No," he granted. "The Bible never says that God created races." His brows skewed. "But he must have, right? I mean, how else could races exist?"

"My sponsors believe that none of the human beings who populate the surface of the earth look exactly like Adam or Eve."

"They don't? So what did Adam and Eve look like?"

"No one knows. When the sons of God took human wives prior to the flood, at least some of their offspring survived and were deemed human, including men referred to as giants, and the Bible also states that such offspring became 'mighty men' and 'men of renown.' There is no mention that Noah and his family were chosen to repopulate the surface of the earth because of genetic purity. Noah was chosen because of his spiritual integrity."

"So you believe that differing races resulted as a consequence of the sons of God mating with human women," Will surmised.

"No," Sheena replied. "I do not believe that different races even exist upon the earth's surface. I simply believe that creatures who were created as candidates in the Creator's quest to find a proper 'help meet' for Adam, meaning that they were created as candidates for becoming a *coequal companion* for Adam, perpetrated a horrendous evil prior to the Great Flood by taking human women as wives and producing offspring. As a result, humans who populate the surface of the earth live within genetically tainted bodies, and they will not be free of such corruption until they receive their immortal bodies in the eternal realm. I do not, however, believe that human beings who dwell upon the surface of the earth are of different races. We are all offspring of Adam and Eve, albeit physically altered, and despite any differences in color and size, I believe we should view ourselves as a single race."

Will took another bite of dessert. Sheena did likewise. "Okay then, let's get back to that last president," Will directed. "It sounds like you were giving clues about a white supremist, a president who did not consider persons who happen to be of darker skin color to be worthy of proper consideration as human beings."

"Quite so, or at least he did not deem it proper for darker-skinned and lighter-skinned members of our race to coexist," Sheena agreed. "He opposed the immigration of darker-skinned people into his home state and supported a state resolution to deny the darker-skinned people the freedom to vote, and he served as a leader in an organized society that raised funds to deport darker-skinned people out of the United States."

"How deplorable," Will responded. A look of inspiration captured his features. "Was he also in favor of shifting power to the central government?"

"You're getting an awful lot of clues for just one president," Sheena chided teasingly. "But okay, the answer is yes. This president hated Thomas Jefferson, who defended states' rights, but he was not above quoting Thomas Jefferson if it served his political ends."

"Woodrow Wilson," Will proclaimed.

A consoling smile preceded Sheena's response. "That's a very good guess."

Will's face sagged. "It's not Woodrow Wilson?" he posed.

"No," Sheena returned, restraining laughter at the look on Will's face. "I'll give you a few more clues." She leaned forward with her forearms propped on top of the table. Her countenance took on a serious demeanor. "Although the vast majority of ministers where this president came from were against his becoming president, and although he reportedly never became a Christian and rarely attended church services, he would still refer to the King James Bible if it served his political ends."

"Sounds like a professional politician. I'll bet he was a silver-tongued orator."

"Indeed so. And the Constitution of the United States was no encumbrance to this president's dictatorial whims."

Will stared at Sheena as if he were attempting to withdraw information from her eyes. "He disregarded the Constitution? How? Can you give some examples?"

"He confiscated firearms from American citizens, which was in breach of the Second Amendment, and he shut down newspapers that opposed him which was in breach of the First Amendment, and although no one would carry out his order, he once issued an arrest warrant for the Chief Justice of the Supreme Court of the United States. Even the Fifth Amendment failed to receive his respect—he wanted to disallow persons the right to remain silent."

"Barack Obama?" Will spoke up.

Sheena responded with a look of puzzlement. "Well, I suppose that's a good guess. But do you really think Barack Obama would have favored the deportation of darker-skinned members of our race? Do you think he was a white supremist?"

"Oh, I suppose not," Will replied sheepishly. "I don't think he would have deported himself."

Sheena smiled at Will's discomfiture. "Do you give up, or do you want some more clues?"

"More clues."

"Very well. But why don't we finish up this dessert before the ice cream melts. We can move into the den after we're done eating and let Mildred finish with the dishes."

Will glanced toward the passageway leading to the kitchen. "Sounds good. And if you don't object, do you think Mildred could sit with us in the sunroom?" He leaned his head over his plate and lowered his voice. "She wouldn't have to strain her ears so hard that way."

"I heard that!"

Chapter 5

Will and Sheena sat in a quaint room with great bay windows. Eastward beyond the windows lay a picturesque lake with a late spring sunset painting a golden band across the blue surface of the water. The atmosphere of the room was enchanting. Live plants hung from urns and vases all about the floor, and tiers of flowering vines grew in baskets suspended below the ceiling. Three marble fountains mimicked the sounds of a babbling brook.

Mildred sat down in a chair facing the petite sofa where Will and Sheena conversed. She had just finished washing dishes. Will had agreed to wait until she joined them before picking back up on the conversation about presidents and American history. Mildred was a member of the local American Historical Society, as was Will, and she had become acquainted with Will soon after he moved to Pineville. Her heart seemed to climb upward into her throat with excitement and anticipation; the most desirable bachelor in town was apparently involved with a beautiful woman from another planet. It was as if she were watching a breathtaking science fiction romance on television and then somehow got sucked into the screen.

"Okay, Mildred's here," Will said. "Let's get to the next clue about the last president."

Sheena reached to a coffee table and picked up her notebook. After perusing several pages, she laid the notebook back down and faced Will. "I would like you to bear with me while I give several more clues about the president who eludes your recognition. I will let you know when I'm finished."

"My lips are sealed until you approve further vociferation," Will declared. He realized that he was enjoying playing the game of clues with Sheena. He was enjoying it very much, and as he gazed upon her face while awaiting the next clue, he could not help but feel that doing anything at all would be wonderfully enjoyable so long as he was doing it with Sheena.

Sheena smiled and then her face became frankly sincere. She glanced toward Mildred and then delved into Will's eyes. "Charles Darwin's *Origin of the Species* was first published in November of 1859 under the title *On the Origin of Species by Means of Natural Selection, or the Preservation of Favored Races in the Struggle for Life*, and it was published in the United States before the close of January 1860. Darwin capitalized the word *Creator* and wrote that the evolution of the human eye was 'absurd in the highest degree,' but then he disregarded this absurdity and fostered an evolutionary theory, a theory that became Satan's tool."

Mildred spoke up, "You betcha it did. All that stuff about men an' women springing up from amoebas an' monkeys has gotta be the hugest heap of stinkin' droppins that ever oozed out from a bushed batch of misfired brain cells."

Sheena smiled and gave Mildred a concurring nod. Then she faced Will. "Some claim that Darwin may have dismissed the theory of evolution altogether if he had known everything about the human eye that our scientists know today, but where I come from, his theory is deemed inexcusably absurd at any point of scientific history."

Will felt his heart and mind drawn into the sincerity and gravity of Sheena's discourse as she continued. "The idea of a master race and the genocide of so-called inferior groups of human beings can certainly be linked to Charles Darwin. Just consider what he wrote in *Descent of Man*, chapter 6:

'On the Affinities and Genealogy of Man, On the Birthplace and Antiquity—At some future period, not very distant as measured by centuries, the civilized races of man will almost certainly exterminate, and replace, the savage races throughout the world. At the same time the anthropomorphous apes, as Professor Schaaffhausen has remarked, will no doubt be exterminated. The break between man and his nearest allies will then be wider, for it will intervene between man in a more civilized state, as we may hope, even than the Caucasion, and some ape as low as a baboon, instead of as now between the negro or Australian and the gorilla.'"

"Jumpin' June bugs!" voiced Mildred. "Sounds like somethin' you'd expect ta' hear from a sadistic scientist whose been sufferin' from mad cow disease!" Her features became solemn. "People are people, all jes the same, no matter if some of em' sunburn easier than others."

"Quite right, Mildred," said Sheena. "Even where I come from—where there actually are different races—we still view all human beings as equally human. My sponsors consider Darwin's proclamation to be an unsound exhibition of wanton arrogance."

"Mmmmm, mmm," hummed Will, keeping his lips together.

Sheena smiled at Will and then looked at Mildred. "I think that means he agrees."

Mildred chuckled.

Sheena shifted positions and again addressed Will. "The president whose identity you have been attempting to guess was reportedly convinced about the idea of evolution after reading a book entitled *Vestiges of the Natural History of Creation* that was published anonymously in 1844 by the Scottish journalist Robert Chambers."

"Lands! You've got all that stuff jes stashed in yer brain?"

Sheena smiled fondly toward Mildred. "One of my classes was solely dedicated to the rote memory of key quotes and facts."

"Oh."

She looked back at Will. "Perhaps it is merely a chilling coincidence that this president was born on exactly the same day as Charles Darwin and lived during the century when Harvard University came up with the branch of study referred to as race science, a branch of study that excused slavery and depicted darker-skinned members of our race as some sort of lesser creatures."

Will's eyes widened.

Sheena's jaw grew firm. "Barack Obama, who you mentioned before, swore into office on this president's Bible, and Adolf Hitler admired this president and even quoted him, a president that introduced total war to modern civilization by attacking civilians as well as military targets."

Mildred spoke up again, "He attacked civilians? You mean like…well…folks like me?"

"I'm afraid so. He launched the bloodiest war that had ever taken place up to that present time, a war you refer to as the Civil War, and he eventually killed more Americans than anyone else in history, including Adolf Hitler."

Mildred's mouth dropped open. She said nothing.

"He was a wealthy trial lawyer who married into an affluent family that owned slaves, and he was an attorney for one of the largest corporations in the world."

Sheena took a couple of breaths. She locked eyes with Will. "He wrote that his objective in the war was not either to save or destroy slavery, and not only did his Emancipation Proclamation limit the freeing of slaves to states that had seceded from the Union, it excluded the freeing of slaves in sections of Louisiana and Tennessee that were under the control of the Northern Army. Furthermore, he actually reversed the freeing of slaves in the border state of Missouri."

"No way," uttered Mildred.

Sheena did not break eye contact with Will. "And I would add that his tactic of offering freedom to slaves amongst enemy forces was not a new war stratagem—Britain pledged freedom for slaves in the American colonies during the Revolutionary War. Yet despite the offer of freedom from slavery, there were slaves who fought for their homeland during the Revolutionary War, just as there were slaves in the South who fought for their homeland during the war that has been named the Civil War. And it is well established that members of our race who you refer to as American Indians fought for the south, and the imperial slaughter of American Indians after subjugation of the south is one of the darkest pages in American history."

Will's lips parted, but then he recalled his agreement to wait until Sheena granted permission for him to speak. He stared into her eyes with a look of startled wonder.

Sheena acknowledged Will's continued silence with a nod and then recommenced speaking. "After launching a bloody war without the approval of Congress, this president imprisoned thousands of northern citizens who did not support his war, and he shut down hundreds of northern newspapers. Prior to the war, he refused to meet with prospective peacemakers from both the Southern Confederacy and France, and during the war, he expressed his opinion that persons who chose to remain silent should be subject to imprisonment. Everyone should either speak out in favor of his imperialistic war or suffer the consequences."

"So it's like ya said before," remarked Mildred. "He didn't want ta let folks have their Constitutional rights—not even that Fifth Amendment right ta remain silent."

"Correct. Mikhail Gorbachev of the Soviet Union demonstrated much more respect for freedom and human life than this American president. When Soviet citizens positioned themselves in front of Soviet tanks and made a stand for freedom, Gorbachev permitted the secession of Soviet States rather than massacring his own people."

Sheena paused long enough to reciprocate the look of concern on Mildred's face, and then she readdressed Will. "The south had every right to secede. The economic oppression inflicted against the South by unfair tariffs was reprehensible, clearly comparable to any unfair taxes King George of England levied against the American colonies. A large percentage of the Confederate Army was made up of soldiers of Irish and Scottish descent who owned no slaves. These soldiers fought on behalf of freedom, not slavery. And you can be absolutely sure that the horrible practice of slavery would have ended without a war that impoverished the wealthiest states in your nation, states where a significant percentage of the darker-skinned members of your nation reside. And if the freeing of slaves in your nation had been permitted to take place over time as it did in other civilized nations, rather than initially being used as a war tactic and then later being used as propaganda to purportedly excuse an inexcusable war, then there would have never been a Ku Klux Klan."

Sheena paused and examined Will's expression before resuming. She noted that he absorbed her assertions with little outward response, but she could sense the intensity of his inner deliberation. "This president first proposed the idea of the Emancipation Proclamation to his cabinet in the summer of 1862. He presented this proposal as a war measure against the Confederacy."

"Ta keep the slaves from fightin' fer the south?" posed Mildred.

"Not only that. England conveyed sympathy for the freedom-seeking south, but England was also known to oppose slavery, so in order to keep England out of the war on behalf of the south, it appears that this president hoped to employ the sentiment expressed by Charles Darwin who wrote the following in June of 1861: 'Some few, and I am one, even wish to God, though at the loss of millions of lives, that the north would proclaim a crusade against slavery.'"

"So Darwin was against slavery?"

"It appears so, but it also appears that he had little regard for the value of human lives, and Mao Tse-tung, who was allegedly the greatest mass murderer of all time with the slaughter some seventy-seven million people, is reported to have said, 'Chinese socialism is founded upon Darwin and the theory of evolution.'"

"I'll be lassoed and tied—I never heard thatin' before."

Sheena continued. "After coming into office, this president threatened war against any state that failed to collect a newly doubled tariff, and it is notable that the Constitution of the United States defines levying war against states of the United States as treason."

"Whoa…hold on thar a minute." Mildred leaned slightly forward. "Are you sayin' that goin' ta war against states of the United States is treason? The Constitution says it's treason?"

"Precisely so, provided that such war is levied by a citizen of the United States."

"So then, Ab…" Mildred caught herself and glanced at Will. "I mean—so then, the president yer givin' out clues about—the one Will's supposed ta guess next—he committed treason against the Constitution of the United States of America?"

"Well, let's figure that out. First of all, did he levy war against states?"

Mildred hesitated. "What does levy mean?"

"In this case, it means *to enlist or call up troops for military service*."

"Well sure, there's no doubt that he did that."

"And secondly, was he a citizen of the United States?"

"Yes."

"Then the answer to your question is yes. And prior to what you call the Civil War, states were fully aware that they were free to secede, and this freedom helped keep the Federal Government from becoming a despotic monster."

"So states were really free ta secede? Did any of em' try it?"

"The first region of the United States to seriously consider seceding from the Union was New England, and there was no question regarding their freedom to secede. The only question addressed by the New England states was whether it was better to secede or to remain with the Union, and they voted to remain with the Union. Even President James Buchanan, who served as president just prior to this president, clearly supported the freedom for states to secede from the Union, as did the author of the Declaration of Independence, namely Thomas Jefferson."

Sheena stopped speaking for a few moments and settled back in the sofa. She relaxed her posture and faced Will. "Are those enough clues?"

"Incredible," Will uttered. He stared at Sheena's face. "Are we talking about the same president who said, 'I have never known a worthwhile man who became too big for his boots or his Bible'?"

"He never said that," Sheena retorted, again straightening and facing Will. "There are several false quotes attributed to this president that make him out as some sort of godly savior; but to the contrary, he is one of the most notorious war criminals who ever lived. The estimated count of those who lost their lives in the war launched by this president rose from 620,000 to at least 750,000, and this increase was largely due to the added inclusion of southern civilian casualties calculated from prewar and postwar population censuses."

A troubled expression creased Will's brow. "Why haven't I ever heard these things about Abraham Lincoln before?"

Sheena drew a deep breath and sighed. "For the same reason that you have never been taught who wrote your Pledge of Allegiance or when it was written or why it was written. A federal empire rose to power and subjected theretofore free states by force of arms, and then that empire proceeded to assume control of public education and to thoroughly brainwash the American populace."

The creases in Will's brow deepened in perplexity. "Someone wrote the Pledge of Allegiance?"

Sheena shook her head before responding. "The thought that someone sat down and wrote the Pledge of Allegiance never crossed your mind before, did it? You were simply raised to think that the pledge always existed, somehow springing into existence while Betsy Ross sewed the first flag."

"I guess so."

"Well, that's not surprising. It's exactly what your federal school system was programmed to indoctrinate within your mind." Sheena stared hard into Will's eyes. "Would it surprise you to learn that the pledge never even existed before the War of Imperial Aggression, the war you call the Civil War?"

Will paused long enough to ponder Sheena's title for the war between the states, namely the War of Imperial Aggression, and then he considered the substance of her question. "It didn't?"

"No. An avowed socialist by the name of Francis Bellamy wrote the Pledge of Allegiance in 1892. His cousin, Edward Bellamy, authored the socialist fantasy novel entitled *Looking Backward*, a book that exalts totalitarian communism. Francis Bellamy hoped the pledge would serve to foster the totalitarian fantasy in America. He did not have 'under God' in the pledge, which was added a few years after the defeat of Adolf Hitler, and he claimed that his idea for the pledge came from loyalty oaths that southerners were forced to take during the War of Imperial Aggression."

"Loyalty oaths?"

"Yes," Sheena replied. "One of my history teachers compared loyalty oaths, namely oaths that were forced upon citizens of the south, to King Nebuchadnezzar's forcing subjugated Jews to bow down to the great golden statue that Nebuchadnezzar constructed in his own image."

"My lands," Mildred muttered.

Will and Sheena both glanced at Mildred, and then again faced one another.

Sheena resumed speaking. "Your victorious imperial government inculcated the Pledge of Allegiance throughout the public school system. And you should see what the children of your nation looked like prior to World War II as they performed the Bellamy Salute, a special salute that was developed to accompany the pledge."

"The Bellamy salute," Will echoed, raising his phone from his hip. "Can I bring it up on the Internet?"

Sheena shrugged one shoulder. "Well, no and yes."

"No and yes?" Will inquired, pausing while holding his phone in one palm.

"The answer would be no, not now that your government has instituted filtering of the Internet. But the answer is also yes, because I can bring up the Internet that was available in this region a century ago."

Will and Mildred both fell silent. Will stared at Sheena's face and finally spoke. "You can travel through time?"

Sheena stared back at Will for a few seconds, and then she smiled and shook her head. "No. I only know of one race that can travel through time, and they live in a different universe."

An audible gasp sounded from Mildred's throat.

Will absorbed Sheena's statement and continued to stare at her face. "Then how can you bring up the Internet from the last century?"

"There are scientists where I come from who have compiled historical data for thousands of years, including information in regard to your state and in regard to your nation." Sheena raised one hand and touched the pearl necklace that lay upon her bosom. "I can connect your communication device to their information banks."

"Really?"

Sheena dropped her chin toward the pearl necklace. "Beshaatah shuntoosi."

The pearls lit up. Will turned his eyes to Mildred; her eyes were fastened upon the necklace, and her face conferred intense anticipation.

"Shuntoosi Sheezaron beshaatah."

Sheena raised her face and met Will's eyes. "You may bring up your Internet as usual," Sheena directed. "You will now be able to access information that your government has deemed to be threatening to your national security."

Will activated his phone and tapped twice on the Internet icon. He looked back at Sheena. "Okay, I've got it."

"Enter the words 'Bellamy salute.'"

Sheena watched as Will keyed the entry into his phone. Then she observed the expression on his face as he stared down at the small screen in his hands. His brow furrowed in curiosity and concern. He looked back up at Sheena. "It's a group of children. They look like a troop of little Nazis."

Sheena first shrugged and then nodded. "Of course. Why should that surprise you? Adolf Hitler admired Abraham Lincoln. They were both proponents of a socialistic totalitarian empire, and like I said before, Francis Bellamy hoped that his pledge would foster the totalitarian fantasy in America, so why wouldn't Adolf Hitler be drawn to Francis Bellamy and his special salute?"

The look on Will's face changed to one of indignation. "So what you said about my government and the school system is true. I've really been brainwashed."

"Yes."

Will's look of indignation transformed to one of indefatigable resolve. "I'll never be able to cite that pledge again," he averred.

Sheena responded by turning back to a blank page in her notebook and handing the notebook to Will. She then picked up a pen from the top of the coffee table and gave it to Will. "I will give you a new pledge, a pledge that acknowledges the nation founded by your forefathers, a nation that everyone who values truth and freedom should strive to renew. From this day forward, whenever you pledge the flag of the United States of America, I urge you to cite the pledge that I am giving you, a pledge that honors the principles and freedoms upon which your nation was founded rather than a pledge born in socialistic exultation over the unfortunate conclusion of an imperialistic, greed-driven, horrendous, and bloody war."

Will positioned himself to begin writing and then nodded.

Sheena began. She spoke slowly and paused between phrases so that Will had time to write down every word. "I pledge allegiance to the flag of the free and sovereign states, bound in service to God and man, with liberty and justice for all."

Will finished writing and then set the notebook and pen down on the sofa and picked up his phone.

"What are you doing?" Sheena asked.

"I'm sending this to my dad. He'll love it. He'll have everyone in the State of Texas reciting it."

Sheena waited as Will prepared a text message for the governor of Texas. She turned her head and looked at Mildred. Mildred addressed Sheena's eyes and proffered an earnest nod of approval. Both women smiled.

"Okay, I've sent the new pledge," Will said. "What next?"

Sheena was still smiling as she looked back at Will. "Thank you," she said. "My sponsors will be most pleased. They have high hopes for your father's assistance, including his assistance in one other matter."

"One other matter?"

The expression on Sheena's face shifted to a look of serious contemplation. "Do you recall the account in the fourth chapter of the book of Matthew where the Evil One tempted God the Son by offering him the kingdoms of the world if only God the Son would bow to him?"

"Yes. It's where Satan tempted Christ."

"That is correct. So then, what does that account reveal about the general condition of nations upon the earth's surface?"

Will's brow crinkled. "What do you mean?"

Sheena did not seem surprised by Will's uncertainty. She responded with unwearied inquisition. "When one considers the fact that all of creation, including the entire earth, belongs to the Creator, then how was the Evil One able to bargain with Christ by offering him the kingdoms of the world? What was Satan really offering?"

Will's crinkled expression gave way to startled comprehension. "The leaders of those kingdoms must have been servants of Satan. Satan was offering to yield his control over the governments of those kingdoms to Christ."

"Indeed," Sheena confirmed. "Human beings are powerless to resist spiritual consumption by the Evil One unless they willingly choose the lordship of the true and rightful God. Governments in your world are typically ruled by persons who either deny God or who serve a false god or who merely acknowledge God's existence without any real submission to his will and authority. Such nations naturally fall prey to Satan. Your nation was once an exception. It was once a nation that truly acknowledged God and sought to foster the ideals of truth and freedom."

"But that's changed," Will inserted.

"Sadly, yes," Sheena affirmed. "The Revolutionary War freed the American colonies from tyrannical rule and established government by consent of the governed, but then the War of Imperial Aggression overthrew government by consent of the governed and reestablished imperialistic tyranny."

"Lawzzy me, that sure enough is sad, downright sad," Mildred bemoaned.

Sheena allowed a few moments of respectful reflection upon a war that spilled the blood of hundreds of thousands of young Americans for the cause of imperialistic domination. Then she addressed both Mildred and Will. "But your founding fathers foresaw the potential for evil to take hold of your central government. In addition to the freedom for any state to secede from the Union, your founding fathers wisely incorporated another means of counteracting the central government."

"They did?" Will prodded.

"Yes. And that is where my sponsors hope for your father's assistance. Three quarters of the states can pass an amendment to the constitution without consent of the central government. The president cannot rightfully veto such an amendment, and the Supreme Court cannot rightfully strike down such an amendment, and the central legislature cannot rightfully resist such an amendment. And my sponsors believe that the men and women who make up your military will join sides with the constitution and the American people rather than supporting a tyrant who would seize weapons from American citizens and wage war against American states and communities."

"I would agree with that," Will acknowledged. "It would be true for anyone I know who's in the military." He paused and lifted his phone, positioning his hands to send another text. "I assume that you would like my father to introduce an amendment to the constitution and encourage at least thirty-seven other states to pass the amendment along with Texas."

"Yes. Your father needs to contact all of the state legislatures and summon them to apply for a congressional convention for proposing amendments. Once he has succeeded in persuading two-thirds of the states to call for such a convention, then the Federal Congress is required by the constitution to respond and carry out the convention. Your father may then attend the convention and propose an amendment to the constitution, and then after three-fourths of the state legislatures approve the amendment, it becomes part of the constitution. Are you ready to transcribe an amendment that will proffer the hope of reviving the freedom that your founding fathers intended for your nation?"

A faint clap sounded from the chair where Mildred was seated. Will and Sheena both glanced toward Mildred, who sat leaning forward with her hands folded on her lap, and then they again faced one another.

"Okay," Will said. "I'm ready."

Sheena reached forward and picked up the notebook from beside Will. She flipped back through the pages until she found the page she was looking for, and then she drew a breath. As when stating the new Pledge of Allegiance, she spoke slowly so that Will could transcribe each word.

> An individual state of the United States of America may secede from the Union of the United States, thus becoming a free and sovereign state with total sovereignty over all territories, possessions, and entities within the outer boundaries of that state, even if such territories, possessions or entities were theretofore possessed by the federal government. The seceded state shall have total sovereignty over all coastal waters bordering that state. The seceded state shall then and thereafter possess all military or federal territories, buildings, bases, jets, ships, submarines, supplies, equipment, and other military or federal items usually housed, stored, positioned, or docked within the borders or in the coastal waters of that state prior to or during secession. Such secession of a state shall be accomplished by a 55 percent or greater vote of the citizens of that state and by a 55 percent or greater vote of the members of the House of Representatives of that state. An equivalent body to a state legislature, serving under a different title, may fulfill the requirement for secession in place of a state House of Representatives. Persons employed in the military at the time of secession may serve in any capacity proffered by any military that persists or arises subsequent to secession and may fulfill any previous military commitment in whichever military they choose and shall be free to choose between proffered positions of military employment for ninety days after the date of secession. Federal employees apart from the military may serve in any capacity proffered by any government

that persists or arises subsequent to secession, and may fulfill any previous commitment in whatever proffered employment they choose, and shall be free to choose between proffered positions of employment for ninety days after the date of secession. Any federal debt or tax owed by a citizen, military member, or any other entity of a seceding state becomes the possession of the seceded state on the date of secession, or within ninety days of secession in regard to military or federal personnel."

Will finished sending the second text to his father, and then he lowered the phone to his lap. He grinned as he faced Sheena. "You won't go off and leave me when my father asks you to join his staff, will you?"

Sheena's face bloomed. She placed the notebook back down on the coffee table without breaking eye contact with Will. "So you think he will like the amendment?"

"He'll absolutely love it. And I have no doubt that he'll do everything he can to get word out to the other states."

Sheena smiled and shook her head. "No, I won't leave you and move to Austin to work with your father, not unless you're moving there with me." Then she shifted to a more leisurely posture, leaning back and resting one arm on the back of the sofa. "So then, how do you think the people of your nation will respond when they learn the truth about the War of Imperial Aggression?"

Will hesitated.

"I'll speak ta that thar' question," Mildred interjected. Will and Sheena both faced her. She scooted forward to the edge of her seat and spoke with the animated accompaniment of open arms and hands. "No doubt both ya'll know enough about world history ta recollect how that thar statue of Joseph Stalin was ripped down in Hungary leavin' nothin' but the boots."

Will and Sheena both nodded as Mildred looked back and forth between their faces.

"Well, the way I figure it, the first thing ta happen will be fer some folks ta tear down that thar Statue of Lincoln that sits in Washington DC and raise up a statue of Robert E. Lee in its place. After all, Robert E. Lee was a Christian gentleman who downright condemned slavery as a 'moral and political evil,' and he turned the slaves his wife inherited plum loose and free. And besides all that, he fought ta uphold the actual words an' the actual spirit of the Declaration of Independence, namely that governments should derive ther just powers from the 'consent of the governed,' not by a tyrannical and unconstitutional war against free states."

Will and Sheena met one another's eyes and smiled, and then they looked back at Mildred.

Mildred was inspired by the looks of approval on Will's and Sheena's faces. "And that ain't all either. I think that thar face of Abe Lincoln that's whittled on the big rock at Mount Rushmore will get carved into the face of Booker T. Washington." She paused and folded her hands on her knees, again looking back and forth between Will and Sheena. "Booker T. Washington was a downright great American that went from bein' a slave ta bein' the foremost educator in the whole country."

"That's right," Sheena chimed in. "Booker T. Washington founded Tuskegee University, and a monument that stands in the center of the university campus is engraved with the following words: 'He lifted the veil of ignorance from his people and pointed the way to progress through education and industry.'"

Will and Mildred both stared at Sheena. They wondered how a woman from another planet was so well versed in American history.

Sheena easily interpreted the looks of awe on Will's and Mildred's faces. "I had a very good history teacher," she commented. "And besides, I had a special interest in American history."

"I'd sure enough guess you did," Mildred said. "You've jes gotta come ta some of our Historical Society meetin's." She glanced at Will and then looked back at Sheena. "Maybe you can tell the society what ya think Texas ought ta do as soon as that amendment clarifyin' the freedom fer states to secede gets passed by thirty-eight of the states."

"That's easy," Sheena responded. "Texas should exercise its First Amendment right to *establish*, and then they should put prayer back in the public schools. If the federal government forbids such action, even though such forbiddance is without doubt in breech of the First Amendment, then Texas can band together with a few other states and threaten to form a separate nation if the federal government doesn't back off and permit the exercise of the foremost right in the Bill of Rights, namely the right to establish."

"The right to establish?" Will queried

Sheena faced Will with a startled expression. "Aren't you familiar with the First Amendment to your Constitution?"

"Well sure, I can quote it," Will affirmed.

"Then what's the very first freedom that the amendment protects?"

"The freedom of religion," Will stated.

"No," Sheena gently chided. "The first freedom protected in the Bill of Rights is the freedom for states to *establish religion*, not just the freedom of *religion*. 'Of religion' is simply an adjective phrase that denotes the specific nature of *establishing* that the states are free to carry out, namely the *establishing of religion*. It is perfectly acceptable, in light of the foremost right in the Bill of Rights, for Texas to proclaim itself a Christian state and to establish Christianity as the official religion of Texas, and to teach Christianity as a required course in every public school within the borders of the state."

"Whoa, whillakers! Now I know you've gotta come ta our meetins," Mildred declared.

Will addressed Sheena's eyes with intent interest. "I've never heard that before. I mean, from what little I know about English composition, I guess it makes sense. But I thought the First Amendment was just talking about freedom of religion, not freedom to establish religion."

Sheena shook her head. "No way. Without the freedom to establish religion, the states would have no freedom of religion at all. Religion would end up being dictated by the federal government."

"Jes' like what's happened," Mildred inserted.

Sheena resumed. "Furthermore, it would make no sense to interpret the phrase 'Congress shall make no law respecting an establishment of religion' as a reference to making laws that pertain to a particular church, rather than to the act of establishing religion. If it meant that Congress could make no law pertaining to a particular church, then that church could own slaves, import and export cocaine, and manufacture nuclear weapons, all of which could be done with complete immunity from any federal laws. It would be insane for anyone to be so stupid as to interpret the First Amendment that way." Sheena's expression altered, and she brought a hand to her breast. "I'm sorry. I hope I didn't offend you. Sometimes I get rather emotional when it comes to certain subjects."

Will laughed. And then he faced Sheena with a look of inspired deliberation. "No. I'm not offended. I'm just dumbfounded to think how hoodwinked I've been. You're perfectly right. The First Amendment's freedom of speech is not just the freedom to give particular speeches, and the First Amendment's freedom of the press is not just the freedom of particular printing establishments, so why should the freedom of religion be the freedom of particular religious establishments? It must be, as you say, the freedom for states to establish religion." Then his brow furrowed. "But if that's true, then what's all the talk about Thomas Jefferson's separation of church and state?"

Sheena swept her arm from her breast and grasped the back of the sofa in a playful gesture of exasperation. "No! Not separation of church and the local state, but rather separation of church and the federal state. The federal government cannot pass any laws that establish religion, nor can the federal government pass any laws that deny the individual states the freedom of establishing religion."

"Wow!" Will said. "Is that really what Thomas Jefferson meant in regard to separation of church and state?"

"Of course. In Jefferson's second inaugural address, he made the following statement:

> 'In matters of religion, I have considered that its free exercise is placed by the Constitution independent of the powers of the general government. I have therefore undertaken, on no occasion, to prescribe the religious exercises suited to it, but have left them, as the Constitution found them, under the direction and discipline of state or church authorities acknowledged by the several religious societies.'

"So in other words, Jefferson clearly stated that the federal government, which he referred to as the general government, could neither establish religion nor interfere with the freedom for individual states to establish religion. He even went on to say that the establishment of religion by the individual states could either be carried out by state authorities or by church authorities."

"Lands ta Betsy!" Mildred exclaimed.

"And Thomas Jefferson did not merely give verbal support in regard to the freedom for individual states to establish religion, he wrote it down in bold ink," Sheena asserted.

"Really?" Will coaxed.

"You bet. Just listen to what he wrote in a letter that was penned on January 23, 1808:

> 'I consider the government of the United States as interdicted by the Constitution from intermeddling with religious institutions, their doctrines, discipline, or exercises. This results not only from the provisions that

no law shall be made respecting the establishment or free exercise of religion, but from that also which reserves to the states the powers not delegated to the United States. Certainly no power to prescribe any religious exercise, or to assume authority in religious discipline, has been delegated to the general government. It must then rest with the states, as far as it can be in any human authority.'

"And I would add that Thomas Jefferson practiced what he preached—he supported a bill that called for a day of fasting and prayer while he served on the Virginia State Legislature, but he shunned such activity on the federal level when he served as president. And Jefferson made it clear that the freedom for individual states to establish religion should not be vulnerable to any alteration or judgment on the part of the United States Supreme Court, a fact that he made clear in the Kentucky Resolutions of seventeen ninety-nine."

"I'll be branded pink," Mildred declared. "Sounds ta me like Thomas Jefferson said the exact opposite of what most of them federal government dictators have been shovin' down our throats. Thomas Jefferson told the federal government ta keep thar grubby hands off the freedom for states ta establish religion, an' that would include the freedom ta be prayin' in public schools."

"Quite right," Sheena affirmed. "Thomas Jefferson's teachings would not only grant states the freedom to institute prayer in public schools, but also the freedom to pass out Bibles and teach Christianity. The overwhelming majority of men who signed your nation's Declaration of Independence were Christian, and the delegate from Massachusetts who introduced the First Amendment to the Constitution, namely Fisher Ames, said that Bible teaching should be in public schools. And besides all that, we should honor and respect our Creator regardless of what our ancestors have done before us, and the Creator should never be banned from any public institution."

Mildred slapped her hands to her thighs. "That cinches it," she said. "I've got the Bill of Rights and Thomas Jefferson both backin' me, not ta mention our Creator, so I'm gonna ask Principal Edwards ta let me give a prayer on the loudspeaker at the school, and jes' let them highhanded feds come an' give me the chance ta announce ta the whole country how we've been bushwangled."

Will looked at Mildred with fond concern. "You're a brave and noble woman, Mildred, but maybe we'd best plan out our strategy for regaining our constitutional freedoms before we make our first move. I'd like to get my dad involved along with us."

Mildred took a deep breath and then sighed. "Okay, but jes' don't be waitin' till I get too old ta crawl outa ma bed an' walk on ma own two feet. I'm wantin' in on this *first move*."

Will and Sheena both laughed. "Don't worry. You're too great a warrior to leave on the sidelines," Will said.

"And while we're on the subject of religions, let me say this," Sheena interposed. "My sponsors believe your states should permit the practice of most any religion in regard to private homes, private schools, and private places of worship. They say this reflects God's respect for the *free will* that he has granted to mankind. After all, God allows men and women to embrace eternal damnation if they so choose."

"So then, the majority of people in a state can select what religion they will or will not establish in public schools, while private schools are free to conduct themselves in an entirely different manner," interpreted Will.

"Yes, that's right. But also consider this—If some diabolical cult from hell poses as the true religion of God, and if that cult promotes the indiscriminate maiming and murder of innocent men, women, and children to an intolerable degree; or in other words, if that cult engages in terrorism to such an extent that people become fearful of leaving their own homes; then states should be free to ban that religion from within their borders on account of public safety—not on account of religion, but on account of public safety."

"I know jes' what cult yer talkin' about," Mildred stated. "I've got a second cousin who's one of 'em. I pray for 'em ever single day."

Will set his eyes upon Sheena. "I couldn't agree with you more, but I believe this conversation got started with how your sponsors, as you call them, want my dad to contribute to our mission—namely the mission to help people who suffer from diabetes."

"That's right," Sheena said.

"Okay then. Your sponsors apparently want my dad to help bring freedom back to our nation."

"Yes."

"Well then, what does freedom have to do with diabetes?"

"It has everything to do with diabetes," Sheena asserted. "My sponsors have sent me to reveal the etiology of diabetes, but what good would it do for me to explain the most prevalent cause of diabetes and how to counteract that cause if your federal government will simply exercise its imperialistic powers to squelch anything that you try to accomplish with that information?"

The room fell to a still quiet, with the trickling of the fountains rising above all other sound. Will and Mildred both stared at Sheena with inquiring eyes. "Do you think that the federal government would actually take measures to keep people from finding out about the cause of diabetes?" Will asked. His voice carried a tone of incredulity.

Sheena countered Will's query. "Would concealing the cause of diabetes be more inconceivable than concealing the origin of the pledge that your government compelled children across your nation to recite? Would it be any worse than glorifying one of the worst war criminals in history to a position of virtual sainthood in order to justify treason against your Constitution and a bloody war against free states? If the release of certain information were to pose a threat to the power and wealth of the ruling hierarchy that constitutes your federal government, then why would it be difficult for you to believe that your federal government would choose to permit people to continue suffering with illness rather than risk the loss of political power and material riches?"

Again, Will and Mildred both gazed at Sheena in silence.

"How could releasing information about the cause of diabetes pose a threat to the federal government?" Will asked.

"What if the cause of diabetes is directly connected with multitrillion-dollar industry that plays a major role in the institution and preservation of your federal government?"

"That 'ud sure do it," Mildred said.

Will studied Sheena's countenance and contemplated the nature of her statement. "It's already happened, hasn't it?" he averred. "I mean, the government has already done something to keep the American people from finding out about the cause of diabetes, am I right?"

Sheena glanced at Mildred and then faced Will with a sober mien. "We are venturing into a topic that could entail danger."

Will followed suit and peered toward Mildred, noting her intense concentration, and then he again faced Sheena. "Okay then, I'm game for a change of subject. So what's the primary cause of diabetes?"

Sheena seemed relieved by the change of subject, but she also appeared to be taken off guard. She addressed Will with uncertain eyes. "Oh, yes, that's a good question," she proffered. Then she paused in thought for several seconds. "My sponsors thought it would be best to disclose the cause of diabetes in a gradual and convincing manner. They were afraid that simply stating the cause of diabetes would put you in a difficult position, given your educational background and training."

Will could not help smiling at Sheena's expression. "Okay, well, I'm not really doing anything else at the moment, so how about getting started with the gradual and convincing revelation?"

"Sure enough, let's do," Mildred encouraged.

Sheena looked at Mildred and Will in turn. She lifted a hand and fondled the pearl necklace that continued to glow upon her bosom. "Okay then. Your communication device still has access to information from my world, information that you could not normally retrieve on your Internet."

Will lifted the phone from his lap. "I'm ready."

"First enter 'chewing tobacco and diabetes' and search for studies that look for an association between the practice of chewing tobacco and acquiring diabetes."

A look of interest seized Will's visage. Several minutes passed as he searched through different sites and even used different search engines. Then a look of puzzlement creased the borders of his eyes as he lowered the phone and faced Sheena. "It looks like there's no association at all. I mean, chewing tobacco or dipping snuff does not appear to increase the rate of diabetes at all."

"Exactly," Sheena said. "Now enter 'cigarette smoking and diabetes.'"

Only a couple of minutes passed before Will lowered the phone and raised perplexed yet intrigued eyes. "Wow. Increased insulin resistance can be measured by the number of cigarettes smoked, and one study concluded that smoking fifteen to twenty-five cigarettes per day triples the rate of diabetes, and another study showed that smoking one pack of cigarettes per day more than doubles the rate of diabetes while stopping smoking drops the chances of acquiring diabetes to only about twenty percent higher than nonsmokers." He pondered the data as he continued facing Sheena. "How could that be? I mean, if chewing tobacco—"

"Now enter 'air pollution and diabetes,'" Sheena said, knowing the nature of Will's question.

Will's intrigued expression intensified. He again surfed the Internet, this time in search of epidemiological studies addressing air pollution and diabetes. Again, only a couple of minutes passed before he lowered the phone and faced Sheena. He gave Mildred a look before addressing Sheena. "There's not merely an association between the degree of air pollution and diabetes, there's a remarkably strong association."

"Correct. Now enter 'nuts and diabetes.'"

About four minutes passed before Will reported his findings. "It appears that mixed nuts score a bit higher than peanuts and peanut butter, but they all lower the incidence of diabetes to a substantial degree. One study concludes that eating an ounce or more of nuts daily, at least five days a week, lowers the incidence of diabetes by thirty percent."

"And nuts contain fat, right?" Sheena asked.

"It must be good fat," Will said. His brows converged questioningly. "But even at that, how would eating any kind of fat decrease the rate of diabetes?"

"Maybe it's not the fat so much as the sulfur-containing amino acids," Sheena posed.

Will stared. He sensed that the conversation was drawing closer to a disclosure. "Okay then, it's the sulfur-containing amino acids that lower the rate of diabetes. But how?"

Sheena peered into Will's eyes and leaned slightly toward him. "Think. Nothing in chewing tobacco increases the incidence of diabetes, but something produced by burning tobacco greatly increases the incidence of diabetes. Whatever that something is, it must also be in air pollution, and that would explain why fat people and pregnant women get more diabetes because both conditions result in increased respiration—they breathe more air." Sheena stopped speaking long enough to lean back and don an expression of inquiry. "So then, why don't persons who exercise acquire more diabetes? Don't they also breathe more air?"

"I give up. Why?" Will asked, anxious to hear Sheena's explanation.

"Among other things, exercise produces lactic acid, and lactic acid is converted to pyruvic acid, and pyruvic acid is an antidote for a poison in air pollution that binds to insulin molecules and deactivates them, thus causing insulin resistance. And that same poison is a beta-cell toxin, gradually destroying the cells in the pancreas that produce insulin, thereby resulting in type 2 diabetes. And that same poison can also bind to the beta cells in the pancreas and trigger an immune response, causing a person's own immune system to attack and destroy the beta cells, thus resulting in type 1 diabetes."

"And besides being neutralized by pyruvic acid, that same poison is neutralized by sulfur-containing amino acids," Will guessed.

Sheena hesitated. "Well, yes, in a way. Organic acids such as pyruvic acid and alpha-ketoglutaric acid bind to the poison and deactivate it, whereas the sulfurs provided by sulfur-containing amino acids are used by the body to metabolize the poison, resulting in a byproduct that is fifty times less toxic."

"Okay. So what poison is it?" Will asked.

The curious look on Will's face caused Sheena to smile as she responded with additional data. "It is a poison produced by many industrial processes, including simply burning gasoline or coal. A heavy-duty truck can emit enough of this poison to kill someone while being driven merely one mile. And the scrubbers typically used on stacks at coal-burning power plants do not destroy this poison. Some passes into the air from the stacks, and some enters the atmosphere from the surfaces of waters where the scrub fluids are discharged. Once the poison enters the atmosphere, 98 percent of the poison remains in the lower atmosphere, namely the portion of the atmosphere that persons on the surface of the earth breathe. And then, as if all of that were not bad enough, the half-life of the poison in the atmosphere is roughly two years, meaning that the poison can encircle the entire earth in less than one half-life."

"So that's why the rate of diabetes shot up in China, even in populations of people who are generally slender and eat healthy diets. They've cranked up a large number of coal-burning power plants," Will remarked.

"Right."

Will and Mildred again faced one another.

"Why don't you ask her this time?" Will suggested, still facing Mildred.

Mildred nodded and then addressed Sheena. "You've explained all this stuff simple enough. Even I understood what you were sayin'. So then, what nasty poison floats around in the air an' makes folks come down with diabetes?"

Sheena faced Will. "I'm not really supposed to tell you until you're convinced that diabetes is caused by an air pollutant. I don't think I've mentioned that vulnerability to this particular air pollutant can be hereditary, explaining why the risk for diabetes is both hereditary and environmental. Do you need some more data?"

"No. I'm convinced. What's the pollutant?"

"The next search will answer your question," Sheena said. "Enter '*Houston Chronicle*, front page, December 18, 1981.'"

A look of astonishment sprang to Will's features. He raised his phone and began entering the search line. He looked up. "What was that date?"

"December 18, 1981."

He looked back down and completed the entry. Then both Sheena and Mildred watched his eyes widen. He read from the screen, "Doctor at odds with city, Heights physician has faith in cyanide diagnosis, God." Then he raised his eyes and faced Sheena. "It's cyanide?"

"Yes, airborne cyanide. One of the most potent poisons known to man."

Will pointed at his phone. "And this doctor knew about it way back in 1981? Why wasn't anything done about it?"

"It's a long story," Sheena replied. "Suffice it to say that when only ten positive tests for cyanide were acquired from a single laboratory, the findings were splashed all over the front pages of newspapers and reported on live television. On the other hand, when a hundred positive tests were acquired from several different laboratories, there was a total blackout—no one reported anything, not a single newspaper and not a single television station."

Will and Mildred exchanged looks of amazed concern.

"Why?" Will asked.

Sheena responded with additional questions. "Why did the first laboratory stop reporting any blood cyanide levels that measured less than ten micrograms per deciliter, even though the first level they reported was only two micrograms per deciliter? Why were the three laboratories in your nation that tested for urine thiocyanate, a metabolite of cyanide, reduced to only one laboratory? And why was the method of testing for urine thiocyanate at that one laboratory completely changed while still using reference values from the old method of testing?"

Will shook his head in concerned bewilderment.

Sheena continued, "Why was testing for immunological sensitivity to cyanide halted, namely testing developed by a microallergist from Johns Hopkins who observed the reaction of patients' white blood cells in a solution that contained cyanide bound to those patients' native proteins? And why was the physician who discovered that airborne cyanide was affecting human health not able to convince any laboratory in the entire Nation to perform simultaneous tests for methemoglobin and cyanmethemoglobin, tests that may have proven very useful for detecting exposure to environmental levels of airborne cyanide?"

Several moments of silent contemplation ensued. "It was a cover-up," Will surmised.

"Yes," Sheena avowed. "It was a cover-up of monumental magnitude. Imagine the untold human suffering that could have been prevented during all the years that have passed since the latter years of the twentieth century—the loss of vision, loss of limbs, painful neuropathies, kidney failures, and untimely deaths."

Will was all too familiar with the relentless disease processes of diabetes. He continued facing Sheena. "The newspaper headline mentioned God. Was the doctor who made this discovery a Christian?"

"Yes. And not only that, he gave God full credit for the discovery."

Will absorbed Sheena's proclamation and presented a look of resolve. "Did he figure out any way to treat people? I mean, there obviously wasn't much done about the air pollution—people apparently weren't even informed about it—but did this doctor figure out any way to help his own patients?"

"That he did," Sheena said. She reached to the coffee table and picked up her notebook. She turned back to a blank page and handed the notebook to Will. Will picked up the pen from the seat of the sofa and positioned himself to write.

Sheena spoke slowly, waiting for Will to write down every word she spoke. "Per compounding pharmacies, injectable vitamin B12 mixed as twelve and one-half milligrams of hydroxocobalamin per milliliter and twelve and one-half milligrams of methylcobalamin per milliliter, for a total B12 concentration of twenty-five milligrams per milliliter. Inject anywhere from 0.3 milliliters every three days, to 0.5 milliliters daily, depending on finances and insurance coverage. It can be injected either intramuscularly or subcutaneously."

"Got it," Will said.

"Then, food grade sodium thiosulfate pentahydrate salt. Take a small pinch, perhaps one sixty-fourth of a teaspoon, either dissolved in a few ounces of water and drank, or simply dissolved under the tongue, every two or three hours while awake."

"Got it."

"Alpha-ketoglutaric acid. Drink one-eighth of a teaspoon dissolved in eight ounces of water in the middle of each meal, three times daily."

"Got it."

"Vitamin B6, either fifty milligrams four times a day, or one hundred milligrams morning and evening, or else fifty milligrams with breakfast, fifty milligrams with lunch, and one hundred milligrams in the evening. Divided doses are better. And also take folic acid, four hundred micrograms morning and evening, and Vitamin D3, one thousand units daily."

"Got it."

Sheena was silent. Will looked up and met her eyes.

"That's it?" Will asked.

Sheena nodded. "Yes. And persons who take the special B12 injections on a daily basis may not need as much sodium thiosulfate or alpha-ketoglutaric acid. While on the other hand, persons who shun needles may omit the B12 injections and supplement full doses of sodium thiosulfate and alpha-ketoglutaric acid with sublingual methylcobalamin tablets or sublingual hydroxocobalamin tablets—at least one sublingual tablet daily, but preferably one tablet each morning and one tablet each evening, with each tablet containing at least 2,000 micrograms of methylcobalamin or hydroxocobalamin, but preferably containing 5,000 micrograms of methylcobalamin."

Will finished jotting down some notes and then rested his hand. He and Sheena addressed one another's eyes in thought.

"Well," Mildred injected, slapping both hands to her thighs. She faced Sheena and smiled. "I bet that's about all the stuff that Will's brain can soak up for one sittin', even if he's the downright smartest man I ever met." She looked back and forth between them. "How about some more of that blackberry cobbler?"

Will and Sheena faced one another with inquiring countenances. Their postures relaxed.

"Sounds good to me," Will said.

Sheena addressed Mildred. "Me too. I think that blackberry cobbler of yours is just about as downright delicious as puca pies back home."

Will smiled.

Chapter 6

Sheena adapted to her new job quickly. Katie, who was used to functioning both as a nurse and receptionist, served as a tutor. The patients were very cordial—news that Dr. Johnson had a new girlfriend who was working in his office circulated throughout Pineville within hours, along with the fact that she was working for free.

"I just can't believe you're doing so well already," Katie said. She had entered the front office and was peering at the computer screen as Sheena entered data. "There's no way I'd have thought you could do all that by the end of your first day."

"Thanks," Sheena said.

Katie handed Sheena a patient chart. "Just one more chart after this. Will's with his last patient. After Wilma's done checking out, I need her chart back in the lab."

"No problem."

Sheena finished checking out an elderly lady with diabetes, hypertension, and hypothyroidism, and then she carried the lady's chart to one of two back rooms in the clinic. The laboratory was to her left; and across the hallway, to her right, was the break room. Katie was seated before a lab computer. The room was stocked with provisions such as needles and syringes, vacuum blood vials, a centrifuge, a microscope, a small refrigerator, specimen collection cups, tourniquets, bandages, rubber gloves, and urine dipsticks. Situated in one wall was a small metal door that opened into a chamber connecting the laboratory with an adjacent bathroom.

"Here's the chart," Sheena said.

"Thank you," Katie replied, laying the chart beside the computer screen.

"You're welcome," Sheena said. She stepped into the hallway and began walking back to the front office.

"No!" came a gruff voice from the exam room nearest the front office.

Sheena stopped and moved close to the exam room door where she could hear the conversation taking place between Will and the final patient that she had checked into the clinic, Dr. Terrance Turner. She recalled that Dr. Turner was a tall, distinguished-looking gentleman wearing a grey suit.

The voice sounded again, though now more subdued. Sheena had to listen closely to hear what was spoken. "As I've told you before, I'm a retired logic professor, and I don't want you or anyone else praying for me. If it was logical to believe in some god that created the universe, then maybe I'd consider it logical to have someone pray for me. But it isn't, and I don't."

A look of sheer amazement passed over Sheena's face. She had been taught that there are men who walk the surface of the earth who deny the existence of a creator, but she found such teaching difficult to believe. Even the wicked inhabitants of Vandolia believe that the earth was created by a god, though unfortunately, they worship a god of lies who cannot grant eternal life to anyone. After a few moments of recollecting her wits and contemplating the matter, she strode to the front office and lifted a small stool with wheels. She carried the stool back to the door to the exam room and set it down before the door. Then she knocked.

"Yes?" came Will's voice.

"Can I come in?"

"Yes."

Sheena opened the door, rolled the stool inside, and then closed the door behind her. She positioned the stool so that she sat between Will and Dr. Turner, with Will seated on a stool and Dr. Turner seated on the end of an exam table. Then she smiled as she looked at both of their faces.

Sheena's appearance and demeanor were spellbinding. She was attired in similar garments to what she wore the previous day, except that the white pearls were suspended above a green satin dress with a golden belt and golden shoes. Her brilliant red hair and striking blue eyes captured the full regard of both men. They just stared with quizzical expressions.

Sheena settled her eyes on Dr. Turner. "Please pardon my intrusion, but I believe I overheard you say that you are a retired logic professor. Is that correct?"

Dr. Turner nodded, and his face brightened. "Yes."

Sheena straightened and clasped her arms to her body in a gesture of enthused interest. "Oh wow, that was one of my favorite fields of interest. I studied logic for quite a number of years." She glanced at Will, who faced her with a curious and amused countenance, and then looked back at Dr. Turner.

"You're hardly old enough to have studied logic for 'quite a number of years,' as you put it," Dr. Turner said. He spoke with obvious condescension, but the tone of his voice revealed that he was flattered rather than annoyed. "I was no doubt studying logic before you were even born."

Sheena smiled. "With all of your experience and training, would you mind my asking you a few questions? That is, if Dr. Johnson does not object."

"No, that's fine. Go right ahead," Will said.

Sheena noted that Will's face evinced expectant interest. She faced Dr. Turner. "I would like to delve into some of the fundamental basics of human logic. In your opinion, can something come into being from absolutely nothing?"

Dr. Turner proffered a smug smile. "Of course not," he declared. "In order for any given thing to exist, that thing must come into being by effect of one or more other things, either by deliberate act or spontaneously."

"I like the way you put that," Sheena said. "You make a complicated issue so conclusively simple."

Dr. Turner's chest swelled as he peered toward Will with a look of self-satisfaction. Will gave no outward response.

"My next question is this," Sheena said, again capturing Dr. Turner's attention. "In order for *something* to exist, is it necessary for that *something* to have a beginning at some point in the spectrum of time?"

"Of course," Dr. Turner replied. "The beginning, persistence, and ending of any given thing is quantified in a progressive linear dimension that we refer to as time."

Sheena raised her hands and then plopped them down on her lap. "Well then, I guess it's final. Nothing exists."

Dr. Turner's chest sank downward as he stared at Sheena with a look of bewilderment. Will dropped his face to hide a smile.

"What?" Dr. Turner managed to ask.

Sheena's face bore an image of simplistic innocence. "Well, it only makes sense that if the beginning of any given thing occurs in the dimension of time, then everything that exists must begin at some point in time. Am I correct?"

"Well, yes."

"And if everything must begin at some point in time, then any two things that exist must either begin simultaneously, or else they must begin in sequence, one after the other. Am I correct?"

"Of course."

"And if that is true, then there must have been *something* that came to exist first, either by itself or in sequence with one or more other *things*, and that something or those things must have come into existence before anything else came into existence. Is that not logical?"

There was long pause. Dr. Turner stared at Sheena's eyes. His brows drew together and the muscles of his face grew slack. "Yes," he spoke softly, and then he spoke again before Sheena had a chance to respond. "And that something or those things, since it or they came into being before anything else, must have come from absolutely nothing, which is impossible, so it is only logical to conclude that nothing exists."

Sheena broke eye contact with Dr. Turner as she shrugged and nodded. Then she reached down to her leg and pinched. "Ouch!" she said, jolting up on the stool and meeting Dr. Turner's eyes. "How is that possible? How could I feel myself pinch my leg if I do not exist?"

Will choked down a chuckle by feigning a cough.

After several moments of staring into Sheena's eyes, Dr. Turner turned his face and looked at Will. Will managed a sober visage, and then shrugged and looked toward Sheena.

"Very well," Dr. Turner said, again meeting Sheena's eyes. No inkling of condescension persisted in his demeanor. He seemed, rather, to bear an expression of awe, as if he deemed Sheena to be an intellectual genius. "You've just proven the very basis of human logic to be illogical. What next?"

"Well, I suggest that we solve the dilemma by means of further logic."

A look of intrigue rose to the logic professor's countenance. "By all means, yes. Please proceed."

Sheena proffered a gracious nod before speaking. "We have logically concluded that one of two suppositions is incorrect. Either, something cannot come from absolutely nothing must be incorrect, or else, everything that exists must have a beginning must be incorrect. The only other conclusion would be that both are incorrect, but I think it would be more logical to conclude that only one of those suppositions is incorrect. Do you agree?"

Will noted that Dr. Turner appeared to comprehend everything that Sheena said.

"Yes," Dr. Turner said.

"Okay then. Which supposition, in the opinion of an experienced logic professor, is most logical to dismiss?"

A few seconds passed as Dr. Turner pondered the matter. Then his lips parted. "Without any doubt, it is more logical to dismiss the supposition that everything that exists must have a beginning. Scientific observation strongly supports the supposition that something cannot come from absolutely nothing, whereas the supposition that everything that exists must have a beginning is more the product of intellectual contemplation."

Sheena granted a smile, resulting in a sigh and a retuned smile on the part of Dr. Turner. "I most emphatically agree," Sheena said. "And this, of course, opens a new and exhilarating world of logic, namely the world of logic that one enters when one realizes that something or some things must have existed without having a beginning."

Dr. Turner turned his head and met eyes with Will. The two men wore similar expressions, expressions of wonder. Then Dr. Turner returned his gaze to Sheena. "You've given an old logic professor much to ponder," he said. "I would assume that you have already given extensive thought to the matter. What are your conclusions?"

Sheena produced a winsome smile. "I am most pleased that you have asked that question. First consider that something existing without having a beginning may as well be someone. This is true for the simple reason that something or someone existing with no beginning is not limited by principles of origin, development, evolution, nutrition, sustenance, or maturation. Would you not agree?"

The look in Dr. Turner's eyes deepened. "Well, yes, that would be logical."

"So then, given the intricacies and complexities of the physical universe and organic life upon the earth, which of these two entities would it be more logical to accept as existing without having a beginning—some sort of inorganic cosmic goop or an intelligent Being capable of creating the universe and everything within it?"

Dr. Turner nearly collapsed. He dropped his face and braced his hands on the forward edge of the exam table. A long minute elapsed. When he raised his face, his visage was wholly altered. He looked at Will for several seconds and then addressed Sheena. "Beyond all doubt, it is much more logical to conclude that an intelligent and capable Creator existed without having a beginning."

"Very well," Sheena pronounced. "And in line with this reasoning, it would be logical to conclude that an intelligent God created mankind, would it not?"

"Yes."

"And given the emotional and personal qualities of human beings, it would be logical to conclude that the Creator possesses emotions and personality, would it not?"

"Yes."

"So then, would it also be logical to conclude that God intended to have some sort of interaction and relationship with mankind?"

"Yes."

"Okay then, would it also be logical to conclude that at least one of the religions known to mankind reflects or contains communication from God?"

"Yes."

Sheena shifted positions on the stool and looked at Will. He stared at her in silence. She turned back to Dr. Turner. "In consideration of all of our logical conclusions, what religion or religions would it be most logical to deem as communication from God?"

Dr. Turner took some time before answering. He broke eye contact and gazed away from Will and Sheena. Then he turned his face back and addressed Sheena. "Only one religious leader claimed to be a person of God and then proved his claims by working miracles and rising from the dead. I've known for a long time that historical records, the fulfillment of prophesies, and the conduct of his disciples all yield strong evidence to the claims of Jesus Christ. I simply could not get past my presumptive opinion that it was illogical to believe in a Creator."

"But now you realize that it is fundamentally logical to believe in a Creator, do you not?" Sheena posed.

"Yes."

"And are you aware that Jesus Christ claimed to be the exclusive avenue to eternal life, thus negating the validity of any religion that proffers eternal life while rejecting the claims of Jesus Christ?"

"Yes."

Sheena peered into Dr. Turner's eyes. "Do you choose life or death?"

Dr. Turner's face took on a look of elation. He faced Will. "I'll see you in church Sunday. I've got to go tell Martha." He looked back at Sheena. "Send me a bill," he said, and then he slid down from the exam table and headed for the closed door to the room.

"Wait!" Sheena voiced.

Dr. Turner pivoted around and faced her.

"What would occur if you were killed in an automobile accident on the way home?"

A look of terror passed across Dr. Turner's features. He knelt to one knee and prayed out loud. "God, I repent of my unbelief and sin. I ask your forgiveness through the blood sacrifice of Jesus Christ, who I wholly choose as my Lord and Savior. I proclaim that you are the true God and Creator, and I rejoice to be your child forever."

Without speaking another word, Dr. Terrance Turner rose and exited the room, closing the door behind him as he departed.

Sheena met Will's eyes. "Martha is his wife," Will said. "She's been praying for him for over thirty years."

"Then her prayers have been answered," Sheena said.

Will rolled his stool forward and positioned himself next to Sheena where he could gaze closely into her eyes. He spoke in a low and sincere voice. "You're more wonderful than I ever dreamed possible for any human being. I love you more than I ever imagined I could love a woman."

Tears glazed Sheena's eyes as she leaned forward and met Will's lips. When their lips parted, the two of them just sat and delved into one another's eyes. And then Will spoke again. "Will you marry me?"

Sheena smiled and continued peering into Will's eyes. And then she thrust forward and clasped her arms around his neck and spoke into his ear. "I love you, William Bartholomew Johnson. And, yes, with all my heart, yes. I will marry you."

Sheena released Will's neck and again gazed into his eyes. They started to kiss again, but then Sheena turned her face toward the door.

"What is it?" Will asked.

"Listen," Sheena said.

There came the sound of footsteps.

"I don't care who you are, you can't just barge—" Katie's voice sounded, but then her speech ceased. A moment later came a muffled bang, a brief groan, and the sounds of something or someone toppling to the floor. Footsteps recommenced.

Will rose from his stool. Sheena also arose. They exchanged looks of puzzlement and alarm. Then the door swung open. Will and Sheena drew close together and took a step backward. A man in a dark suit stood in the open doorway with a raised gun.

"What do you want?" Will asked.

"Dr. Johnson, I presume," the man said. Another man entered and stepped beside the first man. The second man reached inside his suit jacket and withdrew a gun that was identical to the weapon held by the first man.

Sheena looked at both men. She scrutinized their weapons. "Nukemaster derringers," she remarked in a calm voice. Both men's brows rose. Will peered back and forth between Sheena and the two men. "Each pistol holds five darts, and each dart is capable of rendering a victim unconscious within seconds."

The two men glanced at one another, and then the man who was the first to enter faced Sheena and spoke. "These weapons are top secret. How is it that a visitor from Switzerland knows anything about them?"

"I assume you took it upon yourself to eavesdrop on private messages between a son and his father," Sheena stated, seemingly ignoring the man's question.

"When a son's father happens to be a renegade governor, a governor who takes it upon himself to threaten the security of an entire nation, then we make it a point to monitor all communications."

"Governor Johnson is a man who loves freedom and honors the Constitution of the United States," Sheena rebutted. "He's no threat to the homeland envisioned by this nation's founding fathers. You are."

The man's grim expression seemed unaltered by Sheena's proclamation. "You can discuss politics later. Let's be going."

"On what charge?" Will challenged. "You can't just come in here and arrest us without any cause."

"We can take whatever action we deem necessary when it's a matter of national security," the man spoke coolly. "The charge against both of you is intergalactic conspiracy to overthrow the United States of America."

Will faced Sheena. She met his eyes. His countenance bore no hint of doubt or distrust; rather, he held her eyes with a look of grave concern. She absorbed the compassion and apprehension that poured from his eyes and felt her heart throb with fretful affection. Then a sudden recollection rose and captured her mind—she recalled how her mother's life was spared after being incarcerated in Brockman Penitentiary for the purpose of luring the return and capture of a presumed alien from another planet.

Sheena turned her face and peered at the second man who entered, and then she shifted her eyes and addressed the first man. "I am the daughter of Justin Collins, one of the three Quazarian warriors who were murdered by your special forces and whose bodies were dissected by your scientists."

The man shrugged. "I don't know what you're talking about."

"I'm talking about the three warriors, two men and one woman, who had power-generating cylinders embedded across their foreheads." Sheena paused and perused the man's eyes for several seconds. "I understand that your scientists experienced some sort of difficulty when they attempted to analyze the cylinders—something about an explosion."

The man's staid countenance was momentarily swept by a look of incredulity. "Impossible. That would make you well over a century old."

"We age differently where I come from," Sheena said. "I will leave a Buccal smear in the laboratory to prove my claim. I know your scientists have kept record of the DNA composition of my father's body."

The man visually inspected Sheena. "We have this building surrounded. You cannot hope to escape."

"Will," Sheena spoke. She turned her face and met his eyes.

Will stared back in silence.

"My father and mother—namely Justin and Rachel Collins—both grew up in this nation before moving to the place where I was born. I'm 157 years old; but my body, here in this world, has the relative maturity of a seventeen-year-old female, and I will age accordingly. Can you still love me? Can you still love me if I have power-generating cylinders implanted across my forehead? Can you still love me if I return to rescue you with superhuman powers?"

Will glanced down at the white pearls that rested upon Sheena's chest. He wondered if those pearls could somehow transport her body to another location. He then gazed into her eyes. "I already believe that you have superhuman powers. Of course I'd still love you." He shook his head with sincerity while staring into her eyes. "More certain than anything else in this entire world apart from my faith in God, I am certain of this—I love you."

The two men watched in silence, but the man who had spoken leveled the barrel of his gun toward Sheena's shoulder.

"Becoming superhuman is a little complicated," Sheena said, still speaking to Will, but consciously conveying a message to the two men who held raised weapons. "Give me two years. Look for me to liberate you on this very date, two years from today."

A bang and thud sounded almost simultaneously. Will saw Sheena reach for her shoulder and lunge forward, and then he heard a second bang and felt a sting in his upper right chest.

Will became aware of mumbling sounds, and then he realized that it was his own mumbling. His mind seemed a myriad of memories and images that whirled in disconcerted efforts to bring one or more subjects into focus. Then his eyes opened, and he remembered that he and Sheena had been shot with tranquilizing darts. He surveyed his surroundings, a spacious room with furniture that included a sofa near the foot of the bed where he was propped up in a semisitting position. There was a well-equipped kitchen on the opposite side of the room, an open archway to the left of the kitchen that led into what appeared to be a combination bathroom and gymnasium, and a desk with a computer that sat against the wall to his right. The walls were blue, with assorted pictures of farmland, forests, and wildlife. He noted that he was dressed in flannel pajamas with a sheet drawn up above his waist. A man in a brown suit was sitting in a hunched position on the sofa near the foot of his bed.

The man finished typing something on a laptop computer and then glanced up. His head shot back up when he noticed that

Will was awake. For a few moments they stared at one another, and then the man rose and carried the laptop computer to a chair that was positioned to Will's left. He was a small man with a bony frame and short grey hair. He wore wire-framed glasses. After seating himself, he addressed Will with a pointy nose and beady brown eyes.

"I see that you have awakened. Permit me to introduce myself. My name is Professor Edwin Scherzwin. You may address me as Ed."

"Hello, Ed," Will said. "So then, I assume this is Brockman Penitentiary."

Ed hesitated. His face drew into a scrutinizing mask of inquisition. "They told me that you are notably intelligent and that you possess political savvy. Apparently they were correct." He confronted Will with his eyes. "You are in an older section of Brockman Penitentiary, a section that is reserved for special guests. As you can see, your quarters are very accommodating, and in addition to that, they are private. Unlike the newer units of the penitentiary, your unit has no surveillance cameras and no microphones. In fact, the door, walls, floor, and ceiling are all soundproof. Just outside your door, however, are both cameras and microphones, and there are armed guards at either end of the hallway. It is impossible to escape."

"Is Sheena in a room like this one?" Will asked.

The scrutinizing disposition of Ed's visage deepened. "That's something I'm supposed to talk to you about."

"You're supposed to talk to me?"

"Yes." Ed closed the laptop computer and then rose and placed it on a small table beside the head of the bed. He then sat back down and scooted the chair closer to Will. When he spoke next, it was with a heightened tone of confidentiality. "We only have limited knowledge when it comes to extraterrestrials."

Will's eyes narrowed. "Where is she? What are you doing to her?"

Ed settled back in his chair without breaking eye contact. His posture eased. "So what you've told us is true. You really don't know that she escaped."

Will felt a wave of relief ripple through his body. "She escaped?"

"Yes. You were captured two days ago. The agents kept you sedated until you arrived here, and then you were given a medicine that helps you answer questions in an honest and responsible manner. You probably don't remember anything that happened."

"Was she injured? How did she escape?"

"I'll get to that," Ed answered. His face assumed a patronizing expression. "The important thing is to remember everything that you can so that you can tell us anything that we may have missed while you were under the influence of medication." He leaned forward and folded his hands on his lap, maintaining a steady gaze into Will's eyes. "It is difficult to conceive the degree of danger to the human race that advanced life forms from other planets may impose. You revealed quite a lot to us while you were medicated, enough to conclude that you were thoroughly brainwashed."

Will waited several seconds to respond. The words that Ed had spoken and the look in Ed's eyes left no doubt within his mind that he was sitting face-to-face with a dissolute liar. A disturbing sensation tightened his abdomen; he wondered if Sheena had really escaped or if her capture were being kept secret from him. "What more can I tell you?" he asked.

Ed produced a nod and a smile, and then again settled back in his chair. "Do you have any idea why the tranquilizing darts had no effect on Sheena's body?"

Will's brows rose for moment. "No."

Ed shrugged. "Well, that's consistent with what you told us before. And you also told us that you have no idea how she was able to disarm a federal agent, shoot two agents with tranquilizing darts, escape through an air-conditioning vent in the roof of the building, and make her way up the large oak tree that grows at the rear corner of your workplace, all without detection of several agents who were searching inside and outside the building. The only helpful information you were able to proffer was that you figured she was able to see inside the dark attic of the building by causing the pearls around her neck to light up." Ed produced a demeaning smile before adding one more comment. "And we were able to conclude by the evidence we gathered that she was not able to convey her body from one location to another through some magical power of her pearls."

Will deduced that there was nothing within the memory banks of his mind that might not now be on the memory drives of his captors' computers. "She appeared to be quite athletic."

"Superhuman is more like it," Ed asserted. "The Buccal smear she left in the laboratory was botched. She meant for us to think, no doubt, that she botched it accidentally, and that she is the daughter of Justin Collins, a human being."

Will said nothing. There was no doubt within his mind that Sheena was human.

Ed cleared his throat. "One of the agents found a trace of blood in the attic. We were able to run a DNA test on the blood, and not only did the DNA fail to resemble that of Justin Collins, it was not even human." Ed took a breath and lowered his voice to a sincere and sober tone. "You were duped by an alien that came to your clinic during a time when you were emotionally vulnerable, right after your fiancée had broken up with you, and that alien fed false information into your mind for one sole purpose."

"One sole purpose?"

"Yes. To prompt you to encourage your father to foster rebellion against the sacred Union."

"Sacred Union?"

"Yes, the sacred Union—the United States of America. All that stands between the invasion and takeover of our world by alien forces is the supreme military force that is sustained by our great nation. If our nation is dissolved, our military force will be diminished, and our world will be helpless to prevent a takeover by ruthless invaders."

Will was tempted to ask who would defend the citizens of the world against the corruption and lust for power that had taken hold of the central government of the sacred Union, but he refrained. "So you say that I was duped?"

"Sadly so," Ed vouched. "Do you really think the United States government would withhold the underlying cause of diabetes from the American people?"

Will gave no reply.

"Your phone is on the end table, hooked up to your charger," Ed said, pointing to the table where he had set his laptop computer. "Go ahead and bring up the Internet."

Will gave Ed a startled look and immediately picked up his phone and dialed his father's phone number. DISABLED appeared on the viewing screen.

The smug look that came to Ed's face only increased Will's dislike for the man. "I'm afraid that phone services are forbidden to residents here, and the same applies to e-mail services, but you may still access the Internet."

"Does my father know I'm here?" Will asked.

Ed shook his head. "No, but he was told that you escaped apprehension for treason by fleeing the country with a foreign spy, so he has no reason to believe that you are not safe and well."

"He would never believe that," Will said.

"Are you so sure? Didn't you get him to believe that diabetes is caused by an air pollutant?" Ed gestured toward Will's phone. "Check the Internet now. Conduct a search for air pollution and diabetes."

Will worked with his phone for several minutes, searching one Internet site after another. He finally lowered his phone and faced Ed. "It was there before," he stated.

"Sure it was," Ed scoffed. "It was there so long as the alien was present to transmit false data to your phone's receptor. Now try that Bellamy salute she told you about."

Will complied, again without success.

"You see," Ed crooned. "Almost everything the alien told you is false. Abe Lincoln was the greatest and noblest president this nation has ever had, and he never ordered the execution of a single American Indian, and he fought for the equality of all races, and he welcomed the immigration of black people into his home state, namely Illinois. And the Pledge of Allegiance sprang from the hearts of the American people from as far back as the conception of our nation, all except for that 'under God' phrase that got added to the pledge by Eisenhower. And there was never a time that American children were forced to pledge the flag with their arms hoisted up like a troop of little Nazis."

Will sustained contact with Ed's eyes, attempting to withhold any show of expression. He said nothing.

Ed glanced at a watch on his left wrist and then readdressed Will. "It's six o'clock. Kristy should be here soon. I've given you enough to think about for now. I'll come back tomorrow."

"So today's date is May twenty-first?"

"Correct."

"Who's Kristy?"

Ed produced a quizzical smile and gestured with an open palm. "You're a lucky man, that's all I've got to say. I wouldn't mind being a resident here if she were my attendant."

Without further comment, Ed picked up his laptop computer and exited the room. Will slid from the bed and discovered that there were slippers on his feet. He began inspecting his quarters. The refrigerator was stocked with food. The stove, oven, microwave, and toaster were all immaculately clean. The combination bathroom and gym had a tub, shower, sink, toilet, treadmill, and several different workout machines for muscle strengthening. Back beside his bed stood a bookshelf loaded with classic novels. A small closet was built into the corner of the room on the opposite side of his bed from the outside entranceway, but the closet was locked.

Will sat down at the desk and computer, discovering that the computer, like his phone, could access the Internet. He attempted sending a message through the Internet, but a large red DISABLED popped up across the monitor screen. He decided that he would try some different sites later, but first he would eat something. There was a large selection of foods in the pantries and refrigerator. He poured himself a bowl of cereal and a glass of milk and sat down at a small dining table. Another chair was positioned on the opposite side of the table. He offered prayers that included supplications on behalf of Sheena and his father, and then he began eating.

Will placed his spoon beside his plate and wiped his lips with a napkin. He could see the door to his quarters from where he sat, and a woman entered without knocking. She glanced at him as she stepped inside, and then she turned and closed the door. Everything about her was sexually provocative—from her skimpy, tight, red silk dress and black high heels to the manner in which she bent over as she closed the door and gazed back over her shoulder with a seductive smile.

The woman then walked toward Will and sat down in the chair across the table from him. Her hair was wavy and jet black, matching her shoes, and her glossy red lipstick matched her scant attire. She leaned forward and stared at Will with dark, decadent eyes. She placed her elbows on the table and rested her chin on folded hands.

"You must be Kristy," Will said.

The woman answered in a suave tone of voice that matched her demeanor. "Yes, I'm Kristy. I'm your sole attendant, and you're my sole patient. I'll be here for three to five hours each evening or longer if you desire. I know that doesn't sound like a long work day, but I'm well paid. I'm your maid, your cook, your nurse, and I can offer whatever else you may desire that I am naturally endowed to give you."

"I understand," Will said, peering into Kristy's eyes, delving, as it were, into her very soul. No one said a word. A puzzled, uneasy expression gradually replaced Kristy's brazen façade. And then at last, Will spoke again. "I'd only have sex with you if I was married to you, but I'd like to be your friend."

The look that suddenly overcame Kristy's countenance startled Will. She appeared to be intellectually disarmed and emotionally frayed. Her lips trembled and moisture came to her eyes.

"What is it?" Will asked.

When she spoke next, Kristy's voice sounded like that of different woman, or perhaps like the voice of a heartbroken child. "No man's ever looked at me like that," she said.

"Like what?"

She shook her head and started crying. "Like I'm a real person."

"But you are a real person," Will replied. "Or at least you're meant to be a real person."

Then Kristy's crying gave way to outright sobbing. She dropped her face and wept for a full minute, and then she raised an earnest visage and locked eyes with Will. "How? I'm a second-generation prostitute. Even when I was a little girl, men wanted me, and sometimes Mother let them have me." She choked down a sob and managed a more sober bearing. "I've made it big by flaunting my mother's profession in more sophisticated settings than she ever imagined, but my heart feels so worthless that I think about suicide almost every day." She stared into Will's eyes with earnest. "What hope is there for me to become a real person?"

Will looked toward the door and then faced Kristy. "Can we keep speaking out loud? I mean, is it true that this room is not bugged?"

"No, this room's not bugged," Kristy replied. "They guarantee employees like me strict privacy. They don't want us to be inhibited in any way. We're paid bonuses if we can coax information from prisoners that they weren't able to extract with their truth serum."

"Very well," Will said. "Tell me what you know about God."

Kristy obliged, and then she and Will entered into a conversation that lasted well over three hours. At one point, Will found himself repeating everything that he remembered Sheena saying to Dr. Terrance Turner regarding the logical existence of God. And later on in the discussion, he became appreciative for every Biblical course he had ever taken in regard to sharing the good news of salvation through Christ to a person with basically no knowledge of the Word of God. Kristy was receptive, and it was obvious that the Holy Spirit of God was speaking to her heart at the same time that Will addressed her ears. Finally she faced Will and said that she was ready to repent of sin and accept salvation through the redeeming blood of Jesus Christ. Together they prayed, and when their eyes met again, Will realized that he was no longer sitting face-to-face with a lost child of Satan. Rather, he was peering into the eyes of an eternal sister, a born-again child of the living God.

Again Kristy cried, but this time she laughed as she cried. She thanked Will over and over. "And I'll be looking for another job once you're not here anymore," she commented.

"When I'm not here anymore?" Will reiterated. "So you think they're planning to release me?"

Kristy's face grew somber. "I think they're keeping you here in hopes that it will somehow help them capture your fiancée. No one quartered in this room has ever been released. Not ever."

Will read her expression. His chest tightened. "They've all been executed?"

"Yes, unless they died first. That is, all but one. Your fiancée's name is Sheena, right?"

"Yes."

"Well, the only person that ever got out of here alive was your fiancée's mother."

"What? Sheena's mother?"

Kristy nodded. "Yes, that's right. When I was briefed about this assignment, I was told that an alien with superpowers broke into the penitentiary over a hundred years ago and escaped with a female prisoner named Rachel, a prisoner who had been quartered in this very same room for a year. The alien was a man named Justin Collins, and he took Rachel to his home planet and mated with her. Your fiancée is their daughter, or at least that's what they tell me."

"That matches the names Sheena told me. She said that her parents' names were Justin and Rachel Collins." A look of inquiry beset Will's brow. "And whoever briefed you seemed sure that Sheena is their daughter, right?"

"Oh yeah. They claimed that she left a Buccal smear that proved it."

Will's brows flinched. "That's not what Professor Ed told me."

"Of course not. Ed's a professional liar."

Chapter 7

Sheena sat at the meeting table with Dr. Azora, Charftan Yarzon of Southern Ivoria, Golchuron of Quazaria, Terrab of Equavere, Charftan Zimstar of Scintillia, Charftan Nukeel of Cerulea, and Leah, the Southern Ivorian spy. They sat at the same oval table in the Palace Museum where the group had met together prior to Sheena's expedition to the earth's surface. This time, however, there was an additional person seated at the table with them, Moeeta of Quazaria—a female Quazarian warrior. It was the first time that Moeeta had ventured outside the realm of Quazaria since Quazarian warriors waged holy war and decimated a third of Subterrania's population after the Great Corruption, the period of time when evil first entered Subterrania. It was also the first time that Moeeta, in deference to customs outside the realm of Quazaria, had ever donned a tunic.

"But there is still much to consider," Moeeta spoke with force, speaking in the native language of Subterrania. She faced Sheena, who sat across the table from her. "Of course I have no doubt that you can pass the inquisition, especially since I'll be the one serving as your inquisitor and reading the thoughts of your mind, but can you harness the anger that burns within your soul in a sufficient manner to make rapid and crucial decisions in the midst of mortal combat? Leah has confirmed that your fiancé is confined within Brockman Penitentiary, as was your mother, and it may require cool and quick thinking as well as the powers of a Quazarian warrior in order to safely liberate him."

Sheena responded. "It is true that my heart burns with both love and anger, but is that wrong? Is there no place for righteous anger? Was your own heart void of anger when you departed from the sinless world of Quazaria and came to this side of the Dimensional Chasm where your sword wielded justice against the evils that invaded Subterrania from the surface of the earth?"

Tense moments passed with Sheena and Moeeta staring into one another's eyes. The others looked on in silent respect for both women.

"That was a long time ago, before I took the Quazarian Vow, which as you know forbids any further acts of war by Quazarian warriors outside the realm of Quazaria," Moeeta said.

"Yes, but since that vow was taken, three more Quazarian warriors have been trained, and not one of them was required to take the Quazarian Vow."

"True enough, but all three were slain," Moeeta said. Then her face melted in compassion. "I'm sorry. Please forgive my rash decree. Your father was one of the noblest men I was ever honored to befriend. His death was for a virtuous cause, and his name is engraved in the Quazarian Hall of Champions, along with the names of the two Quazarian warriors who died with him, Chad and Ouana."

"I thank you for your kind words," Sheena conferred. "But what you said first is true. All three of the Quazarian warriors who did not take the Quazarian Vow have been slain. Has not the surface of the earth grown sufficiently corrupt to merit a visit from a Quazarian warrior who has not taken the vow?"

Sheena broke eye contact with Moeeta and cast her pleading countenance from face to face about the table. "I told my fiancé that I would return in two years. Three months have already passed, and I have not even started my training. I know the path that I choose is not an easy one, and I know that there is no guarantee that I'll be accepted into the Quazarian academy; but I must try. Please, won't you grant permission for me to begin my quest? What hope do I have if I cannot even gain permission from this council?"

Golchuron, who had listened to all that was said without comment, now addressed the entire group. He was seated to Moeeta's right. "For myself, I have little doubt that Moeeta will permit Sheena's entrance into Quazaria. The two women are so much alike that Moeeta may have difficulty knowing whether she is peering into Sheena's mind or looking back into her own mind."

Dr. Azora, seated to Sheena's left, chuckled, eliciting a reprimanding glance from Moeeta. The look on Moeeta's face educed additional chuckles from Terrab, Charfton Yarzon, and Charftan Zimstar.

"As all of you know," Golchuron continued, "Quazaria is governed by seven Verurs. The Verurs decide whether or not there is any need to recruit and train an additional Quazarian warrior. Presently there are sixty-three Quazarian warriors, and after the deaths of three Quazarian warriors on the earth's surface, the Verurs have decided that, for the present, no additional Quazarian warriors are needed."

"Then I'll have to return as I am," Sheena blurted.

"No," Leah interjected. The others faced her. She was seated farthest to Sheena's right, on the other side of Terrab. She leaned forward and looked past Terrab to address Sheena's eyes. "They not only have your description, but plenty of pictures from surveillance cameras. Even if you shaved your head and wore a wig, they'd identify you. And although their orders are to detain you, they also have orders to kill you rather than to permit your escape. Your only chance to liberate your fiancé, who will eventually be executed unless you are successful, is to consider the words that Golchuron has not yet spoken."

A look of curiosity seized Sheena's countenance. Leah leaned back and looked toward Golchuron. Sheena and the others also faced Golchuron.

Golchuron nodded in Sheena's direction, and then he resumed speaking to all of those at the table. "Recently something occurred that was quite unexpected. The Seruna Savant—the esteemed ambassador between two worlds—was mortally wounded on her home planet and has died."

Gasps and looks of astonishment occurred among all of those who sat at the table with Golchuron; all of those, that is, except for Moeeta and Leah. Golchuron and Moeeta had spoken in confidence with Leah prior to the meeting.

Moeeta set her eyes upon Sheena. "That is why Golchuron and I have urged this council to give us more time," Moeeta said, speaking directly to Sheena. "The Verurs wish to replace the Seruna Savant, namely Scarlita, but none of the remaining Quazarian warriors will even consider replacing her. Besides agreeing to become the adopted child of the king and queen of the Vorsheams, becoming the Seruna Savant requires taking up permanent residence on Planet Seruna." She stared into Sheena's eyes. "If another candidate is found to replace Scarlita, then that candidate would first need to become a Quazarian warrior."

Sheena felt her pulse quicken within her chest. She looked back and forth between Moeeta and Golchuron. "There has never been a Seruna Savant except for Scarlita," she said.

"Correct," Golchuron voiced. "Scarlita became the Seruna Savant thousands of years ago, and there has never been another."

Charftan Nukeel interposed. "Quazarian history was not something I studied in depth. I have certainly heard reports of the Seruna Savant, but can someone explain exactly what it means to be the Seruna Savant?"

Golchuron obliged. "Are you aware that the Quazarian universe has a sun and three planets, Quazaria, Seruna, and Toolemar?"

"Yes."

"Are you also aware that none of the inhabitants of the Quazarian universe have fallen into moral corruption?"

"Yes."

"Well, Seruna is a planet of deep oceans and lofty islands. Two species of spiritual beings inhabit Seruna. First, there are blue dolphins that inhabit the seas. And second, there are magnificent white winged unicorns with golden hooves, golden horns, and golden eyes. The unicorns inhabit the islands, and they can fly from island to island, but they depend upon Quazarian spacecraft when it comes to visiting Toolemar or Quazaria. And unlike all other spiritual beings within the Quazarian universe and within Subterrania, the unicorns and dolphins of Seruna do not speak Subterranian."

"They speak a different language?" Charftan Nukeel asked.

"Not exactly," Golchuron replied. The Vorsheams, as the unicorns are called, communicate with one another by means of mental telepathy, as do the dolphins, and the Vorsheams and dolphins communicate between each other in the same manner. When Quazarians first began visiting Seruna, they were able to deduce that the Vorsheams are intelligent and spiritual beings, but they were at a loss when it came to conversing with them. Then one of the Quazarians got the idea of bringing a Quazarian warrior to Seruna to see if the warrior could read the mind of a Vorsheam through the powers imbued by his or her vermaskian cylinders."

"And that's where Scarlita got involved," Charftan Nukeel surmised.

"Not yet. The first Quazarian warrior to visit Seruna was a man named Efrim, who attempted to read the mind of Shartrandor, king of the Vorsheams. Shartrandor rules the Vorsheams along with his wife, Queen Felores. When Efrim entered Shartrandor's mind, he discovered that the language barrier was still a major problem. Then back in Quazaria, Zingross came up with an idea."

"Zingross?"

"Yes, one of the two surgeons capable of implanting tworshan threads over the surface of an individual's brain in connection with fusion-powered vermaskian cylinders that are embedded across the individual's forehead. This surgery is part of the process of becoming a Quazarian warrior."

Charftan Nukeel nodded.

"So," Golchuron continued, "Zingross theorized that a Quazarian warrior could expand the telepathic pathway between his or her mind and the mind of a Vorsheam by focused use of the vermaskian cylinders. This, he theorized, could take the Quazarian warrior beyond the simple reading of the Vorsheam's mind and open the telepathic pathway so that the Vorsheam could also read the Quazarian warrior's mind. Once this was accomplished, he theorized that a Vorsheam could transfer knowledge, including knowledge of the Vorsheamian language, into the mind of the Quazarian warrior."

"Did his idea work?"

"Eventually, yes. Zingross accompanied Efrim to Seruna, and they revisited King Shartrandor and Queen Felores. With assistance from Zingross, Efrim was able to make the king and queen understand Zingross's idea. The king and queen took the matter very seriously. The only way they would agree to transfer the knowledge of their minds to a Quazarian warrior was if that warrior agreed to become a member of the royal family of Vorsheams and take up residence in Seruna. Efrim was not willing to do that."

"And Scarlita volunteered," Charftan Nukeel guessed.

"That is correct," Golchuron said. "She was a loner, and she loved riding horses and unicorns, and she was enthralled by the idea of riding and flying upon the backs of Vorsheams. And in addition to that, she was greatly flattered by the prospect of being adopted as a Vorsheamian princess. Zingross's idea worked very well. Felores, Queen of Seruna, imparted knowledge to the mind of Scarlita, and Scarlita served as spokeswoman for the Vorsheamian race from that day forward."

"That must have added a whole new dimension to the relationship between Quazarians and Vorsheams," Charftan Nukeel remarked.

"Indeed it did," Golchuron averred. "Vorsheams started visiting Quazaria by way of Quazarian spacecrafts so long as Scarlita traveled with them, and tourists from Quazaria started frequenting Seruna as a favorite vacation getaway. And it became evident that Scarlita had gained more than just the ability to communicate with Vorsheams, she became renowned for her wisdom. The Vorsheams are noble and wise creatures, and the transfer of knowledge from the mind of Queen Felores to the mind of Scarlita apparently imbued Scarlita with noteworthy wisdom."

"So that explains the title by which Scarlita became known, the title of Seruna Savant," Charftan Nukeel deduced.

"Yes."

Charftan Nukeel eased back in his chair and looked about the group. Golchuron nodded to Moeeta, and Moeeta in turn faced Sheena. Sheena could sense an air of drama as everyone else's eyes became fixed upon her.

"How did she die? How did Scarlita die?" Sheena asked, directing her question to Moeeta.

"Seruna, for the most part, is a beautiful and safe planet," Moeeta commenced. "The oceans teem with plants and fish more colorful than a rainbow at sunset, and the islands feature birds and animals too wondrous to describe, and none of these plants or creatures are dangerous to human beings."

"So Scarlita was not slain by a wild creature," Sheena assumed.

Moeeta and Golchuron exchanged glances. "Actually, yes, she was. The Vorsheams are able to use their wings to seemingly fly through the waters of their oceans, and they can then break from the surface of the water and fly through the air. But they are air-breathing beings, and they only swim to limited depths within their seas. But by use of her vermaskian cylinders, Scarlita was able to create an air bubble about her body and generate artificial light so that she was able to course much deeper into the ocean waters than any Vorsheam."

"And there are dangerous creatures in the dark depths of the Seruna seas?"

"No, the oceans are safe. But Scarlita discovered a deep underwater cavern. The opening of the cavern is far deeper than light from the Quazarian sun is able to penetrate. Even the dolphins do not dive as deep as the opening to the cavern. And when she found this opening, she was intrigued to note that faint light shone from the mouth of the cavern, and then she proceeded to explore the cavern. As she continued farther, she discovered that the cavern first wound downward toward the center of Seruna and then rose back upward, coursing upward so high that she deduced that she emerged from the cavern and from the water into a great vault within the heart of a mountain. The ceiling of the vault contained phosphorescent crystal, and the far side of the vault dipped downward into an enchanting underground world."

Moeeta stopped speaking long enough to glimpse around the table. The others were captivated. Golchuron was the only one, besides Moeeta, who knew anything about the cavern.

Moeeta then readdressed Sheena. "Scarlita then ventured into an underground jungle with a solid crystal phosphorescent sky. She surmised that she had discovered an underground kingdom that was similar to the kingdoms of Subterrania on the other side of the Dimensional Chasm, and she began searching the jungle for the presence of intelligent spiritual beings. She was walking past a large boulder, or what she thought was a boulder, when a huge tail whipped out from the body of a gigantic reptile and smashed her body against the trunk of a tree. What she had thought was a boulder rose to its legs and roared, opening a mouth of teeth that looked like rows of ivory sabers, and then it plunged its jowls toward her maimed body."

"It killed her?"

"No. If it had killed her, she would have simply disappeared, and it is likely that no one would have ever known what happened to her. She was able to engage her vermaskian cylinders and ward off the reptile, but she was mortally wounded. She made her way back through the cavern, up to the surface of the sea, and onward to the Royal Cave, a great marble cave wherein the palace of King Shartrandor and Queen Felores is situated. She told them everything that had happened, and then, after conveying her love and appreciation, she died."

Several moments of respectful silence ensued. Everyone began looking from face to face, wondering who would ask the next question or voice the next comment. Golchuron was first to break the silence. "We advise that the next Seruna Savant stay away from the undersea cavern, or at least that she conduct any exploration of the cavern with extreme caution."

The eyes of all the others then turned back to Sheena. It was obvious that she was being asked to consider the possibility of becoming the next Seruna Savant. She met Moeeta's eyes. "Does the Seruna Savant live in the Royal Cave with the king and queen of the Vorsheams?" she asked.

Moeeta nodded. "Living quarters for Scarlita were built into a branch of the Royal Cave by Quazarian craftsmen. The quarters are luxurious, with fountains, baths, a dining area, a spacious kitchen, and a stately bedroom that looks like an exhibit from an art museum. Quazarians were most appreciative for a communicator between the Quazarian race and the Vorsheams, and the extravagance of the home that was built for Scarlita reflects their depth of appreciation. The next Seruna Savant will inherit that living space, and additional bedrooms may be constructed at her request."

"Additional bedrooms?"

"Golchuron and I recommended you to the Verurs, as well as to Zingross and Efrim. We truly feel that you would make an excellent Seruna Savant. Zingross and Efrim, after considerable time and effort in communicating, were finally able to come to an agreement with King Shartrandor and Queen Felores."

"An agreement?"

"Yes. The next Seruna Savant will, like Scarlita, be the adopted daughter of King Shartrandor and Queen Felores, a princess of the Vorsheams. She will take up residence in the Royal Cave, and if she desires, she will be permitted to have a husband who lives with her, as well as children, so long as the children immigrate to another world in order to mate and bear children of their own. And with much persuading, we gained permission for the next Seruna Savant, and any members of her family, to wear clothing, provided that the Seruna Savant herself wears only a brief white tunic with a golden belt and golden slippers. And in addition to that, Queen Felores wanted to know if Zingross could make the next Seruna Savant's vermaskian cylinders golden in color rather than silver like the color of Scarlita's vermaskian cylinders, and Zingross said that it would be no problem to manufacture misprite, the primary element used for the outer surface of vermaskian cylinders, that is as golden in color as the iris of a Vorsheamian eye."

Sheena contemplated the significance of Moeeta's words. She looked at Golchuron, who proffered a supportive smile, and then she looked at everyone else at the table. The looks on all of the faces around her were hopeful and encouraging. She settled her eyes upon Moeeta. "So if he wants to, Will could still marry me, even though I'm the Seruna Savant. And we could even have children."

"Yes, and that brings up one last point in the agreement with the king and queen."

"What is it?"

Moeeta drew and breath and sighed before responding. "Queen Felores says that no Princess of Seruna is venturing to the earth's surface without her mother, even if she is a Quazarian warrior. She insists upon going with you to rescue Dr. Johnson."

Sheena's countenance grew perplexed. "Really?"

"Yes. Zingross argued that it would place you in additional danger to have to protect a Vorsheam while on the surface of the earth, and then he and Felores finally came to a compromise."

"A compromise?"

"Yes. Felores agreed to take orders from her adopted daughter while on the earth's surface and to wear a harness with a special disc that generates a protective force field extending ten feet in all directions. Felores also agreed to give her adopted daughter full control of disengaging the force field. Both Felores and her adopted daughter will be able to turn the force field on, and the force field will protect against any fast-moving projectiles such as spears, arrows, or bullets, and it will also protect against harmful radiation." Moeeta relaxed her shoulders as if she were finished speaking, but a moment later, she raised a finger and drew another breath. "And one more thing. Zingross, at Queen Felores's request, agreed to make the harness golden in color with a red disc that matches your hair."

"They told the king and queen that I have red hair?"

"Of course. All native Quazarians have bronze skin and golden hair, so Efrim and Zingross thought it best to inform the king and queen that you would appear somewhat different."

"Was that all right?"

"Yes."

There were a few seconds of silence. A crease of concern came to Sheena's brow. She continued facing Moeeta.

"I'll be subjected to a Quazarian inquisition when I first enter Quazaria, right?"

"Yes."

"Well, if I become the Seruna Savant, and if Will comes to Seruna with me, will he also be subjected to an inquisition?"

Moeeta shook her head. "No. We have heard very good things about Dr. William Bartholomew Johnson, and if you bring him into the Quazarian universe as your husband, then we will make a second exception—he will not have to face the Quazarian inquisition."

"Second exception?"

"The first exception was your mother. She did not have to face the inquisition when she entered Quazaria with your father."

Sheena's face evinced several seconds of reflective contemplation, and then her visage transformed into an image of resolute determination. "Okay then. I'll do it."

"Whoppin' Whiplash!" Chirra exclaimed. "That's one fine-looking getup. I can just see you wearing that outfit while sailing through the air on a flying unicorn." She lifted her face dreamily and raised an open palm. "There's your thick red hair streaming back behind you while the unicorn's white tail sails below like a silk banner."

Sheena rolled her eyes and shook her head, and then she turned and faced Verma and Treshonda. All four women were standing in the living room of the cottage that Sheena inherited from her mother. Verma and Treshonda were wearing blue tunics while Chirra was dressed in a black bathing suit. Sheena spoke, "Magnificent job on the white tunic, Verma. And you did a wondrous job on the golden slippers and golden belt, Treshonda."

"Treshonda made an extra belt and an extra pair of slippers, and I made three tunics," Verma spoke up. "It hardly took more silk fabric than a single tunic, as skimpy as you said I needed to make them. And since that's the only clothing the king and queen of Seruna will let you wear, we figured you'd need extra outfits to wear while you were washing your other clothes."

Sheena laughed. "Thanks. From what I understand, though, they'd think nothing of it if I went naked while I was washing my clothes."

Treshonda muttered something and shook her head. "That's two reasons why I'd never visit Quazaria. First you have to pass through the Dimensional Chasm and let some stranger read your mind while you're worrying about your body being vaporized. And then, if you're still alive, you end up in a world where people go around naked."

Sheena laughed again, and this time Chirra laughed along with her. Then Chirra faced Sheena with a look of concern. "You'll come back to visit now and then, I mean, after you become the Seruna Savant, right?"

"Of course, I'll come visit," Sheena replied. "And I'll bet Queen Felores will come with me."

"A Vorsheam?" Chirra posed with excitement.

"Yes, the Queen of the Vorsheams."

"Oh my, how wonderful," Verma inserted. "I've always wanted to see one of those flying unicorns. My mother used to read me a story about a Vorsheam when I was a little girl. It was a story about a little Vorsheam named Flutterwings that made friends with a dolphin named Splishyfins."

Another look of concern came to Chirra's face. "Won't it take years for you to complete your training as a Quazarian warrior?"

"Yes, but remember that time passes ten times faster on the other side of the Dimensional Chasm. I can train for twenty years there, and only two years will pass here."

Chirra inquired further, "Okay, but how will we know that you weren't vaporized when you first entered Quazaria? I'm going with you to the Dimensional Chasm, but I won't be able to see or hear anything that takes place on the other side."

Sheena thought for a few moments. She noted a bracelet of small black pearls around Chirra's left wrist, and then she faced Chirra. "Moeeta is the name of the woman who will be conducting my inquisition. You can loan me your bracelet, and then I'll have Moeeta pass the bracelet back to you as a sign that I've passed the inquisition."

"Okay. That sounds good," Chirra said. And then she glanced at the closed door to the cottage before readdressing Sheena. "Let's go to the lake and show Twishell your outfit. Tomorrow's the big day, and Twishell wanted to see your outfit before you left, remember?"

Sheena smiled. "Sure, I'll go to the lake with you. And I think you'll be coming back here to visit, even when I'm in Quazaria. I've never seen anyone make such close friendships with the mermaids within a few days."

Chirra was obviously pleased by Sheena's comment. She gestured with open palms and a shrug of her shoulders. "I know it. It's almost like Twishell and I are long-lost sisters."

"And besides the mermaids, this cottage may get lonely for some company now and then after Verma and Treshonda move back to Scintillia," Sheena added.

Verma and Treshonda looked at one another, and then Verma motioned toward a sofa and two lounge chairs that were arranged around a multicolored rug in the center of the room. Sheena and Chirra glanced at one another with questioning eyes, and then they succumbed to Verma's gesture. After everyone was seated, Verma folded her hands on her lap and faced Sheena. Chirra looked on with silent curiosity.

"After your mother's funeral, it did not take long for news to spread throughout all of Southern Ivoria about your father," Verma said.

Sheena nodded, maintaining eye contact with Verma.

"Well, people have started talking about turning this cottage into a museum, a memorial to the only Quazarian warrior that ever lived in Southern Ivoria."

"Really?"

"Yes. And now, if you end up becoming the second Seruna Savant, there's no doubt that this cottage will become a museum. It will be renowned as the place where the wife of a Quazarian warrior raised a Seruna Savant."

Sheena dropped her eyes and pondered Verma's proclamation. Then she looked back up. "My mother is a wonderful woman, and I have no doubt that my father is a wonderful man. It would be an honor to donate this cottage as a museum." Verma's face bloomed, and Sheena returned Verma's smile. "I would like to maintain ownership of this land, though, in case one of my children chooses to live in Southern Ivoria, provided that I have any children. He or she could build a house someplace near here, perhaps near the shore of Lake Veroona."

"Oh, that would be wonderful," Verma said. She turned her head and met eyes with Treshonda, and then she again addressed Sheena. "Treshonda and I have fallen in love with this community. We'd like to remain living here as hostesses and custodians of the museum."

Sheena leaned back and lifted a hand to her breast. She looked back and forth between Verma and Treshonda. "Do you really mean it?" she asked.

Both women nodded.

"With all our hearts, yes," Verma avowed.

"It would be an honor and a joy," Treshonda added.

"Of course you can stay. I'd love for you to stay. You can each keep your bedroom as your private quarters, and you can exhibit the remainder of the cottage as a museum, and of course, you can still use the kitchen and bathrooms." She peered at a picture of her father. "I just wish there was a picture of my father without a bandana covering his vermaskian cylinders."

Verma leapt up. "Wait here," she said, and then she dashed from the room.

Sheena and Chirra shared inquisitive glances, and then both girls faced Treshonda. Treshonda folded her hands on her lap and smiled. For a while, she said nothing, and then she finally commented, "I hope she brings my favorite one."

Seconds later Verma returned to the room toting a large picture mounted within an intricately engraved wooden frame. She stood on the rug and held the picture where Sheena could view it.

"Whoppin' Whiplash!" Chirra exclaimed.

Sheena rose and knelt on the rug, staring at the picture. The look on her face grew intense. The man whom she knew to be her father was suspended in midair with one hand on his hip and with his opposite arm embracing a beautiful young woman with soft brown hair—her mother. Her mother wore a golden dress that flowed downward to her ankles like an angel's satin gown, while her father was dressed in sleek black slacks and a black shirt with a silver belt and silver shoes. Across her father's forehead lay a band of silver cylinders that sparkled like the stars she observed in the clear night sky above Texas.

Sheena reached up and touched the picture. Her eyes were teary as she raised her face to address Verma. "This has been right here, in this cottage, all of my life?"

"Yes, dear one," Verma answered. Her voice quaked. "The doctors said that we should keep certain things hidden and secret due to your mother's illness."

"And there are more pictures?"

"Yes."

Sheena rose to her feet. "Can Chirra and I look at them after we get back from the lake?"

"Of course. Treshonda and I will start getting supper ready, and then we can all sit down on the rug and look at pictures after we eat."

"That sounds wonderful. Thank you."

There were few words spoken as Sheena and Chirra left the cottage and began hiking down the pathway to the lake. Chirra sensed that Sheena's mind was embroiled by the spectacle of a Quazarian warrior holding the woman he loved. Chirra's mind, meanwhile, shifted between thoughts of having a friend who was the Seruna Savant and thoughts of becoming better acquainted with Twishell. She wondered if Twishell might someday escort her into the Vault of Wonders, the marvelous cavern where human girls are temporarily transformed into mermaids while mermaids are transformed into humans.

As they drew near the lake, Sheena became more attuned to her surroundings. She noted that the trees, shrubs, and grasses of Southern Ivoria looked similar to botanical species that she saw on the earth's surface, albeit scenery in Southern Ivoria appeared more vibrant and untarnished. There were no brown or wilted leaves on the trees in Southern Ivoria, and perpetual flowers sprung up among the grasses and bedecked the shrubs and trees. She and Chirra stepped down a grassy embankment to a white sandy beach and then walked across the beach to the edge of a great blue lake. Sheena remained at the edge of the water while Chirra waded into the lake and knelt to her knees.

Popping sounds were emitted into the atmosphere as Chirra slapped cupped palms against the surface of the water. She continued whopping the water for about ten seconds and then waited in still silence, gazing out over the lake. Soon a head popped out of the water several yards in front of Chirra. It was the head of a merman with curly orange hair and blue eyes. He stared at Chirra for several seconds and then turned his eyes to Sheena.

"Hi, Sheena," the merman said. It was obvious that he was visually scrutinizing her attire.

"Hello, Sherdallo," Sheena replied. "How are you and your family?"

"We do well."

"I am glad. Can you summon Twishell for us?"

"Yes, she has been expecting you. She's keeping an eye on a spawn of lostwirsta to show her new friend." Sherdallo turned his face to Chirra. "You must be Chirra of Arulia."

"Yes."

"Twishell speaks highly of you. I will send her to you." He turned his face back to Sheena. "I will report that the new Seruna Savant looks magnificent in her white and golden garbs."

"I'm not the Seruna Savant yet," Sheena said.

Sherdallo merely smiled at Sheena's reticence and dropped below the surface of the water.

Chirra twisted around and met Sheena's eyes. Her face bore a look of excitement. "He knew my name."

"I think you are going to be quite popular with the merfolk," Sheena remarked.

Chirra's look of excitement heightened. "The merman mentioned a spawn of lostwirsta. What are lostwirsta?"

"Lostwirsta are emerald-colored fish that swim in schools in open waters. They are beautiful, but they are rarely seen up close. They come to the Bed of Wesheria to spawn, and their fry are amazing."

"Really? Why?"

"They have big glowing red eyes, and they swim in a ring around their mother like a glittering ruby halo. Now and then, they all dart inward to their mother and eat a special slime that she produces on the surface of her scales, and then they all zip back out and reform the ring."

"Wow, I've got to see that," Chirra remarked. "And the Bed of Wesheria is amazing itself, even without any lostwirsta. I've never seen such a beautiful collection of tiny flowers, and the green stems and leaves coat the floor of the lake like a plush carpet."

"A very thick carpet," Sheena averred. "I was only seven years old when I decided to investigate the length of the stems. Verma was swimming with me. She nearly died of fright when she saw me disappear beneath the flowery surface of the Bed of Wesheria, and she must have ripped up a thousand flowers looking for me."

"Were you okay?"

"Sure, other than for the fact that I was not permitted to swim in the lake for a whole week after that. The stems are about nine feet tall."

Sheena's gaze shifted to a point beyond Chirra. Chirra turned back around. A mermaid smiled as Chirra espied her. Her head and the tops of her shoulders were visible above the water. Long silver hair complemented her brilliant green eyes.

"Welcome, Chirra," the mermaid said. "Are you ready to swim with me and see something wondrous?"

"I'd love to," Chirra said. She again twisted around to face Sheena. "Would you mind if I swim with Twishell for a while?"

"Of course not," Sheena replied. "I'll go back to the cottage and see what Verma and Treshonda have to show me. Take as much time as you like."

While Chirra and Sheena conversed, the mermaid perused Sheena's golden belt, golden slippers, and white tunic. "Most magnificent," Twishell said, addressing Sheena after Sheena finished speaking to Chirra. "You will look stunning alongside a Vorsheam, or perhaps mounted on its back, provided that such creatures truly exist."

"Truly exist?" Sheena retorted. "Why would you question the existence of Vorsheams?"

Twishell swam closer to shore where she could brace her hands on the floor of the lake as she faced Sheena. "Well, the history of Quazaria and Quazarian warriors is considered factual amongst merfolk, and we also believe that one of the female Quazarian warriors became known as the Seruna Savant. But the existence of flying unicorns with snow-white fur and golden eyes that communicate with their minds is generally thought to be a myth."

"Is that so?" Sheena posed. Her face assumed an expression of amusement. "Perhaps it would interest you to know that humans inhabiting the surface of the earth generally consider the existence of merfolk to be a myth."

An astonished look of disbelief besieged Twishell's countenance. "No. Why? How could that be?"

Chirra reacted to Twishell's discomfiture. "Do not take it to heart," Chirra said, addressing Twishell. "Many of the humans on the surface of the earth are like Vandolians. Their beliefs are warped. Some even think that the earth created itself, and that mud, fire, and water somehow merged to form living creatures."

Twishell's face went blank for several seconds. She stared hard at Twishell. And then she dropped her head back and laughed merrily. Chirra and Sheena glanced questioningly at one another. When Twishell's laughter eased, she again faced Chirra.

"You are a gifted teaser," Twishell said. "No doubt I will find our friendship to be most entertaining."

"Gifted teaser? What do you mean by that?" Chirra queried.

Twishell laughed again. "Life from mud, fire, and water? Will you deny that you jest? Even young children in the Vault of Wonders would not be so stupid as to believe such nonsense."

Chirra turned to Sheena. "Tell her I speak the truth."

"I'll have to agree with Twishell," Sheena teased. "Little merfolk would surely know better than to believe something like that."

"Never mind the little merfolk," Chirra rejoindered. "I'm not talking about little merfolk, I'm talking about the humans on the surface of the earth."

Sheena smiled at the expression on Chirra's face, and then turned to Twishell. She managed to bring a degree of sobriety to her visage. "Although I agree with you that Chirra is a gifted teaser, what she says is true. Some humans on the earth's surface believe that nonliving matter, in and of itself, somehow produced life apart from the Creator. Some of them even deny the Creator's existence."

Twishell's features grew stern. "Then some of them are truly like Vandolians, or even worse."

"I'm afraid that is true."

A period of silence elapsed as Twishell and Sheena gazed into one another's eyes. Twishell broke the silence. "Okay. Perhaps the Vorsheams really exist. So then, I would be honored and grateful if you would someday bring a Vorsheam to the shore of this lake for me to see."

Sheena pondered Twishell's suggestion. "The Vorsheams are good swimmers, so perhaps one day you'll turn around and discover me swimming toward you on the back of a Vorsheam."

Twishell drew back and brought a hand to her chest. She smiled. "Oh my, what a marvelous thought." She looked at Chirra and then again faced Sheena. "The Creator be with you and yours."

"And the Creator be with you and yours," Sheena returned.

Twishell motioned for Chirra to follow her. Chirra nodded toward Sheena and then swam after Twishell.

Sheena paid little attention to the environment during her walk back to the cottage. She thought about the picture of her father and mother, with the two of them suspended in midair, and she wondered what other pictures had been hidden away. Her thoughts also dwelt upon Will. What sort of treatment was he receiving in Brockman Penitentiary? Did he still want to marry her? Would he want to marry her if it meant migrating from Planet Earth to a planet where he and his wife would be the only two human inhabitants?

"Welcome home," Verma said as Sheena entered and then closed the door to the cottage. "Where's Chirra?"

"She's visiting with Twishell," Sheena answered. She stood and stared down at Verma and Treshonda. The two women sat on the rug in the center of the room with a large open photo album lying between them.

"We've been refreshing our memories," Verma said. Treshonda, who was also facing Sheena, smiled and nodded. "It's been many years since your mother showed us these pictures and told us about them."

Sheena sat down on the floor with Verma and Treshonda and flipped back to the front of the album. The pictures in the album were large, with only one picture per page. The first page held a smaller version of the picture in the wooden frame with Sheena's father and mother suspended in midair.

"You can turn the pages," Verma said, peering at Sheena's face. "I'll try to answer any questions."

Sheena flipped the page. The next two pictures were similar to the first picture, but now her father and mother were farther away, and there was a large silver disc in the air above them. A light shone from the bottom of the silver disc and illuminated her father and mother. "Dr. Azora told me that Golchuron was a member of the crew that brought Father, Chad, and Ouana to Brockman Penitentiary to rescue Mother," she commented. "He said they traveled from Quazaria to Brockman Penitentiary in a Quazarian spacecraft, passing through the second Dimensional Chasm. And he said that the second Dimensional Chasm leads from a mountain cave in Quazaria to an undersea cave in the deepest realm of the ocean on the earth's surface."

"Well, I know that they flew in a Quazarian spacecraft," Verma acknowledged.

Treshonda looked on and listened. She was a woman of few words, contrasting with Verma's talkativeness.

Sheena peered back down at the silver disc. It was apparently a Quazarian spacecraft. Then she turned to the next two pages and perused two more pictures. The picture on her left was that of a white marble mansion built into the side of a mountain, and below the mansion lay a picturesque lake. On the right was a picture showing a green lawn below the porch of the marble mansion, and on the lawn stood her father and mother, both dressed in white tunics, and they were accompanied by a large tiger that stood next to her father. Sheena gazed upon the images of her father and mother, noting the band of vermaskian cylinders across her father's forehead, and then her eyes became fixed upon the tiger. A curious wrinkle emerged upon her brow. She raised her face and looked back and forth between Verma and Treshonda.

"Are these pictures from Quazaria?"

"Yes," Verma affirmed. "The mansion is where your parents lived until your mother was several months pregnant. Then they moved here."

"They moved here because members of races who age and die are not permitted to reproduce and raise children in Quazaria," Sheena stated.

"That is correct. If Will accompanies you to Seruna and the two of you bear children, as I know you hope to do, then you will become the second woman from this side of the Dimensional Chasm to give birth to a child on the Quazarian side of the Dimensional Chasm."

Sheena looked back down at the picture of the tiger. "The first woman was Shareesha, the original Shareesha the Tiger Queen," she said. And then she paused and faced Vera. "And Shareesha gave birth to a little girl while living in Quazaria—a little girl who she named Sheena."

"Yes," Vera affirmed. "And you were named in honor of that little girl."

Again Sheena peered down at the tiger. She placed a finger on the tiger's image. "Gwarzon," she declared. She looked back up at Verma and Treshonda. "When Chirra and I had breaks between our courses of study in Equavere, we loved to visit the Hall of Memories, which as you surely know is the renowned museum in Urmoonda. The bottom chamber in that museum is dedicated to Shareesha the Tiger Queen, and there are pictures both of Shareesha and of the tiger. And there are also pictures of that same tiger in the Palace Museum, right here in Southern Ivoria, for it was that same tiger who fought at the side of the second Shareesha the Tiger Queen, namely Princess Alania."

"Yes," Treshonda spoke up. It was apparent that the subject of Gwarzon stimulated her. "Many of the animals in Quazaria are spiritual beings. Gwarzon is a ceremony master, a legendary spiritual leader who conducted the marriage between Zake the Son of Sir Marticus and Princess Alania, the second Shareesha the Tiger Queen. And the marriage took place in the Royal Gardens of Equavere, the most marvelous setting for a wedding in all of Subterrania."

Vera smiled at Treshonda's enthusiastic proclamation. She then spoke in confidential tones to Sheena. "Treshonda was very young at the time, barely having reached womanhood. She was an adventurous poet and writer, and she was selected as one of six Scintillians who were flown across the desert Kingdom of Draskar on the backs of skargs to attend the wedding."

Sheena gasped and faced Treshonda. Her eyes widened. "You were at the wedding? You witnessed the marriage?"

Treshonda straightened and folded her hands in her lap. For a few moments her eyes seemed to drift. A wistful, pleasurable expression took shape upon her countenance. "Yes." She shook her head as if the memory were more than her mind could fathom. "There are no words to tell you how I felt when Zake and Alania kissed. I tried to write about it, and I did write about it, but I knew that there was no pen in any universe that could transcribe the spiritual and emotional sensations that pervaded the hearts, minds, and flesh of all who witnessed that kiss."

Sheena felt her pulse quicken. "Treshonda, that's wonderful. Why have you never told me about this?"

Again, Treshonda shook her head, though this time with a look of empathy. "Zake and Alania both migrated to Subterrania from the surface of the earth."

"Oh," Sheena said. "You were worried about Mother. You were afraid that bringing up the wedding would cause Mother to have one of her spells."

"Yes."

The room grew quiet. Sheena looked back down at the album and turned through the remaining pages. There were no additional pictures of Quazaria. Most of the remaining pictures featured a baby girl—sometimes in her mother's arms, sometimes in her father's arms, sometimes with Vera or Treshonda, or with a pet, and sometimes all by herself. She noted that the baby girl was almost always smiling or laughing.

Tears came to Sheena's eyes. She closed the album and faced the two women who had cared for her since infancy. She smiled.

"Thank you so much," Sheena said. She did not have to explain that she was thanking Vera and Treshonda for being her surrogate mothers, for such thanks was proffered by her eyes. "I love both of you dearly."

Neither Vera nor Treshonda could hold back tears. "We love you too."

Several seconds passed, and then Sheena placed an open palm on the cover of the album. "I want to marry Will in the Royal Gardens of Equavere, and I want Gwarzon to conduct the wedding."

The mood in the room transformed instantly. Vera and Treshonda faced one another with looks of gleeful anticipation.

"The marriage of a man from the surface of the earth to the first female to win the Challenge of Kingdoms, a female who also happens to be the second Seruna Savant, will no doubt arouse all of Subterrania," Verma declared.

"Especially if Gwarzon emerges from Quazaria for the first time since the marriage of Zake and Alania," Treshonda added.

"Yes, well, except for the time he accompanied Zake and the others who traveled through the second Dimensional Chasm in a Quazarian spaceship to rescue Zake's sister, namely Colesia, the only daughter of Sir Marticus the Avenger," Vera pointed out.

"True enough," Treshonda said.

Vera turned her eyes to Sheena. "I never knew that the little girl who Treshonda and I taught to swim and ride horses would someday have such big plans," Vera said.

"Neither did the little girl," Sheena replied.

Treshonda and Vera both laughed.

"Well, I guess tomorrow begins your quest," Vera said. "Treshonda and I will ride Pucabit, and you and Chirra can ride Windfeather. That way, Treshonda and I can ride both horses back home while Chirra returns to Arulia."

"Thank you," Sheena said.

Then all three women turned their heads toward the door. They were drawn to the sounds of Chomper's excited whimpers.

"It must be Chirra," Sheena said.

Chapter 8

Sheena, Chirra, Vera, Treshonda, and Terrab walked deeper into the Tunnel of Transformation. It was the only passageway into Diamond Mountain, a great dome of unknown substance rising like a colossal crystal turtle in the heart of the Equaverian jungle. Outside the entrance to the tunnel stood Charftan Yarzon and Dr. Azora, keeping watch over four horses. Two of the horses were Windfeather and Pucabit.

"This floor feels smoother than the tip of a dog's wet nose," Vera remarked. She was trying to say something casual, something that would loosen the knot that was tightening within her abdomen. She peered at the whitish translucence of the vaulted walls that rose to either side of her, rising higher than Terrab could reach and forming a flawless domed ceiling. "And it smells cleaner than a stack of freshly washed dishes."

"I feel like I've been swallowed by something," Treshonda responded. Her comment did nothing to loosen the knot in Vera's abdomen. Terrab, Sheena, and Chirra all laughed. Terrab had passed through the Dimensional Chasm a number of times during past years, and although neither Sheena nor Chirra had ever passed through the Dimensional Chasm, they had both ventured to the mysterious blue wall at the end of the tunnel while attending the acastoria in Equavere. For Vera and Treshonda, however, entering the Tunnel of Transformation was a new venture.

"We don't get transformed in here, do we?" Vera asked.

"No," Terrab answered. "The tunnel was named the Tunnel of Transformation because it leads to the Dimensional Chasm."

The group grew quiet as the thickening darkness began yielding to faint blue light. The light grew brighter as they continued walking, and ahead of them appeared an arched wall that seemed the surface of molten blue glass encasing a blazing moon. They halted twenty feet away from the blue wall.

"It's beautiful," Treshonda said.

Vera's abdomen eased. Although her heart held a thousand apprehensions in regard to Sheena's impending venture, there was something about the essence of the blue wall that settled her nerves. "You can feel the goodness," she said.

"Indeed," Terrab averred. "On the other side of that blue barrier is a universe that has never been tainted by evil."

Vera clasped her arms around Sheena in a motherly embrace. "The Creator be with you. I love you dearly."

"The Creator be with you also. I love you, and I thank you for everything you've done for me and Mother," Sheena said.

A like hug and similar words then passed between Treshonda and Sheena. Next, Terrab stood before Sheena and raised his right hand with an open palm, the formal manner of salutation in Subterrania. "It is my honor to bid farewell to the champion of the Challenge of Kingdoms, to a special friend, and to a woman who walks in unreserved determination to fulfill the Creator's calling for her life," he said.

"Thank you," Sheena said.

Terrab dropped his hand and stepped aside. Chirra replaced him. She removed a bracelet of small black pearls from her wrist and fastened it around Sheena's wrist. "Remember to send it back. I'll hardly be able to breathe until I know that you haven't been vaporized."

Sheena smiled. "How could I forget? You've reminded me three times since we left the cottage."

Then the two girls, one with golden skin and coal black hair and the other with fair skin and blazing red hair, stepped forward to the surface of the mysterious Dimensional Chasm. They stared into one another's eyes with the endearment of avowed sisters.

"The Creator be with you," Chirra said.

"And the Creator be with you," Sheena said.

Sheena broke her gaze with Chirra and lunged forward into the blue wall. Suddenly she was nowhere, or perhaps everywhere. Her body seemed surreal, swirling through scintillating mists. Every smidgeon of flesh in her body pulsed and tingled, yet she experienced no pain. And then she was standing on solid ground.

A breath of wonder filled Sheena's lungs. In the distance rose a magnificent wall of great trees with sprawling, intertwining limbs. The leaves of the trees blended together in colorful shades of green, blue, and violet, while the roots of the trees rose above the ground and adjoined themselves in a fence of woody lace and spirals. At the foot of the trees lay a beautiful meadow. Wavy blue-green grasses covered the floor of the meadow along with patches of colorful flowers, and eye-catching birds of various sizes and hues flitted and chirped both in the meadow and amidst the branches of the trees. And in the middle of the meadow lay a great silver disc, identical to the picture of a Quazarian spacecraft that Sheena viewed in the picture album while sitting on the floor of her home with Verma and Treshonda.

Sheena's eyes became affixed to a creature dashing toward her from the direction of the spacecraft. It was a deer with silver antlers, ochre fur, and silver hooves. Then her eyes were averted to an opening that appeared in the side of the spacecraft. Someone was stepping out onto the meadow; it was a woman wearing a white tunic. The deer stopped a few feet in front of her. Its large eyes appeared as silver discs that matched its antlers.

"My name is Astrogan," the deer stated. "This meadow and the surrounding woods are my home, and I have become the official greeter of those who pass through the Dimensional Chasm."

Sheena was fully aware that many of the animals in Quazaria are spiritual beings that can talk. Nonetheless, she found herself staring at Astrogan in wonder. "I'm Sheena," she managed to utter.

"Yes, I figured that," Astrogan said. "You fit your description, and you arrived just when we expected."

Sheena turned her eyes toward the woman who had exited from the spacecraft. The woman was walking briskly across the meadow toward her. Astrogan turned his head back to follow Sheena's gaze.

"That's Moeeta," Sheena said.

"Yep," Astrogan conferred, returning his eyes to Sheena. "And this will be the first time I've ever seen her conduct an inquisition with clothes on." He looked Sheena over. "It's also the first time I've ever been told that the inquisition is basically a formality. It has already been determined that you will not be vaporized. At the very worst, you'll just be sent back."

"Thank you, Astrogan," Moeeta spoke as she drew near enough to overhear what was spoken between Astrogan and Sheena.

Astrogan bowed his head and strode several yards away. Then he turned and watched. Moeeta stopped about six inches in front of Sheena and stared into Sheena's eyes. Since she was of average height for a Quazarian female, about five feet tall, her head was tilted upward to meet Sheena's eyes. Then the silver cylinders across Moeeta's forehead began to sparkle.

Sheena lost cognizance of the environment surrounding her. She sensed her thoughts, memories, ambitions, desires, and fantasies laid bare, an open book for Moeeta's perusal. Time seemed to lose dimension. And then she sensed a compelling curiosity, and suddenly she was touching Moeeta's inner being. Untainted purity pulsed through Sheena's heart and mind, impregnated with memories of holy war, endearing love, heartrending pain, enduring gratitude, and allegiance to the Creator.

The sparkling across Moeeta's forehead ceased. She took a step backward and stared at Sheena's face. "That's never happened before," she said.

Several seconds passed before Sheena responded. It was all she could do to keep tears from glistening her eyes. "I'm so sorry," she said. "What was your husband's name?"

"Verktor," Moeeta replied. "Three of us were slain during the cleansing of Subterrania that followed the Great Corruption—namely my husband Verktor, Irtevia the wife of Alzor, and Carniazon, a young Quazarian warrior who was engaged to wed a Quazarian maiden named Marseena."

Sheena stood in respectful silence and then slowly shook her head. "You are such a wonderful person. I had no idea—"

Moeeta raised an open palm and halted Sheena's speech. "Thank you. I feel the same about you." She dropped her hand and looked at Sheena with a quizzical expression. "Quazarian warriors never enter one another's minds without permission, and a Quazarian warrior has never entered the mind of a native Quazarian without permission. But what you just did, entering my mind while I was examining your mind, is presumably impossible for any human being apart from a Quazarian warrior." Moeeta stared at Sheena a few more seconds. "Entering one another's minds, such as we just did, is the way that Bushworls and Vorsheams communicate on Planet Seruna."

"Bushworls?"

"A Bushworl is one of the native dolphins of Seruna. They are spiritual beings."

"And they communicate like we just did?"

"I suppose," Moeeta said. "But like I said, it has never before happened between two human beings unless both of those human beings were Quazarian warriors. I've conducted inquisitions ever since the Great Corruption, and I've conducted a great number of them, but no one else has ever been able to mentally harness the power of my vermaskian cylinders and enter my mind. I sense that you have a strong will, and you must also have a special gift."

"A special gift?"

"Yes. It seems that you possess an innate ability, an ability that I've never before encountered."

Sheena turned her eyes to Astrogan. He was staring hard, and his ears were perked up toward her and Moeeta. "The deer seems friendly."

Moeeta turned to Astrogan. "Thank you, Astrogan. You may be dismissed."

Astrogan bowed his head and then trotted away.

Moeeta turned back to Sheena. "Yes, he's very friendly; and he's also very nosey."

Sheena smiled.

"Very well," Moeeta said. "Are you ready to petition the Verurs?"

"I hope so."

"I believe you will do well. Come with me to the spacecraft."

"We're traveling in the spacecraft?"

"Yes."

Sheena removed the bracelet of black pearls from her wrist and held it up in one hand. "I'm supposed to send this back through the Dimensional Chasm to show that I wasn't vaporized."

The silver cylinders across Moeeta's forehead sparkled and the bracelet rose into the air. Then it zoomed back and disappeared into the surface of the Dimensional Chasm. Sheena noted that the Dimensional Chasm appeared the same in Quazaria as it did at the end of the tunnel in Equavere, only now it was centered in the foot of a towering grey cliff. She turned back to Moeeta. "Thank you."

"You are welcome. Shall we proceed?"

Sheena and Moeeta walked side by side toward the spacecraft.

"Given your background and your plan to liberate Dr. Johnson and bring him to Seruna, the Verurs have decided that those persons assigned to interact with you will wear tunics, including the Verurs themselves," Moeeta remarked as they walked. "Furthermore, if you are to raise children in Seruna and if those children will one day migrate to a realm where nakedness is deemed socially unacceptable, then those children should be trained to wear clothing."

"I quite agree," Sheena said.

Moeeta glanced at Sheena's face and then resumed speaking. "Queen Felores has already been transported to Laquistar."

"The capital city?"

"That is correct. If you are accepted by the Verurs, then Felores will be summoned to meet you. She will be accompanied by Efrim, and Efrim will assist with communication between you and Felores. If Felores also accepts you, then you will begin training as a Quazarian warrior with the goal of becoming the next Seruna Savant."

"And rescuing Will," Sheena added.

"Of course."

As the two women neared the open hatch of the spacecraft, a Quazarian man wearing a silver tunic emerged. "You must be Sheena," he said, facing Sheena.

"Yes," Sheena replied.

"My name is Albruxt, and it will be my pleasure to transport you to Laquistar."

"Thank you."

Albruxt nodded, and then Moeeta and Sheena followed him up an inclined metallic plank that led into the spacecraft. The interior of the craft was very different than Sheena had anticipated. Eight lounge chairs were evenly spaced around the periphery of a round table, and there were cabinets and small refrigerators positioned within four of the openings between the chairs. There were no other occupants apart from Sheena, Moeeta, and Albruxt. One other chair, a control chair, was positioned near one side of the craft, to Sheena's left, and there was a walled-off compartment to Sheena's right with a single, central door—obviously a toilet, remindful of the toilet in the Ivorian module, where she sat with other competing champions while awaiting her turn in the Challenge of Wits.

A buzzing sound ended with a click as the doorway closed and sealed. The interior of the spacecraft presented confluent

A look of concern came to Moeeta's face. "Yes. But you must never try to pass through the second chasm unless you are in a spacecraft such as this one. The pressure at the bottom of the ocean where the second chasm opens on the earth's surface would smash most aircraft, and any occupants would be killed."

"I know," Sheena said. "I learned about the second Dimensional Chasm while I was studying the history of Quazarian warriors at the acastoria in Equavere."

Moeeta nodded. Then she peered back down at the tabletop. "I love the Poranian Forest," she commented.

Sheena gazed downward with Moeeta. A sandy shore passed beyond view as the spacecraft flew over the heart of a great forest. The landscape within the forest was charmingly capricious, featuring colorful bluffs, scenic lakes, quaint meadows, and majestic trees. Occasional structures began to appear as the spacecraft continued its flight toward Laquistar. Sheena surmised that these attractive edifices—composed mostly of white stone walls beneath steeped roofs, and embellished with outdoor decks and huge windows—were homes; and she noted that the structures were generally situated near the shore of a lake or at the edge of a meadow.

The mountain had changed little, but now Sheena espied lofty towers that rose toward the sky, towers that were situated upon the landscape south of the mountain. The towers were arranged in concentric rings.

"Those are the central towers of Laquistar," Moeeta said. "The tallest, the tower in the very center, is the tower where the Verurs conduct official business. Their meeting room is on the hundredth floor. There's a landing platform adjoined to that floor, and that's where we're headed."

"How many towers are there?"

"Seven towers surround the central tower, and twelve towers surround the seven towers."

The forest topography on the tabletop gave way to a level plain. White streets interconnected and fed into major roadways. Buildings, some large and some small, became more and more numerous. There were many trees, but they appeared cultivated rather than natural. Orchards appeared now and then, as did stadiums and swimming pools.

"It looks like the people of Laquistar like sporting events," Sheena said.

"Oh, they do," Moeeta averred. "Practically every sport that has ever been conceived upon the earth's surface or in Subterrania has been introduced to the Quazarian people, and we also have some unique sports of our own."

"What's that building?" Sheena asked, pointing to a gold and white structure that rose in the shape of an enormous seashell.

"Tohonla Hall," Moeeta replied. "It's an auditorium for symphonic, orchestral, ballet, and theatrical performances."

Sheena moved her eyes over the surface of the tabletop with an appreciation for the symmetrical beauty of Laquistar. It seemed that she could sense harmony and happiness permeating the atmosphere, emanating from the heart of a sinless city—a city with no thievery, no murder, no sexual debauchery, and no political corruption. The first tower appeared, and then a second tower. She looked up at the nearest tower. It was huge, with smooth white walls and many rows of evenly spaced windows and balconies.

People, most of them naked, waved from volleyball courts and a swimming pool as the spacecraft passed over the top of the tower. People also waved from lounge chairs where they sat beneath shapely little trees or around small fountains.

"Can they see us?" Sheena asked.

"They cannot see us, but they know that we can see them," Moeeta answered.

"So is that a recreational tower?"

"No, the outer towers are residential. People live in them." Moeeta noted a look of inquiry on Sheena's face, and then she resumed speaking. "You can find recreational facilities within the inner circle of towers, and those towers also contain schools, libraries, research laboratories, and some workshops."

Sheena peered forward. "And what about the tallest tower in the center? What's in that tower besides the meeting room for the Verurs?"

"All kinds of things go on in there," Moeeta answered. "Some people live there, including most of the Verurs, and there are schools, shopping areas, gymnasiums, theaters, auditoriums, communication centers, and every type of restaurant you could imagine. And on the very top of the tower sits the Quazarian observatory, a place where folks can view the planets and moons in our solar system."

Sheena peered up at a humongous white dome atop the central tower. Then the spacecraft slowed as it approached the side of the tower. Numerous balconies jutted outward from the exterior wall, some large enough to feature pools, fountains, and gardens. People waved. The spacecraft glided through a large opening and came to rest on a marble floor.

"Disengaging flight power," Albruxt said.

Suddenly the outer world disappeared. A buzzing sound commenced. There was a soft thud when the buzzing ceased, and then Albruxt led Moeeta and Sheena out of the spacecraft.

"Greetings, Albruxt and Moeeta," spoke a young woman who walked toward them. They stopped as she reached them. "You must be Sheena." She raised her right hand with her palm outward. "My name is Velta, and I welcome you."

"Thank you," Sheena replied, returning the formal gesture of raising and then lowering her right palm. She noted that Velta was attired in a white tunic like that worn by Moeeta. She was much the same size as Moeeta, but her golden hair was much longer than Moeeta's hair, draping downward over her shoulders and hanging midway down her back.

"Follow me," Velta said.

Velta led Albruxt, Moeeta, and Sheena to a doorway through the inner wall of the vast room. The walls, floor, and ceiling of the room all appeared to be smooth, white marble. They passed through the doorway and then through a wide hallway with potted plants, elegant statues, crystal chandeliers, marble benches, and petite fountains, and then Velta directed them through a second doorway at the end of the hall.

"I wish you well," Velta said. She closed the door as she departed.

The meeting room of the Verurs was spellbinding. Memories of trekking through the Equaverian jungle with Chirra came to Sheena's mind as sounds of trickling water played upon her ears and scents of healthful verdure filled her nostrils. Rising before the bases of the walls were plants and flowers growing from engraved marble troughs, and above the plants were eye-catching aquariums that surrounded the room. The lighting in the room was provided by the aquariums, and soft, harmonious music played in the background. The music sounded like a distant symphony orchestra accompanying breathtakingly beautiful female voices, voices that easily contested the voices of the Silkatta Sisters of Scintillia.

Lounge chairs were positioned around a round wooden table with a crystal dome rising from the center of its surface. A ring of smaller crystal domes surrounded the center one. Above the table hung a large inverted hemisphere, appearing like the inside of a gigantic hollow egg. Sheena glanced about the room for a few seconds, and then her eyes moved from face to face at the persons who were seated in the lounge chairs. One of those persons, a man wearing a silver tunic, stood up on the far side of the table.

"My name is Karnor, and I welcome you," the man who had risen said. "The other Verurs are Chasira, Jakarto, Loa, Machiello, Sweensa, and Albruxt."

Each of the two men and three women who were seated nodded toward Sheena as they were introduced. Albruxt, who was standing to Sheena's left, simply grinned when Sheena looked at him. Sheena turned to Moeeta, who stood to her right, with a look of startled inquiry. Moeeta leaned and whispered into Sheena's ear. "Albruxt doesn't like anyone mentioning that he's a Verur."

"Very well then," Karnor spoke up. "Please be seated. We're ready to begin."

All the women wore white tunics and all of the men wore silver tunics. After everyone was seated, Sheena noted that the men and women, despite all having bronze skin, golden hair, and blue eyes, presented strikingly differing hairdos and appearances.

Karnor faced Sheena. He was seated directly across the table from her. "We are well versed in regard to your intentions and qualifications, and we count ourselves most fortunate to have such an outstanding candidate for becoming the next Seruna Savant. We would like to show you some images of Planet Seruna as well as images of the cave where the new Seruna Savant will reside. Do you have any questions before we proceed?"

"Well, I do have one question," said Sheena.

"Please ask," returned Karnor.

"Those voices, they're so lovely. Whose voices are they?"

Karnor turned his face to Loa, who sat two chairs to his left. She was squatter than most Quazarian females, with a rounded face, shoulder-length curly hair, and large blue eyes bordered by thick golden lashes. "Loa is a renowned vocalist," he said, glancing toward Sheena, "and she is responsible for providing the beautiful recordings of mermaids singing in accompaniment with the reed flutes of mermen and a Quazarian orchestra."

"That's right," acknowledged Loa. She faced Sheena. "The recordings were made at the shores of Iquamer on Planet Toolemar. Iquamer is a beautiful tropical island on a planet that is otherwise ocean." She peered at Sheena with a look of interest for several seconds before again speaking. "The Vorsheams are very musical, playing ingenious musical instruments with their hooves, wings, and mouths; but they cannot sing. They hoped that Scarlita could persuade some merfolk to migrate to Seruna so that they could produce music in accompaniment with singing by the merfolk, but it never happened."

"Because Scarlita was killed?" asked Sheena.

Karnor interposed, "Scarlita was fonder of flying and swimming than she was of music. The Vorsheams hope that the new Seruna can be more persuasive in her invitation for merfolk to migrate to Seruna."

Sheena smiled and shook her head. "No fear. I love music. If I'm the next Seruna Savant in place of Scarlita, then my plea for merfolk to migrate to Seruna will be most genuine."

There were numerous nods and smiles, and then Karnor turned his face upward toward the hollow hemisphere. "Holostar impromptu," he spoke.

The inner surface of the hemisphere, as well as the crystal domes atop the table, began glowing. A slowly rotating planet appeared in mid-air between the hemisphere and the domes. Azure oceans were dotted with pristine islands that sparked Sheena's sense of adventure. Closer views revealed that islands situated near the equator were tropical, like the Subterranian Kingdom of Equavere, whereas islands farther north and south presented forest landscapes. There were three islands near the northern pole of Seruna, and these islands wore white mantles that Sheena knew to be snow, though she had never touched real snow. Karnor explained that the largest island, Sprumora, is a forest island—the island where a mountainside cave contains the living quarters for the king and queen of the Vorsheams as well as the living quarters for the Seruna Savant. He remarked that the mountainside cave is known as the Royal Cave of Seruna.

Sheena observed that phosphorescent lighting in the marble caverns of the Royal Cave illuminated walls and ceilings with surreal magnificence. Living quarters for the king and queen presented simple elegance while quarters for the Seruna Savant featured artistic extravagance. She brushed a tear of hope from her cheek as she envisaged herself sitting with Will at the marble table that was pictured in the dining room. She imagined Will chasing a toddler around the table while she sat and laughed. It seemed almost unfathomable that, after living more than one hundred and fifty years in Subterrania, her heart panged over a man who she had known only briefly—a man who she met in a kingdom called Texas upon the surface of Planet Earth.

When the last image above the table faded away, Sheena sensed a change in the mood of her environment.

"Holostar, terminate," Karnor said. The inner surface of the overhanging hemisphere dulled to the appearance of solid ivory and the crystal domes on the surface of the table soon held only reflected light from the aquariums.

Sheena glanced about the table. The faces of the others were all directed toward her, and every face presented a serious mien.

"We hope you like what you have seen of Planet Seruna and your intended abode," Karnor said, speaking in solemn tones.

"Yes, of course, it's lovely," Sheena responded. She could not help but feel nervous about the change in everyone's demeanor.

"So you are still of a mind to become the next Seruna Savant?"

"Yes."

"Very well." Karnor paused and looked in turn at all of the others, and then he again addressed Sheena. "Only one other person from outside Quazaria has ever been endowed with the abilities and training of a Quazarian warrior, and as you know, that person was your father."

"Yes."

Karnor leaned forward with his forearms on the table and peered into Sheena's eyes. "After your vermaskian cylinders are implanted and your training is completed, you will have the ability to defeat the entire military force of any nation within Subterrania or upon the surface of the earth. Your powers will be tremendous. If you ever became something evil, then only a band of other Quazarian warriors could hope to vanquish you."

Sheena felt overwhelmed by Karnor's words and by the expression in his eyes, and she was about to express feelings of inadequacy, but then an image of Will arose within her mind and stilled her tongue. She simply nodded.

"We have learned all that we can learn about you, and we are willing to give you our full trust. But there is one thing that we must ask in return before we go further."

"Okay," Sheena said. She had no idea what Karnor was about to request, but she sensed that it would be something crucial.

"In order to proceed with your introduction to Felores, we must have your sincere assurance that you will serve as the Seruna Savant after being empowered and trained as a Quazarian warrior, even if your fiancé chooses to remain upon Planet Earth after he is rescued and even if he pleads for you to remain with him."

Sheena stared at Karnor with a look of dismay, and then she dropped her gaze downward. The soft sounds of trickling water coming from the surrounding aquariums pervaded the otherwise silent room. Moeeta and the Verurs scarcely breathed as they gazed upon Sheena's bowed head. Then Sheena raised her eyes.

"I have already given much thought and prayer to this matter," Sheena said. "It will take a miracle to liberate my fiancé, and I believe that the Creator has commissioned me to be that miracle. I will serve as the Seruna Savant so long as God grants breath to my mortal body, and I will do so whether or not Will chooses to return to Seruna with me."

The postures of those gathered about the table eased.

Karnor turned his face toward Moeeta. "Moeeta, please summon Queen Felores and Efrim."

these thoughts and images played upon Sheena's cognizance while her heart embraced the depth and passion of Vorsheamian life. Communication was mutual. Sheena held back nothing—her deepest passions and utmost convictions poured from her eyes and were absorbed by the empathetic golden orbs that cuddled her soul.

There was no doubt in Sheena's and Felores's minds that they had explored the depths of one another's hearts, and that they adored one another. Sheena stepped forward and embraced Felores's neck. Then she withdrew her arms and turned to face the others. Felores likewise positioned herself to visually address the group. Efrim stepped around the table and whispered into Karnor's ear.

Karnor broke the intense silence, speaking to Sheena. "It appears that you possess an innate ability that none of us have ever witnessed or even known possible. You could serve as the next Seruna Savant without even having to become a Quazarian warrior."

A look of near panic sprang to Sheena's features. Her intention to become the Seruna Savant was rooted in her desire to rescue Will, and rescuing Will depended upon the abilities she hoped to acquire as a Quazarian warrior. And in addition to the fact that she loved Will and hoped to marry him, she also felt responsible for the fact that he was imprisoned. She sensed Felores mentally inquiring about the nature of her altered mood, and she peered into Felores's eyes for several seconds before glancing at Moeeta. Moeeta's face wore an expression of strong objection, and Sheena easily perceived that Moeeta shared her emotional reaction to Karnor's declaration.

Sheena, Moeeta, and Felores all turned their eyes upon Karnor, and Felores shook her mane and stomped a hoof against the floor.

Karnor had no problem interpreting the response to his words. "Of course," he said, looking at Sheena, Felores, and Moeeta in turn, "the Verurs have already granted permission for

Sheena to train as a Quazarian warrior, and we will not retract this permission unless Sheena approves of such a retraction."

The Verurs all faced Sheena, as did Efrim. Sheena again peered into Felores's eyes, and then addressed the others. "I will train as a Quazarian warrior, and then I will serve as Seruna Savant."

Moeeta smiled. Karnor faced Sheena with a look of serious contemplation for several seconds, but then his features yielded to an expression of acquiescence. "Very well," he said. He looked about the group. "Let's take our seats. The time has come to introduce our new Seruna Savant to her instructors."

Sheena then discovered what the face of a Vorsheamian looks like when wearing a smile. She broke eye contact with Felores and sat down, and Felores walked nearer to the edge of the table and stood between Sheena and Albruxt. Efrim sat down in the chair to Karnor's left, and the others all situated themselves in their former seats.

"Holostar impromptu," Karnor spoke.

Again, the inner surface of the hemisphere above them began softly glowing, as did the crystal domes atop the table.

"Quazarian training camp," Karnor cued.

Sheena glanced at Felores and then stared ahead. She knew that ten years of time pass in Quazaria for every year that passes in Subterrania, and she figured that she was about to see images of the place where she would be residing for about twenty Quazarian years. Mount Solm appeared, rising from the center of the table, a blue-green cone with a white tip. Then those surrounding the table seemed to zoom in to the north side of the mountain. Natural terraces and forestland came into view, with red granite cliffs adorned by crystalline waterfalls that plunged downward into charming pools and with rippling brooks that wound between the feet of soaring evergreens.

Nestled within the mountain forest was a valley with cultivated trees, level fields, neatly tiled pathways, and numerous buildings. The buildings were intriguing, varying from primitive log huts to futuristic structures that seemed, to Sheena, like something she would expect to see in an advanced alien world, but then, as she thought about it, she was, in fact, in an advanced alien world. And in addition to that, she was destined to become a permanent resident of yet another alien world. She imagined herself turning her head and staring into Will's eyes as he rode with her on the back of a flying Vorsheam, and then she drew a breath and focused on the scene before her.

Brilliantly colored birds swooped between branches and serenaded passersby, and Sheena had occasional glimpses of furry arboreal creatures and woodland deer. Then the image above the table took the observers into a cedar structure the size of a small auditorium. Inside was a stylish classroom with several desks arranged in a semicircle so that they all faced a central podium, and behind the podium stood a Quazarian man wearing a silver tunic, a man who Sheena recognized as Golchuron.

Karnor spoke again, addressing the entire group. "Golchuron will be Sheena's primary lecturer, though there will be several others. In deference to the customs in Sheena's homeland, all of her instructors will wear tunics."

Sheena met eyes with Felores and relayed Karnor's message. She discovered that she and Felores could communicate much more rapidly than persons using verbal language. It seemed incredible that the two of them had just met. They both looked back above the table, and as further dialogue ensued, Sheena silently translated all that was spoken, looking from time to time into Felores's eyes.

"This is Keema," Karnor said. The image had transformed into a gymnasium where a petite female Quazarian warrior stood beside a mat on the floor. Her hands were propped on her hips. She wore a white tunic, and her long golden hair was pulled back in a pony tail. "Keema has less natural strength than any of the other Quazarian warriors, and yet her skills in the martial arts are so refined that she can usually defeat any of them in hand-to-hand combat." Karnor paused and peered at Sheena before continuing. "She is fully aware of Sheena's previous training and accomplishments, and she will begin Sheena's martial arts training at an advanced level."

The gym was replaced by the single image of a male Quazarian warrior. His tunic was silver, and the silver discs across his forehead were twinkling. His thick hair was trimmed so short that it gave the impression of a golden helmet. He was gaunt and tall by Quazarian standards, standing five feet and seven inches in height, and his facial visage seemed to exude intelligence. His image slowly rotated so that everyone at the table was able to see his contemplative expression.

Karnor resumed speaking. "Zemo is the only Quazarian warrior who has mastered the skill of reading the minds of other persons by simply gazing upon them, without even making eye contact. He will attempt to coach Sheena into developing the same skill. And in addition to reading minds, Zemo has mastered the skill of causing persons to fall into a deep sleep for various periods of time, periods ranging from as little as three minutes to as long as five hours."

When Sheena next communed with Felores's eyes, Felores conveyed that she was impressed by Zemo's ability, and she wished Sheena good luck in acquiring Zemo's skill. Then both of them looked back above the table as a new image appeared. This time the image was accompanied by unusual humming sounds that reminded Sheena of bees. Another male Quazarian warrior was presented, again wearing a silver tunic. He stood on a grassy field and faced three large boulders that were suspended in midair, aligned side by side.

Suddenly, there was a cracking sound like the sound of a nearby bolt of lightning striking the ground prior to the arrival of subsequent thunder. Only half of each of the two boulders that were suspended to either side of the center boulder remained, and those two halves came to rest on the ground on either side of the center boulder. The center boulder was rounded off, and it appeared to have an opening on top. "This is Shandor," Karnor said. His voice carried an air of respect. "He is more proficient in directing the energy of vermaskian cylinders than any other Quazarian warrior who has ever lived, and you just witnessed him vaporize one-half of two separate boulders at the same time that he rounded off and hollowed out a boulder that was suspended between them."

Sheena stared at the transformed remnant of the central boulder in spellbound wonder.

Karnor rested both palms on top of the table and glanced about the group. "Shandor has expressed his determination to foster exceptional capabilities within the new trainee—namely, the trainee destined to serve as the sole Quazarian warrior that will be free of the Quazarian vow." He leveled his eyes upon Sheena. "He says that he wants her skills with vermaskian cylinders to exceed his own."

Sheena's eyes widened and she turned her head to convey Karnor's proclamation to Felores.

I know little about the surface of planet earth, but I have no doubt that the next Seruna Savant will be something that the surface of that planet has never envisioned, Felores averred.

"Holostar, terminate," Karnor said.

Sheena and Felores faced Karnor along with the others. He spoke again when all was still and quiet. "I believe we are all in agreement. Shall we proceed with the commissioning?"

The other Verurs nodded in unison.

Karnor faced Sheena. "On behalf of the Verurs of Quazaria and having been granted such privilege by the king and queen of Seruna, I offer you the position of Seruna Savant. If you accept this offer, then you will be transported to the training camp for Quazarian warriors. After two Quazarian years of training, you will return to Laquistar where Zingross will implant tworshan threads over the surface of your brain and connect them with golden vermaskian cylinders that will be embedded across your forehead. You will then return to the camp and train as an individual warrior for ten additional years. When those years are completed, Felores will begin training with you. You will learn to ride and fly and how to coordinate the use of the red disc that Felores will wear on her chest so that a protective force field can be generated around her body. What is your response?"

"I accept."

"We're all here," Golchuron said. He glanced about the table at Dr. Azora, Charftan Yarzon, Terrab, Professor Trathbor, Charftan Zimstar, Charftan Nukeel, Moeeta, and Leah. They sat at the oval table in the meeting room of the Palace Museum in Southern Ivoria, the same table where they sat when Sheena was first confronted with the idea of becoming the next Seruna Savant. Almost two years had passed, as measured by Subterranian time, since they last met together. Leah had returned from the earth's surface with information that resulted in a summons to all of those in attendance—a summons that compelled the group to assemble somewhat earlier than they had originally planned.

"So where's Sheena?" Charftan Zimstar asked. He sat on the south side of the table.

Moeeta, who was seated across the table from Charftan Zimstar, answered. "She and Felores are paying a brief visit to a mermaid named Twishell. They should arrive soon."

"And Felores is—" Charftan Zimstar began, then his mouth froze in a half-open position. His eyes grew large as he peered past Moeeta and stared out a wide window that provided a view of Lake Ultreelle. The others all turned their eyes and followed his gaze, and most of them exhibited similar looks of startled wonder. Charftan Zimstar finally managed to recapture use of his vocal cords. "Bellowing berquhors," he uttered, voicing an expression of awe that was indigenous to Scintillia.

Golchuron and Moeeta were the only ones who had ever beheld the spectacle that mesmerized everyone else at the table. Great white wings were widely spread, fluttering in flight to either side of a lovely creature with golden hooves, golden eyes, and a golden horn that extended outward from the creature's forehead. Felores glided downward to the surface of the lawn that stretched from the northern porch of the Palace Museum to the shore of Lake Ultreelle. Riding on the creature's back was a woman of stunning appearance, a woman with long red hair streaming down her back. She wore a white silk tunic that draped over her shapely figure from her shoulders to the tops of her thighs. Golden slippers clad her feet, complemented by a golden belt around her waist and a band of golden cylinders that were aligned across her forehead like a natural tiara.

The queen of the Vorsheams and the Seruna Savant came to rest on the lawn, and then after Sheena dismounted, they both began walking toward a door that opened from the meeting room to the northern porch. Everyone rose from their chairs as Felores entered. Then Sheena stepped into the room and closed the door behind her. Despite the beauty and magnificence of Queen Felores, the eyes of those standing about the table were drawn to Sheena. An aura of purpose and power permeated the room

"We welcome you," Charftan Yarzon said.

Sheena glanced into Felores's eyes, and then Felores tapped one hoof against the floor and nodded her head. "Thank you," Sheena returned, looking about the room.

Everyone sat down. Sheena seated herself to Moeeta's right, and Felores took a position in an empty space between Sheena and Golchuron. Dr. Azora, who sat directly across the table from Sheena, folded his hands atop the table and drew everyone's attention. The others faced him.

"You have all been informed that a matter of urgency has arisen in the nation where Sheena hopes to liberate her fiancé," Dr. Azora said.

The others nodded. And as would occur from time to time throughout the discourse, Sheena glanced briefly into Felores's eyes.

Dr. Azora gestured to Leah, who sat to his left, and then he spoke again. "Our spy to the earth's surface has returned with news that prompted this gathering." He turned his face toward Leah. "Please tell us what you have learned."

Leah looked about the table, holding her gaze with Sheena longer than with the others. "I have a number of things to tell you. To begin with, I have been exchanging information with a woman who has direct access to Dr. Johnson within the confines of Brockman Penitentiary. I befriended this woman where she attends church, and I am convinced that she is altogether trustworthy." The look on Sheena's face intensified. "The woman's name is Kristy O'Dell. She's a nurse of sorts, and she and Dr. Johnson have become very close friends."

There was a faint flickering of the golden cylinders that were aligned across Sheena's forehead. Hairs rose upon the napes of necks. Leah fell silent, and the eyes of all the others become fixed upon Sheena's face.

"I will rescue Dr. Johnson nonetheless," Sheena spoke coolly. "He may then choose whatever future he desires."

Felores looked upon Sheena's countenance with an expression of apprehension. There was a general sense of uneasiness.

"No," Leah said, peering into Sheena's eyes. "It's not like that. Kristy has informed me that Dr. Johnson wants to marry you regardless of where the two of you will live and regardless of what kind of superwoman you have become. And Will has been fully informed that you have become both a Quazarian warrior and the Seruna Savant." The expression on Leah's face softened with sincerity. "Kristy and Dr. Johnson are close friends, but that's all, just friends."

A slight blush passed over Sheena's visage. She smiled and peered into Felores's troubled eyes. Then both Felores and

Sheena turned relieved faces toward Leah. The postures of the others eased.

"What additional news do you bring?" Sheena asked.

"A number of things. First, thanks to the woman named Mildred Purser—a woman who you met in Pineville, Texas—a medical center in Houston, Texas, has begun testing patients for blood levels of methemoglobin and cyanmethemoglobin. The same medical center is treating patients with antidotes for cyanide. The results of the medical tests and treatments support what you told Dr. Johnson regarding the primary underlying cause of diabetes and how to prevent and treat diabetes."

"Thank goodness," Sheena expressed.

Extolling grunts and other affirmations of approval were voiced about the table.

"Your father and mother would be most pleased," remarked Dr. Azora.

"Indeed that is so," Terrab confirmed.

Sheena looked around at the commending facial expressions. "Thank you," she said.

A few respectful moments of silence lapsed, and then Sheena spoke again. She leveled her eyes upon Leah. "Why are we here?"

Leah relaxed her neck and shoulders as she collected her thoughts, and then she faced Sheena. "Governor Pete Johnson, who as you know is your fiancé's father and the governor of Texas, has called for a Constitutional Convention, and he has acquired the support of more than two-thirds of the states. The Federal Congress responded appropriately by setting a date for the convention, but then the delegate to the United States House of Representatives from the District of Columbia, namely Delegate Darrell Schnard, somehow filed a lawsuit that declared the Constitutional Convention as being unconstitutional, and he somehow got the United States Court of Appeals for the District of Columbia Circuit to directly appeal the lawsuit to the United States Supreme Court on the grounds that the lawsuit is a matter of public interest that requires expeditious determination. And then the Supreme Court declared that the Constitutional Convention must be delayed until they have time to rule upon the matter."

The room grew ponderously silent. The eyes of all the others became fixed upon Sheena's face. The golden cylinders across her forehead were scintillating like sparks from a crackling fire. "How can the Supreme Court interfere with the constitutional right for the states to amend the Constitution?" Sheena asked. "There are no legal grounds for such debauchery."

"Oh, I totally agree," Leah concurred. "But it has been many years since the government of the United States has felt any real need to follow the precepts of the Constitution. Remember that a bloody war was fought to establish federal rule over the states, and as you are no doubt aware, that war was both sacrilege against the Constitution and sacrilege against the freedoms embodied by the Declaration of Independence."

Sheena's eyes narrowed, and the intensity of her scintillating cylinders increased. Queen Felores looked upon the face of her adopted daughter with concern.

"If the liberties established by the founding fathers of the United States were stolen away by war, then war can win them back," Sheena spoke in calm syllables that contrasted with the fierce look of resolve that beset her countenance.

Leah fell to startled silence as she looked upon Sheena's indomitable visage.

Moeeta intervened. "Sheena," she voiced with urgency, capturing the regard of all the others. Sheena met Moeeta's eyes. "I have studied the history of the United States of America just as thoroughly as you have. The founding fathers of that nation did not intend for persons to be governed through force of arms, but rather by consent of free citizens who abide in sovereign states."

"Yes, I know. But the War of Imperial Aggression desecrated such freedom," Sheena said.

Another few seconds passed.

Moeeta managed a smile. "I do not like to call it the Civil War either," she said, and then her face sobered. "And yes, I agree with you: the War of Imperial Aggression struck down the most vital precept for maintaining freedom within the United States, namely the freedom for a state to secede from the Union." She paused and looked about the table. "Thomas Jefferson, the third president of the United States and the author of the Declaration of Independence, made it clear that a state has the option of leaving the Union if there is no other means of working out that state's objection to a federal law. He described this option in detail in the Kentucky Resolutions of 1799. I hope that Sheena can point out Thomas Jefferson's clear teaching on this matter to governing authorities of the United States."

Sheena rejoindered, "But if the federal government of the United States was willing to commit treason against their own Constitution and wage war against free states, then why would should we believe that the federal government will honor the teachings of their third president?"

Again, Moeeta locked eyes with Sheena. "I can make no guarantee as to how the federal government of the United States will respond to a diplomatic plea to permit a Constitutional Convention. But if you hope to honor the legacy of such men as Thomas Jefferson, George Washington, and Fisher Ames, then I believe that you should pursue a peaceful resolution."

"Moeeta is right," Dr. Azora interjected. He leaned forward with his hands clasped on top of the table and peered into Sheena's eyes. "You have been endowed with great powers, and you are expected to exercise those powers with great wisdom. The founding fathers who brought free states together in a voluntary union known as the United States of America did not intend for a bloody war to decide whether or not states would remain within that union. I quite agree that the War of Imperial Aggression violated the principle of government from the consent of the governed as set forth in the Declaration of Independence written by Thomas Jefferson, but nonetheless, it would be a very good thing if that violation could be remedied through peaceful measures rather than by waging a second war."

"Yes," Moeeta agreed, speaking to Sheena. She motioned across the table toward Leah. "And Leah has some additional information that lends feasibility to a peaceful remedy for reestablishing the constitutional rights of individual states, including the most critical right of them all, namely the right to secede from the nation."

Sheena turned her eyes toward Leah.

Leah glanced about the table and then returned Sheena's gaze. "That's correct. It concerns Dr. Johnson."

"Will?" Sheena responded.

"Yes, Will."

"Go on."

"Well, Dr. Johnson hopes to persuade the Supreme Court Justices to rule against Delegate Schnard's lawsuit and decree that the states may proceed with a constitutional convention. He hopes to do this by appearing before the justices in person and by pointing out the constitutional freedom for states to request such a convention, and he hopes that you can use your superhuman powers to help him gain access to the courtroom."

Several seconds of thoughtful contemplation passed with Sheena and Leah locked eye-to-eye. Sheena then asked, "How could a peaceful court session possibly take place if I use superhuman powers? Wouldn't police and military forces be summoned to battle against me?"

Again, Moeeta intervened. "I have given considerable thought to that very question, and I have discussed the matter with Golchuron." She faced Sheena and opened one hand in a gesture of inquiry. "You know what a force field generator is, and you have been trained in its use, am I correct?"

"Yes."

"Very well." Moeeta relaxed her hand and continued speaking with a look of finality. "A force field generator can be adjusted to the dimensions of the Supreme Court building, and it can be equipped with a compass that aligns with the magnetic field of Planet Earth. You can position it on the center of the roof prior to entering the building. The force field will block communications, and it will render anyone who touches it unconscious. This should provide Dr. Johnson with the opportunity to interface with the Supreme Court justices without interference."

Sheena turned to Felores. Felores met her eyes for several seconds and then nodded. Sheena then queried Leah. "When is this hearing before the Supreme Court supposed to take place?"

"In three days."

Sheena turned back to Felores. The others watched in silence as steel-blue eyes and soft golden eyes conversed in a language that produced no sound. And then Sheena broke her gaze with Felores and looked about the table.

"We will seek a peaceful resolution," she said.

Kristy O'Dell paid the taxi driver and then took hold of the handle to her suitcase. She slid outside and closed the door.

"Are you sure about this, lady?" the taxi driver asked through his open window. "Hardly anybody ever comes down this road. It could be days if whoever's supposed to meet you doesn't show."

"Yes, I'm sure. Thank you."

Dust rose and then dissipated as the taxicab drove off down a gravel road and disappeared into a thick grove of trees. Kristy walked to a grassy bank on the east side of the road and laid her suitcase on its side. She sat on it facing eastward and gazed out over a small meadow covered in wild grasses and dotted with springtime flowers, all basking beneath a clear sky and midmorning sun. She wore her nicest blouse and slacks—it wasn't every day that she was scheduled to meet several aliens, one of them a unicorn with wings. She lifted her eyes and scanned the horizon, looking for any sign of a spacecraft.

Kristy mused over her invitation to flee the outer world and live in a new home in Southern Ivoria. She had accepted the invitation with hardly a second thought. Leah only requested one favor in return: for Kristy to guide Sheena and Felores to Will's room in Brockman Penitentiary. At first the request was terrifying—seemingly a sure ticket to death—but then Leah convinced her that Sheena could provide protection against an entire army, having become some sort of superwarrior. Kristy recalled listening to Leah's explanation of how she would be transported to her new home: a special aircraft, one that could fly through outer space and also pass through the depths of seas, would take her through a magical passageway at the bottom of the Pacific Ocean. They would emerge from the passageway into a world called Quazaria and then fly to a second magical passageway where they would exit the aircraft. They would then walk through the second passageway into Subterrania—the underground world wherein lies the Kingdom of Southern Ivoria.

A deep breath of country air filled Kristy's lungs and brought a smile to her lips. She was alive, alive to a degree she had never imagined possible before meeting Will, and she loved her new life. Sometimes she had to fight the impulse to be jealous— Sheena was a most fortunate woman to be Will's intended bride—but then, she had received more from Will than any man could provide through marriage, for Will had shown her the way to eternal life and to fulfilling spiritual begottenness with her Creator.

The spacecraft appeared suddenly, zooming into view from above the tops of trees that grew along the eastern edge of the meadow. It seemed that an invisible giant slung a colossal silver disc that suddenly materialized as it passed over the border of the meadow, making no more sound that the hum of a honeybee.

Kristy gasped, standing to her feet. "Oh my. A flying saucer," she uttered to herself. She watched as it landed about thirty yards in front of her. Then an opening appeared, and a metal plank extended downward to the ground. A woman stepped out, a woman more stunning in appearance than any human being she had ever envisioned, and following behind the woman paced a creature that seemed to emerge from the page of a fantasy magazine. "Awesome," she whispered. Leah had told her that Sheena would be accompanied by a spiritual being in the form of a winged white unicorn, but Leah had not mentioned that it would be the most beautiful living thing that Kristy's eyes had ever beheld. The woman came forward and stood before her.

"I'm Sheena, and you must be Kristy," Sheena spoke.

"Yes, ma'am."

"I am honored to meet you." Sheena turned slightly and motioned back toward Felores. "This is Felores, my dear friend and adopted mother. I do not think it will be necessary for you to fly with her when we rescue Will, but in case such necessity arises, I'm going to let you practice. I'll take care of your suitcase.

Kristy's lashes parted widely as she watched her suitcase zip through the atmosphere and disappear through the opening in the spacecraft. She noted glittering in a golden band across Sheena's forehead, and then, as the glittering faded, she drew a breath of sheer wonder. Felores reared and pawed the air with golden hooves as great white wings spread like clouds of feathers to either side of her body. Then she dropped her front hooves to the ground, galloped forward with open wings, and rose into the air within three strides. She flapped her wings and glided in a circle around the circumference of the meadow, and then she dropped gently to the grassy bank and folded her wings against her body as she knelt to her knees.

"Felores does not speak our language, but you may ask me any questions," Sheena stated. "She is ready for you to mount."

Kristy had done little horseback riding, and certainly never bareback. She wanted to make a good first impression, however, so she acted as though flying through the air on the back of a winged unicorn was second nature. Felores's thick mane was easy to grip, and she felt fairly secure as she straddled Felores's back and positioned herself just behind the mane.

"Now slip your legs beneath the wings," Sheena instructed.

A faint blush passed through Kristy's cheeks as she positioned her legs and feet beneath Felores's wings while imagining how she would have toppled over backward if the wings had spread open when her legs were positioned on top of them, but then any feelings of embarrassment gave way to exhilaration. She clung to the thick mane as Felores stood, spread her wings, launched forward, and rose into the air. The smooth dips and thrusts as Felores flapped her wings and the even sailing when Felores extended her wings and glided through the atmosphere were very different from the jarring trots and clops she recalled from horseback riding, and the sheer sensation of flying infused her entire body with breathtaking elation. Felores circled the meadow three times and then lighted gently upon the ground near the opening into the spacecraft. Then Felores faced Sheena, who was now standing beside the spacecraft. Sheena smiled as she met Felores's eyes, and then she addressed Kristy.

"She says you fly very well," Sheena said.

Kristy released a good-natured chuckle. "She did the flying. I was just hanging on," she said as she dismounted and then stood facing Sheena.

Sheena laughed in return, and then motioned toward the opening into the spacecraft. "Well, it's time. Let's go get Will."

Despite Sheena's confident and casual manner, Kristy felt a shiver of apprehension pass through her body. She was fully aware that the military soldiers who were commissioned to prevent anyone from escaping from Brockman Penitentiary were instructed to use lethal force without hesitation.

"Sure," Kristy said.

Sheena read the appearance of concern on Kristy's face. She glanced into Felores's eyes, telling Felores to go on ahead into the spacecraft, and then she walked forward and placed a hand on Kristy's shoulder. "Don't worry, I'll protect you," she said.

Kristy smiled and shrugged. "I believe you. I mean, I believe that you would protect me with your life. I don't know if either one of us will come out of this alive, but that's okay, because I'm ready to face my Creator, thanks to Will, and I have no doubt that you're ready."

Sheena peered into Kristy's eyes for several seconds before speaking again. "You know what, I really think that I can find Will without—"

"No," Kristy interrupted. "I know what you're about to say, but I really believe that I'm supposed to serve as your guide, and I would hate to think how I would feel for the rest of my life if I chickened out. Leah told me the plan for rescuing Will, and I want to do my part."

"And I'm pleased to have your assistance," Sheena assented, dropping her hand from Kristy's shoulder and smiling. "After you," she said, again motioning toward the opening to the spacecraft.

Kristy stepped up the silver plank and passed through the opening. Her eyes were immediately drawn to a woman who rose from a chair and approached her. She was different from any human being she had ever seen. The woman was petite, with bronze skin and golden hair, and she was wearing a white tunic. Beyond the woman, Kristy noted that Felores had knelt to the floor outside the periphery of a circle of lounge chairs that surrounded a table. None of the lounge chairs were occupied, but Kristy glanced about her surroundings and espied a man wearing a silver tunic who was sitting and staring at her from a solitary chair positioned near the wall to her left. The woman drew closer and stopped, facing Kristy with vibrant blue eyes.

"Welcome. My name is Moeeta, and I'm a native Quazarian," the woman spoke.

"Thank you, I'm Kristy O'Dell."

Moeeta raised a hand and pointed toward the man in the solitary chair. "This is our captain. His name is Albruxt, and he is quite personable, but he does not speak English. In fact, he speaks no language other than Subterranian."

Moeeta faced Albruxt and spoke a few words in the Subterranian language. Albruxt rose and bowed toward Kristy, and Kristy curtsied in response.

"Very well," Moeeta said, looking at Sheena who had entered behind Kristy. "Court should be in session soon."

"We're ready," Sheena said.

Moeeta nodded and spoke to Albruxt. She then addressed Kristy and Sheena. "Prepare for flight."

Kristy followed Sheena's lead and sat in a lounge chair. She was positioned between Sheena and Moeeta. There was a buzzing sound and click as the doorway closed and sealed. Sheena and Moeeta both observed the astonished expression on Kristy's face as the silver interior disappeared and the sights and sounds of the outdoor environment became perceptible.

"No way," Kristy uttered. She looked back and forth at Sheena and Moeeta. "Leah told me this would happen, but it's...well, it's hard to believe I'm not dreaming."

"We'll be there in a few seconds," Sheena said, facing Kristy as the spacecraft rose into the air and an image of the landscape beneath them became visible on the surface of the table. "Let's review our plan. First, the spacecraft will set down beside your usual entranceway at the penitentiary. You, Felores, and I will exit, with you riding Felores and with Felores's protective force field activated. I will lead the way, and you will give me directions as you ride behind me, and then we will rescue Will. After the rescue, all four of us will flee back to the spacecraft."

"Right. And my job is simply to give you directions to Will's room."

"That is correct. And once we get back to the spacecraft, you will reenter the spacecraft while Will and I head for the Supreme Court building with Felores. The spacecraft will fly back to the meadow by a circuitous route, cloaked from visual and radar detection, and then it will remain in the meadow until Will, Felores, and I rejoin you. Any questions?"

"No," Kristy replied, staring down at the image of Brockman Penitentiary that was televised upon the surface of the table.

"And Will knows the plan, right?" Sheena asked.

"Yes, I told him yesterday," Kristy affirmed.

The spacecraft landed. The interior transformed to opaque silver. Felores rose to her feet. The buzzing sound came again, this time ending in a faint thud. Moeeta secured a silver cylinder to the harness on Felores's chest, positioning it above the red disc.

"Yahweh tun sacka," Albruxt spoke, turning his chair around and facing the women.

"God be with you," Moeeta said.

"Thank you," Kristy said, speaking to Moeeta and then turning her face toward Albruxt.

Moeeta translated Kristy's words to Albruxt, "Buquaw taun."

Albruxt smiled and nodded.

"Yahweh tun sacka," Sheena said, looking at Moeeta and Albruxt. Then she faced Kristy. "Duck your head when you ride out. It's time."

Kristy stepped past Moeeta and mounted Felores's back, securing her legs beneath Felores's wings. She noticed, in passing, that the ruby-like gem affixed to Felores's breast was gleaming, and she had already noted glittering in the golden band across Sheena's forehead. She drew a breath and then exhaled, trying to settle her nerves. She figured this was by far the most dangerous thing she had ever attempted, but she was determined to see it through or else die in the attempt.

"Very well. Follow me," Sheena said. She stepped down the plank and was immediately confronted by two military soldiers holding automatic weapons. They both raised the barrels of their guns toward her chest and stared with widened eyes and open mouths, and then their expressions evinced even more amazement when Kristy and Felores exited the spacecraft and halted behind Sheena. Sheena stared at each of the soldiers' foreheads for several seconds, and then addressed both of them. "Bernard, Stephen, I greet you."

The two soldiers looked at one another, and then looked back at Sheena.

"We're in a hurry to rescue an innocent man, and I believe that both of you would agree that an innocent man should be set free. Therefore, I request that you lay down your weapons and permit us to pass."

Bernard spoke up. "I'm sorry, ma'am, but we cannot do that. Perhaps I can arrange a meeting with a warden."

Sheena glanced at Felores, communicating what Bernard had spoken.

Kristy looked on. Her heart was thumping. Leah had informed her that Sheena and Felores communicated with one another by means of mental telepathy.

The roof is high, and they cannot fly, Felores conveyed.

Good idea. And I'll let them sleep up there for a while so they don't draw attention, returned Sheena. She turned back to the soldiers. The vermaskian cylinders across her forehead brightened, followed by a crackling sound. The rifles held by the soldiers vanished.

"What the?" Bernard stuttered, looking down at his empty hands.

"Woahahoo," Stephen exclaimed, clawing aimlessly as his body rose into the air. Bernard rose along with him. Seconds later they were both asleep, lying side by side atop the roof, five stories above.

Sheena stepped forward and reached to open the door.

"It must be locked," Kristy remarked.

There was another crackling sound, and the door swung open. Kristy provided guidance as they made their way to an older section of the penitentiary that was enclosed by more recent construction. Several guards and employees were left sleeping on the floor behind them. And then finally, they arrived at the door to Will's quarters.

Felores and Kristy both stared at Sheena in silence as Sheena stood facing the closed door. She appeared more nervous than she appeared when automatic weapons were aimed toward her chest. Her hand quivered as she gently knocked. The door opened. It was Will.

They found one another's eyes. Seconds later, without a word yet being spoken, all doubts, qualms, and queries regarding their feelings toward one another were forever dispelled. Tears came to Sheena's eyes. Will stepped forward and embraced her. They were not yet settled within their new abode on Planet Seruna, but they were in one another's arms, and therefore, they were home.

After releasing their embrace, Sheena and Will again gazed into one another's eyes.

"You're wearing the same clothes you had on the last time I saw you," Sheena teased.

Will perused Sheena's striking garbs and vermaskian cylinders. He smiled. "Your wardrobe seems have drifted toward the eclectic."

Sheena responded with a look of self-conscious concern.

"I love it. You look beautiful," Will said.

Sheena smiled.

Chapter 10

Cars, taxis, and buses all came to sudden stops as passengers scrambled outside to look upward. The spacecraft had vanished almost as soon as Kristy boarded, but Felores and her two riders, Sheena in front and Will holding onto her from behind, were strikingly visible as they sailed above the landscape of Washington, DC. The red disc on Felores's breast glowed like a flaming ruby that complemented her beautiful white wings, white body, golden hooves, and golden horn. Sheena looked like a mythological goddess from Mount Olympus, and Will's presence behind Sheena seemed to embrace the hustle and bustle of a mundane morning within the arms of tantalizing fantasy.

"It's that white marble building there, the one with all the columns," Will said, pointing downward toward the Supreme Court building. He had toured the Capitol with his father on two occasions, and both he and his father had sat in the courtroom during a public hearing.

"So do you like flying on a Vorsheam?" Sheena asked.

Will perceived the underlying substance of Sheena's inquiry. "Very much so, but doing anything with you in my arms is sheer heaven, whether or not I'm flying on the back of a Vorsheam. I hope the king and queen of Seruna don't mind seeing the Seruna Savant being hugged."

Will could not see the smile that came to Sheena's face, but he could sense the affection that poured from her soul.

"It looks like quite a crowd gathered outside the main entrance. I'll leave you there with Felores while I activate the force field," Sheena said.

"There may be armed guards."

"Yes, I know. I may have to leave some persons sleeping for a while."

"Like you did with the attendants and guards at the penitentiary," Will surmised.

"Yes. Stay on Felores's back. That way you'll be protected within the force field that surrounds her."

"What about you?"

"I have my own force field."

Sheena patted Felores's neck and tugged on Felores's mane. It was difficult for Sheena and Felores to make eye contact while Sheena flew on Felores's back, but Felores had trained Sheena regarding how to navigate with pats and tugs such as those used by the previous Seruna Savant. They came to rest amidst the crowd on a wide patio below marble steps that led upward to a marble porch and bronze doors. Tall marble columns were aligned along the forward edge of the porch. Exclamations of astonishment arose among the onlookers.

Two soldiers wearing combat gear stood before the bronze doors. One of the soldiers reached to his belt and then raised a phone to his lips, but before he spoke a single word, the phone vanished. Then both soldiers dropped softly to the porch and lay still.

A hushed scream issued from a woman in the crowd, and several of the onlookers reached for phones and cameras. Sheena raised both hands as the vermaskian cylinders across her forehead brightened. Glowing clouds enveloped everyone in the crowd, and every onlooker crumpled gently to the patio. Then Sheena dismounted and unfastened the cylinder from Felores's breast. She moved swiftly.

"I'll be right back," Sheena said. Her body rose and disappeared over the upper edge of a sculptured façade above the columns. Seconds later, a translucent blue dome appeared, arching downward from above the courthouse and resting upon the ground like a giant umbrella. The entire courthouse was encased within the blue dome, including the patio where Will sat on Felores's back.

Sheena reappeared and dropped to the ground. She spoke to Will, also looking into Felores's eyes. "The force field blocks all communication. Hopefully the justices won't know anything has happened. I checked the rest of the area within the force field. There were two other guards that I put to sleep, and a third guard touched the force field, so he's also asleep, the force field is adjusted to render anyone who touches it unconscious for three hours."

Will felt a wave of nervous anticipation sweep through his heart. He had prepared for his confrontation with the Supreme Court justices for many hours, days, and months, and now, within a matter of minutes, all his preparation would be weighed in the balance of established justice. He glanced toward the bronze doors that opened into a legal sanctuary where the founding fathers of the United States undoubtedly expected the Constitution to be respected and upheld. "There will probably be more guards inside," he commented.

"I expect so, darling," Sheena said.

Will met Sheena's stare with startled eyes. She smiled. His uneasiness dissipated from his body, and he smiled in return. He was not confronting the highest court in the United States on his own. With him stood a woman far more imposing than the great female statue positioned beside the steps—the Contemplation of Justice.

"Felores will follow me," Sheena said. "She will have no problem on the steps. Just stay on her back."

They climbed the steps. Will peered ahead as Sheena parted the huge bronze doors without even touching them. There were four military guards, two just inside the bronze doors and two positioned before closed oak doors at the end of a spacious hall that was aligned on both sides with sculptured busts of former chief justices. Rifles were raised by both of the nearest guards, but then the rifles vanished and all four guards dropped gently to the floor. Sheena entered, followed by Felores and Will, and then the bronze doors closed.

When they reached the oak doors, Sheena moved the bodies of the guards to one side and then turned and looked into Felores's eyes. Will gazed between them as Sheena and Felores communicated without making a sound.

You should remain out here where the justices cannot see you. Move to one side when I have the door open.

Felores pursed her lips. *How will I know if you need me?*

Sheena shrugged. *I will cause some object to fly and bang against the door.*

Felores looked at the closed doors and then looked back at Sheena. *As you wish, my daughter. My prayers are with you.*

Thank you, Mother Queen.

Sheena raised her eyes to Will. "Are you ready?"

Will nodded. "I have prayed, I have studied, and I have peered into the eyes of a dauntless woman who stands by my side. Insofar as I know possible, I am ready."

"Very well. Felores will step to one side when you dismount so that the justices will not see her. If you wish to call on me for any sort of assistance, just tug on one of your earlobes. And remember that I can read a person's mind, even if I do not have direct eye contact with that person. But I will not read your mind without your permission."

An amused expression came to Will's face. "Tug on an earlobe? What gave you that idea?"

"My extensive study of American history included the subject of American sports, including baseball."

Will chuckled. Then he faced the oak doors. His expression grew sober and intense. He dismounted and walked to the door.

"I'll follow you and close the door," Sheena said.

Will reached to the handle of the door but then paused. A strident female voice rose and became audible through the closed doors. "But why even consider such an argument? Wasn't a war fought to settle the question of secession? Didn't hundreds of thousands of young men spill their blood during the Civil War? Doesn't the blood of those young men give just cause for heeding Delegate Schnard's request?"

Sheena witnessed a look of resolve take form on Will's face. He opened the door and entered the court chamber. Sheena followed and closed the door and then hurried to catch up.

"Your Honorable Justices of the court, it is only too true that a war was fought to preserve those freedoms embodied within the Declaration of Independence," Will spoke boldly as he strode past empty benches and then continued up an aisle to a lectern that was centered before the justices. "That war was also fought to uphold the protections and rights granted by the Constitution."

A man wearing a dark three-piece suit stepped to one side as Will approached. The man stared at Will with an expression of wary alarm, and he also glanced back at Sheena. The justices all watched in silence. Will stood behind the lectern and continued, "And I would add that it was not only the blood of young soldiers that was spilled during that war but also the blood of freedom-loving civilians. But unfortunately, the noble cause of that war was lost. Those who fought for freedom were defeated by a power-grasping dictator who launched a war without approval of Congress and who committed treason against the Constitution, namely breaching article 3, section 3, which states, 'Treason against the United States, shall consist only in levying war against them, or in adhering to their enemies, giving them aid and comfort.'"

"Strike the intruder's comments from the court record," a shrill female voice commanded. Will and Sheena both recognized the voice as the same voice they overhead while standing outside the oak doors. They looked, along with everyone else, at a woman wearing a black robe with a frilly white collar. The woman was tall, with blond hair, and appeared to be about fifty years of age. She sat in the center chair of three chairs to Will and Sheena's right, and she spoke to the court clerk, who sat at a desk to the left of the justices.

"Wait!" Will interrupted. His forehead skewed with perplexity as he noted that the desk to the right of the justices, the desk of the court marshal, was empty. It further perplexed him to note that, apart from the justices and the court clerk, there was no one present in the court chamber other than himself, Sheena, and the man wearing the three-piece suit. "I have come to serve as a codefendant for the right of the states to hold a Constitutional Convention," he declared. Then he met eyes with the man wearing the three-piece suit. The man was six feet tall with short black hair and wiry glasses. "Who are you?" Will asked.

"The gentleman you are addressing is Darrell Schnard, delegate to the United States House of Representatives from the District of Columbia," the woman who had spoken previously cut in. "Now, unless you can give us some reason why this court should permit your interference, you may leave, and the woman standing behind you needs to exit the court immediately. She is not dressed appropriately to be present within the court chamber."

Everyone watched as Sheena walked calmly around Delegate Schnard and positioned herself before the woman who had requested her departure. She stared into the woman's eyes in silence. It appeared certain that Sheena would speak, and everyone waited in silence to hear what she would say. After nearly a minute, the woman produced an annoyed and condescending expression and addressed Sheena, "Are you going to leave on your own, or do I need to call for assistance?"

Sheena turned her face just long enough to wink at Will and then again faced the woman. "Justice Perle Stalina Steinyetz, daughter of Joseph Lenin Steinyetz and Miriam Bertha Todd Steinyetz, I am certain that you are aware that justices of this court may invite guests to court sessions and that those guests may be seated in the red benches to my right. I respectfully request that you invite me to attend this court session as your guest."

Justice Steinyetz's eyes appeared startled for a few seconds, but then they recaptured their former look of condescension and annoyance. She replied, "I am quite aware of the policies that govern this court, but it is presumptuous for you to think that I would invite you as a guest simply because you have researched the names of individuals in my ancestry, especially when you enter the court chamber dressed like some actress in a Hercules movie. Again, I must ask you to leave the court chamber."

Will observed a wry smile take shape on Sheena's face as she shrugged one shoulder.

"You're questioning my attire?" Sheena posed. "When one considers the getup you wore to General Breckman's party last Halloween, then doesn't my attire seem quite modest."

The atmosphere in the court chamber transformed into a milieu of inquisitive tension. All of the other justices, along with Will and Delegate Schnard, focused on Justice Steinyetz's face. The skin on her cheeks blanched, and she stared blankly at Sheena's eyes. "There is nothing immodest about a trench coat," she proffered.

"Trench coat?" Sheena rebutted. "I'll grant that you wore a trench coat when you entered General Breckman's home, and I acknowledge that you wore it at all times when you mingled with guests on the first floor of his home, but what about the outfit you wore while mingling with elite guests on the second floor? Don't you recall the festivities in the game room where the large portrait that you gave to General Breckman hangs on the wall, the portrait of Major General August Willich? It's the portrait that hung in your parent's home, the portrait that Grandma Bertha used to point to when you were a little girl and say that you were a direct descendent of one of the greatest generals of the Civil War."

There was no mistaking a look of anxious fright that swept through Justice Steinyetz's features, intermixed with indications of astounded wonder. After several silent moments of gazing upon Sheena's face as if trying to remember something, she managed to generate the semblance of emotional composure. She peered about at the others in the room and then looked back at Sheena. "Well then, it seems that you and I are mutual friends with General Breckman, and I do remember Grandma Bertha talking about the portrait. She used to say that I was genetically inclined to victory, given that my ancestors had a knack for fighting on the winning side." She paused long enough to again look about at the others and then nodded to Sheena. "I suppose our mutual friendship with General Breckman warrants an invitation. You may seat yourself in one of the red benches."

Will surmised that Justice Steinyetz had yielded to Sheena's request as a matter of self-preservation. He knew that the Constitution states that justices may be expelled from office for bad behavior, and he could only imagine what sort of behavior Sheena had discovered while scanning Justice Steinyetz's memory. He expected Sheena to act upon her successful bid to remain in the court chamber and retreat to one of the red benches designated for invited guests, but she surprised him.

"Thank you, Justice Steinyetz, but before I sit down, I would like to clear up a misconception. May I speak?"

An awkward slant captured Justice Steinyetz's lower lip. "Well," she stuttered, "the court is in session."

"Understood," Sheena said. She then turned to her left and walked to a position just in front and to the right of the lectern where Will stood. This put her directly in front of Delegate Schnard. She met eyes with the grey-haired justice who sat in the center chair. For a while Sheena and the justice looked into one another's eyes, and then Sheena spoke. "Chief Justice Wilford Turner, I congratulate you on becoming the chief justice with the second longest tenure of all chief justices who have ever served on the Supreme Court. Only Chief Justice John Marshall had a longer tenure, having served for thirty-four years, five months, and eleven days. As you surely must know, Chief Justice Marshall occupied your seat prior to the election of Abraham Lincoln, serving during the first half of nineteenth century."

"Yes," Chief Justice Turner responded, nodding at Sheena with a look of approval in regard to her compliment and with obvious admiration of her knowledge.

Sheena nodded in return and smiled. She spoke again, "No doubt it disturbed you greatly to be confronted with the possibility of hearing a case with no representation on the part of the defense. In all your years of service, you have never held such a hearing. Justice Steinyetz persuaded you to proceed with the hearing even though the counsel for the defense was unfortunately detained. She accomplished this deed by arguing that the hearing is a matter of public interest requiring expeditious determination. To your credit, it was with reluctance that you granted her request."

Chief Justice Turner looked toward the closed oak doors, as did Delegate Schnard and a number of the other justices. Then he again addressed Sheena. "You must have exceptional hearing ability," he remarked.

"I am thankful for all of the abilities the Creator has given me," Sheena replied. "And now, I would like to introduce an educated physician who has prepared himself to represent the states. He is poised to defend the freedom for the states to hold a Constitutional Convention. His name is Dr. William Bartholomew Johnson."

"Your Honorable Chief Justice!" Justice Steinyetz interposed. She opened her mouth to continue speaking. Her eyes met Sheena's. Her speech halted.

Several tense seconds passed as Sheena and Justice Steinyetz stared into one another's eyes. The expression on Justice Steinyetz's face altered from one of defiance to one of resignation. She turned her face back to Chief Justice Turner.

"Did you have a question? Or did you wish to make a comment?" the chief justice asked.

"I have no objection to the doctor standing as counsel for the defense," Justice Steinyetz said.

"Do any other justices object?" Chief Justice Turner asked.

Several of the Justices shook their heads.

The chief justice faced Sheena. "Your request is granted."

"Thank you, Chief Justice. And now, before taking my seat on a red bench as a visitor of Justice Steinyetz, may I please share a few words with Justice Steinyetz?"

Chief Justice Turner looked at Justice Steinyetz and then faced Sheena. "Granted, but please limit your comments to no more than ten minutes."

Sheena curtsied and then walked back to her former position where she stood and faced Justice Steinyetz. "You mentioned how your Grandma Bertha used to point to the portrait of Major General August Willich and say that your ancestors had a knack for fighting on the winning side."

"Yes, that's right."

"I would like to make two points," Sheena stated. "First, Major General August Willich came to the United States among thousands of revolutionary immigrants who fled Germany and Europe after the failed European Social Revolution of 1848. This new wave of immigrants was very different from previous German immigrants who came to the United States to flee religious persecution or simply to make a new home. This new wave of immigrants was largely comprised of influential atheists and agnostics who transplanted their radical social movement from a lost war in Europe to a new political fighting grounds in the United States. Your ancestor, namely Major General August Willich, was deemed a brilliant Union officer and was referred to by Karl Marx as a communist with a heart."

The justice sitting to the left of Justice Steinyetz grunted. Sheena glanced at the justice for about five seconds, long enough to read his present thoughts and to decipher his name, Justice Luke Hadsly. She perceived that he was surprised by what she had just spoken. It was information he had never heard before. She looked back at Justice Steinyetz.

Sheena resumed. "These radical socialists worked hard to put Lincoln in office, and he very probably would not have won the presidency without their support, especially when one considers that Lincoln won a narrow victory with less than 40 percent of the popular vote. At least ten of these immigrant socialists served as officers in the Union army, and one of them served as a New York presidential elector for Lincoln in 1860, namely Frederich Kapp. A key element in the thinking of these immigrant socialists is summarized by a statement made by Frederich Kapp. He stated that America 'will occupy a decidedly higher place as soon as it gets rid of Christianity.' And it is notable that, years later, a subsequent president would swear into office on Lincoln's Bible and then proclaim that the United States of America was no longer a Christian nation—namely, Barack Obama. This kind of thinking contrasts sharply with the devout Christian beliefs of the majority of the founding fathers of the United States. George Washington made a statement that strongly opposes the statement made by Frederich Kapp. He said that 'of all the dispositions and habits which lead to political prosperity, religion and morality are indispensable supports.' And along that same line, the second president, namely John Adams, said, 'Our Constitution was made only for a moral and religious people. It is wholly inadequate to the government of any other.'"

Justice Steinyetz's eyes narrowed as she stared at Sheena. "I'll concede that some of the founding fathers were, to some extent, deists," she said.

"Deists?" Sheena retorted. It was obvious that Justice Steinyetz's remark perturbed her. She looked across the faces of the other justices and then peered into Justice Steinyetz's eyes. "Thomas Jefferson penned the following words on the front of his Bible:

> 'I am a real Christian, that is to say a disciple of the doctrines of Jesus. I have little doubt that our whole country will soon be rallied to the unity of our Creator and, I hope, to the pure doctrine of Jesus also.'"

She met eyes with several justices and then continued addressing Justice Steinyetz. "And George Washington wrote the following words in his personal prayer book:

> 'Oh, eternal and everlasting God, direct my thoughts, words, and work. Wash away my sins in the immaculate blood of the lamb and purge my heart by the Holy Spirit. Daily, frame me more and more in the likeness of thy son, Jesus Christ, that living in thy fear, and dying in thy favor, I may in thy appointed time obtain the resurrection of the justified unto eternal life. Bless, O Lord, the whole race of mankind and let the world be filled with the knowledge of thy son, Jesus Christ.

"And our first court justice, John Jay, said, "When we select our national leaders, if we are to preserve our Nation, we must select Christians." And John Quincy Adams, the sixth president of the United States, who served as chairman of the American Bible Society like his father, said, 'The highest glory of the American Revolution was this: it connected in one indissoluble bond the principles of civil government with the principles of Christianity.' And James Madison, the principal author of the Constitution, said, 'We have staked the future of all our political constitutions upon the capacity of each of ourselves to govern ourselves according to the moral principles of the Ten Commandments.'"

Will observed that the color seemed to be draining from Justice Steinyetz's face. He noted that she did not budge and scarcely appeared to be breathing. She was held motionless by Sheena's eyes.

Sheena resumed speaking, "And I believe it is noteworthy that 106 of the first 108 universities founded in America were Christian. Harvard University was chartered in 1636, and the first rule in the Harvard Student Handbook was that students seeking entrance must know Latin and Greek so that they could study the Scriptures, and for more than one hundred years, over half of all Harvard graduates were pastors." Sheena paused and took a breath, never breaking eye contact with Justice Steinyetz. "Fifty-two of the fifty-five signers of the Declaration of Independence were Christians—not deists. *Christians*. And consider what Patrick Henry wrote in 1776:

> 'It cannot be emphasized too strongly or too often that this great nation was founded not by religionists, but by Christians; not on religion, but on the Gospel of Jesus Christ. For that reason alone, people of other faiths have been afforded freedom of worship here.'"

A glance at Justice Hadsly made Sheena smile. His widened eyes were fixed upon her as if he were in a state of shock. The room was utterly silent. Sheena scanned the faces of several other justices, and they all presented similar visages to that of Justice Hadsly. She then returned her gaze to the face of Justice Steinyetz.

"It is commendable to oppose human slavery," Sheena said. "But the founding fathers would have strongly opposed the idea of turning the entire populace of the United States into slaves to the federal government rather than preserving the freedoms granted to the individual states by the Constitution. Slavery was ended in over ten countries and several colonies during the nineteenth century, beginning shortly after the turn of the century in Haiti and ending as late as 1880 in Brazil, and war during that century was connected with the ending of slavery in only one place in the entire world—the United States. Slavery would have ended in the United States, like the rest of the world, without war. The Civil War was fought on behalf of the inflammatory cause that was borne to the United States by radical socialists, the cause of establishing a federal empire that serves the rationale of socialistic atheists and agnostics." Sheena paused and peered deeper into Justice Steinyetz's eyes. "Is it not peculiar that atheists are highly motivated to gain power over social establishments that, by logic of their own beliefs, are ultimately meaningless and eventually achieve nonexistence?"

Justice Steinyetz returned Sheena's gaze in silence. She said nothing.

Sheena continued, "So my first point is that your ancestor, Major General August Willich, was on the losing side in a war prior to his ever coming to the United States. Unfortunately then, he led his forces to a victory in the United States, and after that, like many of his socialistic comrades, he returned to Germany. And in Germany, as you surely know, another strong federal government would arise under the rule of another dictatorial leader who, like the Lincoln he admired, would wage *total war*, inflicting death and mayhem upon civilians as well as soldiers."

Justice Steinyetz's face revealed little emotion. But what semblance of expression emerged upon her countenance seemed a mixture of astonishment and hatred. Sheena was fully aware, as she peered into the eyes and mind of the eminent woman seated before her, that Perle Stalina Steinyetz was not altogether opposed to the ideas and philosophies promulgated by Adolf Hitler.

"The second point I would like to make is that atheists and agnostics have, by default, made themselves the greatest of losers," Sheena said. "What greater loss could there be than the loss of one's own soul. Our Creator permits free choice. He grants eternal life to all who will repent of sin and receive spiritual cleansing through the blood sacrifice of Jesus Christ, accepting his lordship in their lives. The only other spiritual father of human beings, besides our Creator, is Satan, and Satan will readily claim the souls of all who reject salvation through Jesus Christ. Satan, motivated by unmitigated hatred, manipulates the hearts and minds of his subjects, and that explains why persons with totally meaningless belief systems may exhibit zealous determination to achieve governmental dominance and may strive to exercise unlimited control over other human beings."

There was no verbal response to Sheena's final statement. She stepped back and turned to Chief Justice Turner. "Chief Justice Turner, I thank you for the opportunity to speak. I will now be seated."

Silence persisted until Sheena sat down on a red bench behind a row of black chairs that were situated to Will's right. Then the Chief Justice faced Delegate Schnard and posed a question, "You have presented your case as counsel for the plaintiff. Do you have anything else to say before we hear from the counsel for the defense?"

"Just a reminder, Your Honor," Delegate Schnard answered. His voice sounded a little shaky. "I previously presented just cause for expediting this hearing, and I have requested that a decision be made by open vote prior to dismissal of this session. Nothing has changed in that regard. I still contend that the Civil War dissolved any question of freedom for states to secede from the Union, and I still argue that no movement or meeting of any kind should be permitted to reverse or challenge the solidity of the Union. I ask for a final pronouncement on the issue without delay."

"Understood," Chief Justice Turner said. "You may take a seat."

Delegate Schnard seated himself at a table situated behind and to the right of the lectern. Chief Justice Turner then addressed

Will. "Dr. Johnson, do you agree to an open vote by the justices prior to dismissal of this session."

"Yes, Your Honor," Will answered.

"You may now present your case. Be informed that Delegate Schnard has established that a war was fought to preserve the unity of the states, and that victory was achieved in favor of such unity, and that this victory prohibits a Constitutional Convention that would propose an amendment to grant states the freedom to secede from the Union."

Will took a few moments to steady his nerves. He rested his hands on the lectern. "Your Honorable Justices of the Supreme Court," Will began. He paused and scanned the faces of all nine justices, finally settling his eyes back on Chief Justice Turner. "It is beyond question that our founding fathers would have strongly objected to an act of war determining the outcome of disagreements between the federal government and one or more states. The brief description of treason in the Constitution clearly defines the term *treason* as the act of levying war against states."

Will paused and faced Chief Justice Turner.

"Acknowledged," the Chief Justice said, glancing and nodding toward the court clerk and then looking back at Will.

Will relaxed his posture and removed his hands from the lectern. He continued, "I contend, therefore, that any political or governmental consequence resulting from war against the states on the part of the federal government should be deemed null and void." He drew a breath and quickly resumed speech. "Thomas Jefferson averred that a state can legitimately leave the Union because it freely entered the Union as a preexisting sovereign state. He clearly delineated the steps to be taken if the federal government and a state cannot come to terms in regard to a federal law, and the final step he advised, if other terms of agreement cannot be reached, is for the state to secede from the Union. One can find Thomas Jefferson's clear instruction in this matter by examining the 1799 Kentucky Resolutions. And I would add that Thomas Jefferson was not the only governmental leader who clearly substantiated the freedom for states to secede from the Union, another such leader once sat in the very seat occupied by Chief Justice Wilford Turner."

The Chief Justice's brows rose with interest. Will looked at Sheena, who smiled, and then he again faced the chief justice.

"The lady guest who sits on the red bench has already mentioned Chief Justice John Marshall, who served as chief justice longer than any other individual in history," Will said. "It was under Chief Justice Marshall that the Supreme Court established the unmistakability doctrine, a doctrine clarifying that the sovereignty of states cannot be granted to the federal government unless such transaction is accomplished in unmistakable terms. Nowhere in the Constitution is the sovereignty of any State turned over to the federal government in unmistakable terms, so one must conclude that each state retains its sovereignty and is therefore free to secede from the Union. And I would add that several of the states actually included statements clarifying freedom to secede from the Union when they joined the Union, and since all states that join the Union are deemed to have equal rights and privileges with states that already exist within the Union, it stands to reason that all states in the Union have the right to secede from the Union."

Will again looked at Sheena, who gave him an encouraging nod. Then he again faced forward.

"There were five former presidents of the United States who were still alive at the time that Lincoln took office," Will stated, primarily addressing Chief Justice Turner, though he proffered occasional looks at the other justices. "Notably, not a single one of these former presidents approved of Lincoln's treasonous war against the southern states. In regard to three of these presidents, Franklin Pierce opposed the war so openly that he feared imprisonment by Lincoln. The elderly Martin Van Buren supported the idea of meeting together with the other former presidents in order to issue an appeal for peaceful negotiations, and Millard Fillmore sided against Lincoln throughout the war. And in regard to James Buchanan, this former president maintained that the Union could not be cemented by the blood of its citizens, and when it came to the federal government declaring war against a state, he wrote that no such power has been delegated to Congress or to any other department of the federal government. And then finally, and very notably, former president John Tyler voted for Virginia's secession from the Union, and then he was elected to serve in the Confederate Congress, and he died in 1862 while serving in the Confederate House of Representatives."

At this point, Will took a hiatus and perused the facial expressions of the justices. Chief Justice Turner's level gaze evidenced keen surprise and interest, whereas most of the other justices displayed looks of bewildered wonder; in fact, the justice seated to the left of Justice Steinyetz stared at Will with widened eyes, a slacked jaw, and an open mouth. But in contrast to the other justices, Justice Steinyetz's visage carried no element of surprise at all; rather, her visage seemed one of infuriated chagrin. Will also took another look at Sheena, and he felt his heart rise as she threw him a kiss. He steadied himself by briefly grasping the lectern, and then he drew a breath as he again faced Chief Justice Wilford.

"The idea of denying a Constitutional Convention, on the grounds that the Civil War forbids the freedom for a state to secede from the Union, is without merit," Will declared. "To begin with, the Civil War was illegal and un-American. Lincoln desecrated the Declaration of Independence by disregarding the principle of government by consent of the governed, and this is clearly demonstrated by the fact that citizens of theretofore free and sovereign states were willing to sacrifice their very lives to defend themselves from subjection to his dictatorial bureaucracy. In addition, his war wreaked treason against the very system of rule he pledged to uphold, trouncing the Constitution by conducting warfare against states. And Lincoln's call to arms totally disregarded an essential freedom set forth by our founding fathers and known to exist prior to the Civil War, namely the freedom for a state to secede from the Union."

Will stopped long enough to collect his thoughts. He was presenting his case without any notes. As he looked from face to face, he realized that he had the full attention of everyone in the courtroom, and that he was speaking words that most of the justices had never before heard spoken, despite the fact they had been educated in institutions such as Harvard and Yale.

Will resumed speaking, "Thomas Jefferson said that 'when the people fear the government, there is tyranny. When the government fears the people, there is liberty.' Our nation was changed from a land of liberty to a land of tyranny by a bloody, imperialistic war. Prior to the war, the federal government had to be wary of excessive federal taxes, tariffs, and meddlesome laws because if they pushed a state too far, the state might choose to secede from the Union. After the war, the federal government evolved into a voracious, manipulative monster, having demolished one of the most crucial of all our nation's freedoms—the freedom for states to secede from the Union. With the loss of freedom for states to secede, the United States of America, plural in essence, were replaced by a Federal Empire of Servile States, a solitary nation under federal control."

Another smile from Sheena emboldened Will's next words. "When President Jefferson Davis wrote to Pope Pius IX in 1863, he expressed his heartache and woe over the horrors of the war, and he shared how Southerners, who desired none of their enemy's possessions, were threatened on the very hearths of their homes, and he expressed his hopes and prayers for peace. And when Pope Pius IX wrote to President Davis in return, he addressed him as 'Illustrious and Honorable Jefferson Davis, President of the Confederate States of America, Richmond.'" Will stopped speaking long enough to scan all nine of the justices with his eyes. "Pope Pius IX was correct," he averred. "Jefferson Davis was the president of a legitimate nation that was composed of freely united, sovereign states. And I contend, with good basis and just reason, that the Confederate States of America suffered vicious military defeat by an imperialistic, power-seeking, treasonous, neighboring country that introduced the terror of total war to modern civilization."

No one spoke a word or made a sound in response to Will's declaration. He had effectually drawn back a carefully contrived curtain to reveal a terrible and monstrous truth.

And then Will spoke again, "The Civil War in no way prohibits the states from calling for a Constitutional Convention because the war was altogether illegitimate. But apart from any consideration of the war, the states should still be allowed to convene for a Constitutional Convention because the very purpose of a constitutional amendment is to change the Constitution, either by adding something to the Constitution or by altering something that already exists in the Constitution. Even something that has previously been forbidden by the Constitution may be permitted by an amendment to the Constitution. So in consideration of the fact that our forefathers were wise enough to establish the freedom for states to amend the Constitution without consent of the federal government, and given that they were thorough enough to engrave this freedom within the main body of the Constitution, I contend that no agency or component of the federal government has any legal authority to interfere with the states' right to conduct a Constitutional Convention. I plead for the justices of this Supreme Court to rule that states may convene for a Constitutional Convention separate from any opinion or preference on the part of the federal government."

Quiet followed. The court clerk, who had busily recorded everything Will said, rested his hands atop his desk. There were numerous glances between the occupants of the room. Then the chief justice faced Delegate Schnard.

"Any further comment on behalf of the plaintiff?" Chief Justice Turner asked.

Delegate Schnard stood up and looked toward Justice Steinyetz who in turn looked toward Sheena. Sheena and Justice Steinyetz met one another's eyes for several moments, and then Justice Steinyetz looked back at Delegate Schnard and shook her head.

"No more comments, Chief Justice," Delegate Schnard spoke in a subdued tone of voice.

"Very well," the chief justice said. He looked between Delegate Schnard and Will. "The defense counsel and the plaintiff's counsel may be seated."

Delegate Schnard sat back down in his former seat, and Will sat down at the opposing table to Chief Justice Turner's right.

"Before we cast our votes, I want to clarify the substance of our vote," Chief Justice Turner said, looking first to his right and then to his left. "We are not voting as to whether or not the Civil War accomplished treason against the Constitution. Rather, we are voting as to whether or not the Constitution grants the right for states to call for a Constitutional Convention, even if the focus of that convention is an amendment that grants and delineates the freedom for states to secede from the Union. Any questions or further discussion?"

There was silence.

"Very well," Chief Justice Turner pronounced. "All in favor of the plaintiff, thereby denying the freedom for states to hold a Constitutional Convention in regard to secession, raise your right hand."

Will felt his heart rise and thump against the wall of his chest. After passing his eyes from left to right across the justices, he met Sheena's gaze. She leaned toward him and smiled. Not a single hand was raised, not even the hand of Justice Steinyetz.

Chief Justice Turner's voice sounded again, "All in favor of the defendant, thereby granting the right for states to hold a Constitutional Convention in regard to secession, raise your right hand."

It was several seconds before Justice Steinyetz's right hand rose in unison with the other eight justices.

"This case is dismissed in favor of the defendant," Chief Justice Turner concluded.

Treshonda looked out over the crowd. It was the largest gathering she had ever seen in the beautiful Royal Gardens of Equavere, the most awe-inspiring environment for conducting weddings in the entire realm of Subterrania. She scanned the natural walls of continuously flowering trees that enclosed the glade below her, and then she gazed upward at blossom-filled vines suspended above the glade, a hanging ceiling that dipped between the high branches of bordering trees. The atmosphere was permeated with such intense excitement and anticipation that her skin tingled, remindful of sensations she experienced as she sat among guests in the wedding between Zake, the son of Sir Marticus and Princess Alania, the second Shareesha the Tiger Queen. Her eyes bore witness to the presence of members from every race in Subterrania, including merfolk, who raised their heads and shoulders from a stream that flowed along the back margin of the glade.

Visitors from Quazaria sat in company with Furshea, the wife of Gwarzon the Tiger, who was conducting the wedding ceremony. Kristy O'Dell was seated on the front row beside Furshea. Along the eastern edge of the glade knelt a group of Vorsheams. It was the first time that Vorsheams had ever attended a wedding outside Planet Seruna. Treshonda was one of five bridesmaids, who stood with other members of the wedding party upon the natural shelf of white onyx that served as a ceremonial platform.

Chirra stood as maid of honor, followed by Verma, Treshonda, Moeeta, and Mildred of Texas. All the bridesmaids wore long white gowns with golden belts and golden slippers that matched the outfit worn by the Seruna Savant bride, and the groom and groomsmen, namely Horado, Terrab, Yarzon, Golchuron, and Albruxt, were dressed in matching attire, with white shirts, white trousers, golden belts, and golden shoes.

The ceremony was mesmerizing. The Silkatta Sisters of Scintillia sang with heartfelt passion, and Gwarzon the Tiger implemented precisely the same wedding vows as those exchanged between Zake and Alania several centuries before. Moeeta sat down with Mildred after the wedding and translated everything that was spoken. And later, after being transported back home, Mildred was able to reiterate the wedding vows that took place between Will and Sheena almost word for word as she spoke to the Historical Society in Pineville, Texas. Bill Peebles was among the members of the Historical Society who attended Mildred's speech, and he listened with a visage of amazement as Mildred told about her ride to the bottom of the ocean in a flying saucer and about wondrous worlds that existed on the other side of a mysterious blue wall that shone like a starlit sapphire at the back of an undersea cave.

—⚜—

"I thought I'd have to die before going to heaven," Will said. He walked hand in hand with Sheena on the clean white sand of the shoreline surrounding Sprumora. Now and then, he gazed downward at the protuberance of her abdomen. Two years had passed since their wedding in Equavere, and Sheena was due to deliver their first baby within the next few days.

"They make such beautiful music together," Sheena commented, referring to the orchestra of Quazarians, Vorsheams, and mermen that performed in company with a choir of mermaids. "I'm so glad we decided to spend our honeymoon on Iquamer. I think it helped persuade the merfolk to expand their habitation to include our planet."

Will walked in thoughtful consideration of Sheena's words. "Speaking of our planet," he began, pausing and again looking at Sheena's abdomen, "I suppose that, whenever our child reaches an age to consider marriage, he or she may have to migrate to Southern Ivoria."

Sheena squeezed Will's hand and smiled as she glanced lovingly into his eyes. "Or maybe Texas."

Appendix

Amendment to the Constitution of the United States

―⚯―

An individual state of the United States of America may secede from the Union of the United States, thus becoming a free and sovereign state with total sovereignty over all territories, possessions, and entities within the outer boundaries of that state, even if such territories, possessions or entities were theretofore possessed by the federal government. The seceded state shall have total sovereignty over all coastal waters bordering that state. The seceded state shall then and thereafter possess all military or federal territories, buildings, bases, jets, ships, submarines, supplies, equipment, and other military or federal items usually housed, stored, positioned, or docked within the borders or in the coastal waters of that state prior to or during secession. Such secession of a state shall be accomplished by a 55 percent or greater vote of the citizens of that state and by a 55 percent or greater vote of the members of the House of Representatives of that state. An equivalent body to a state legislature, serving under a different title, may fulfill the requirement for secession in place of a state House of Representatives. Persons employed in the military at the time of secession may serve in any capacity proffered by any military that persists or arises subsequent to secession, and may fulfill any previous military commitment in whichever military they choose and shall be free to choose between proffered positions of military employment for ninety days after the date of secession. Federal employees apart from the military may serve in any capacity proffered by any government that persists or arises subsequent to secession and may fulfill any previous commitment in whatever proffered employment they choose and shall be free to choose between proffered positions of employment for ninety days after the date of secession. Any federal debt or tax owed by a citizen, military member, or any other entity of a seceding state becomes the possession of the seceded state on the date of secession, or within ninety days of secession in regard to military or federal personnel. (Note: The author, Timothy R. Oesch, hereby releases this proposed constitutional amendment as well as the new pledge of allegiance that appears on the back cover of this novel for both public and private use, free of any copyright law or other restriction.)